Also by Nikki Turner

NOVELS

Ghetto Superstar
Black Widow
Forever a Hustler's Wife
Death Before Dishonor
(with 50 Cent)
Riding Dirty on I-95
The Glamorous Life
A Project Chick
A Hustler's Wife

EDITOR

Street Chronicles: Christmas in the Hood
Street Chronicles: Girls in the Game
Street Chronicles: Tales from da Hood
(contributing author)

CONTRIBUTING AUTHOR

Girls from da Hood
Girls from da Hood 2
The Game: Short Stories About the Life

BACKSTAGE

NIKKI TURNER

PRESENTS

BACKSTAGE

STREET CHRONICLES

8472182

8472183

ONE WORLD TRADE PAPERBACKS

BALLANTINE BOOKS | NEW YORK

A One World Trade Paperback Original

Copyright © 2009 by Nikki Turner

Street Chronicles copyright © 2007 by Nikki Turner
Introduction ("The Day I Signed . . . ") copyright © 2009 by Dana Dane
"I'm Good" copyright © 2009 by Krista Johns
"Chasing the Ring" copyright © 2009 by Harold L. Turley II
"Stolen Legacy" copyright © 2009 by Allah Adams
"Lose to Win" copyright © 2009 by Lana Ave
"Gun Music" copyright © 2009 by Nikki Turner
"Outro" copyright © 2009 by Styles P

Published in the United States by One World Books,
an imprint of The Random House Publishing Group,
a division of Random House, Inc., New York.

ONE WORLD is a registered trademark and the One World
colophon is a trademark of Random House, Inc.

ISBN 978-0-345-50429-6

Printed in the United States of America

www.oneworldbooks.net

2 4 6 8 9 7 5 3 1

Book design by Laurie Jewell

*This book is dedicated to every person
who has ever had a dream to make it big!
Dreams do come true!*

DEAR LOYAL READERS

First, I would like to thank you so much for all of the ongoing support that you, my readers, give to all of my Nikki Turner Original novels as well as my Nikki Turner Presents!

It took me a while to decide on a theme for this edition of my Street Chronicles series. Then one day, I got a call from an artist insisting that I come and hang out at his show. I agreed not realizing how much I would be inspired by that night's events. The show was fantastic, and I enjoyed it from my seat out front before venturing backstage after the show. This wasn't my first time backstage but it was the first time that I really observed how the front of the stage was the polar opposite of what was going on backstage. Everything is picture perfect (most of the time) from the fans' point of view, but backstage it is a horse of a different color. It's like an underworld of some sort. Nothing is too strange or too bizarre. From half dressed, low self-esteemed girls looking to get "wifed" up to aspiring artists looking to get put on and everything in between (feel free to let your imagination run wild). And the most insane part of it all is that the people backstage treat this world as normal, as if nothing strange is going on.

In the days, weeks and months that passed, I got acquainted

with some of the power players and became friends with various people from all aspects of the music industry. I was able to get an inside glimpse into that world and realized that behind-the-scenes of the business was more treacherous than backstage of a concert. This was a side of the business that some of my readers may never get to see. That's when a light bulb went off: I wanted to try to put together five different short stories, each giving different points of view of some of the things we, the fans, may not get a chance to see: the love, the hate, the struggles, the highs, the lows, the snakes, dreams coming true and dreams being destroyed . . . all in the blink of an eye.

Now that I had my direction all I had to do was come up with the right combination of authors and/or musicians to complete the task at hand. I began to think . . .

I wrote "Gun Music" around the time I wrote *A Project Chick*. "Gun Music" is far from my regular style of stories but at the time I felt like I needed something gangsta in my life. When I was given the opportunity to work with 50, I thought it would've been the perfect fit, but 50 wanted a female main character, so "Gun Music" was once again tucked away into my files. That was until now; this was the perfect time and place for the story that was waiting to be heard.

KRISTA JOHNS is a really sweet girl I met at Book Expo of America. She sent me her novel and Young Buck called me up to profess that she was nothing short of the truth and I needed to check out her book right away. I did, and I gave her my vision for her story and she rocked it.

HAROLD TURLEY II and I have been great friends from the early days of our careers and he was just a phone call away.

LANA AVE is a close friend of my homeboy and radio personality, Mike Street. He asked me to mentor her and I agreed, and we clicked immediately. I shared this project with her and she had a story a week or two later.

ALLAH ADAMS is a guy that I met at a friend's birthday party. Once he heard I was going to be there, he was there with two books in hand. Because he is an aspiring rapper, I thought his experience would add flare to the project.

I would like to take this opportunity to thank all of the authors involved in this project for being so patient and easy to work with. And Dana and Styles P for putting your pieces together so quickly for me!

Now the moment you've all been waiting for: here is the All-Access, VIP Pass into the entertainment world. Feel free to rub it in your friends' faces or pass it on so that they can share the experience with you as well.

Enjoy!
Much Love,
Nikki Turner

CONTENTS

Introduction

THE DAY I SIGNED . . .

When Nikki asked me to write the intro to this book I was a little reluctant. These stories hit home for me because I know what it's like to be in the unforgiving world of the music and entertainment business. At first I attempted to write a short story to add to the book, but with the intense preparations for the release of my debut novel, *Numbers,* time slipped away from me. But Nikki and I felt it was my duty to provide some insight into my thoughts as a young aspiring rap artist. In essence, take you backstage.

I vividly remember the day—more than twenty years ago—I signed my first recording contract. It was summer in the mid-1980s. I was barely out of my teens when I went to the lawyer's office to put my John Hancock on the recording agreement with an independent record label that was as they put it "taking a chance with rap music." No, I do not remember the lawyer's name; in fact, he wasn't my lawyer. He represented the man (we'll just call him "Sir") who procured the record deal opportunity for me. I didn't know much of anything about the music business at that time except for what Sir had taught me, and that was virtually nothing for the most part. I probably could have learned more about the business if I'd done my research and/or if Sir knew more about the music business, but I didn't and he didn't. Or maybe he did and provided me with as much information as he wanted me to have. There are some people in this business who want artists to have only limited knowledge in order to take advantage of them. Even worse, they may not be very knowledgeable themselves and perpetuate ignorance.

The day I signed my recording contract, I was young and naïve and without a doubt eager to make a record. I didn't understand the price of fame, I didn't know much about double-talk, and I surely didn't understand the pitfalls of the music game. All I did know for sure was that I wanted to put out a record, I wanted to hear myself on the radio, and I had my own distinct flow. My naïveté led me to believe that when people said, "Trust me," they really meant, *Don't worry; I've got your back.* I found out later that "Trust me" in this business of music means, *I'm going to try to exploit you for all you're worth and give you as little as possible in return.* It also meant, *As long as you don't know, I can take advantage of you.* The mind-set was "You're the artist. You've got us around to take care of the business aspect of your career. You just take care of the creative side."

"Hey"—I can still hear their voices in my ear—"we wouldn't lead you wrong, Dana, we're in this together . . . *trust me.*"

"Is this a good contract?" I inquired. There were no negotiations; the lawyer and Sir had me believe it was this contract or nothing (which might have been true). They explained that this was the standard contract (remember youngins: There is no such thing as a standard contract). The lawyer went over the contract with me briefly. It took all of ten minutes. Of course, after the very short 600 seconds, I still didn't understand the magnitude of the paperwork I was about to sign. But it wasn't too hard to convince me to sign since I was unaware of the value of my name, likeness, and music.

I could never have imagined that after that day my career would be such a crazy roller-coaster ride. I could never have thought that not long after my song "Nightmares" was the "World Premier" on one of the hottest hip-hop shows in NYC, the "Mr. Magic Show," with Chuck Chillout and Red Alert, it would become an instant hit and classic. I could never have imagined two years later when my first LP, "Dana Dane with Fame," was released it would be one of the fastest debuting hip-hop albums of its time—going gold and selling 500,000 units in a little over three months, all without a video.

When I think back to the day I signed my first recording contract almost two decades ago, I would never have thought that I would still be trying to get royalties due to me from that agreement. I could not have fathomed that in the year 2000 other rap artists would be performing covers and remakes of my songs without compensating me. I would be lying if I said I didn't feel used and betrayed by that record label and my other handlers, but at the same time I'm not wasting my energy holding grudges. I was afforded an opportunity of which most people only dream. I appreciate the good and the bad people who have crossed my path in the past; they've helped mold me into the great man I am today. Everything has not always been good, but the experience has been great! Hey, I wouldn't have been able to share this scenario if it wasn't for the day I signed my first recording contract.

There's not much integrity in this business of music. But you can find that out for yourself, you don't have to trust me.

I hope I've shared enough to enlighten someone, but let's now look to the present . . . the future . . . the next installment of Nikki Turner's *Street Chronicles: Backstage.* It's time to turn up the volume, time to make it move, time to make it shake. Although the stories depicted in this book are fictional, they do have merit. And it is my sincere belief that you will be thoroughly entertained, but it is also my hope that you will be enlightened as well.

Nikki is a powerful storyteller and has the great ability to locate exceptional writing talent.

So the dressing rooms are stocked with all the rider requirements, the lights are cued, the sound check is complete, and you've got your VIP pass. It's finally time to take you *Backstage*!

—Dana Dane, hip-hop icon and author of the novel, *Numbers*

BACKSTAGE

Mic Check . . . One Two . . . One Two
Let's Take It from the Top
Coming to the Stage . . . Krista Johns

I'M GOOD

by Krista Johns

ou ready to rip it, Yummie?"

"What the hell you mean? That's all I know how to do."
My face twisted up like the nigga had shit on his face or he
was speaking foreign.

He said, "Then get your doodie ass and let it do what it do.
Talking to me like I'm a nothing-ass nigga. This ain't yo daddy."

"Who the hell you think you talking to? Nigga if it wadn't for
me yo mama would still be selling fish sandwiches out her house
to pay her seventeen dollars a month rent that she stay being late
on, hollering it's hard times."

Ziggy usually would go on and give me what I wanted: ammuni-
tion. That's how we did before every show, straight shit-talked. I
always wanted him there. Anybody else—like my nigga, Bone, or
my bitch, Kai—would come with that gay-ass shit like "Let it do
what it do." And that's cool, but why did "I love you," always have

to follow? I ain't singing R&B, I be coming with that gangsta rap. By no means did I want that soft shit before a show. I grew up with Ziggy, and he could destroy someone's self-esteem—have you round here ready to kill ya self. *BOOM!*

I stood onstage and my eyes zoomed on Winky who was in VIP where I knew he'd be. His face seemed different tonight. He looked like he had something on his mind, but who don't? I was so high that I could have stood there in a zone and tried to figure out what's wrong with ole boy, but I caught myself, even though the weed that I had been blowing was so good that I could have forgot all about the crowd that paid fifty and better to see me and some other cat.

Some people look at me and say I'm acting sadity
'Cause I'm pretty but they don't know I'm putting dope in my city
I'm too shitty to be confused with an everyday bitch
Flip the script to get my chips
'Cause my goal's to get rich kind of quick

The crowd went bananas. I did eight of my best songs and walked the stage just like a man. And I had lyrics like a man, but I was too beautiful and feminine to reach down and shift balls that were without question not there. I walked in my heels like they were a pair of Air Force Ones. The iced-out hand medallion around my neck revealed a middle finger that swung like "fuck you, fuck you, and fuck you, too!" The world wasn't ready for me. BET had seen a few imposter broads claiming they were 'bout the business but there were always rumors they had ghostwriters. Their careers flashed so quickly that they were invisible just like their writers leaving you with thoughts of a Boost Mobile: *Where you at?* Me . . . I was too serious about this to be a memory.

I walked to my dressing room with an entourage like a heavy-weight champion. They were screaming my name, "Yummie! Yummie!" My face softened like an R&B singer. Oooh! I loved that! I closed the door behind me and found my room flooded with roses. You would think I had a bunch of admirers but that wasn't the case. I only had two who competed with each other for my love. Male and Female. Bone and Kai.

I smiled without bothering to read their deepest feelings on the little itty-bitty pieces of paper that accompanied the flowers although I was curious about who had won by sending the most. But there were too many bouquets, and they all looked alike. After all, roses are roses.

Winky had abandoned the VIP and was now in my dressing room. He was a big light-skinned dough boy. There was nothing sexy about him, not even his smile—his teeth were stacked on top of one another showing every bit of his thirty-two teeth.

"Yummie, your lyrics are getting tighter and tighter. Most rappers rappin' another niggas' lifestyle. Not you, Yummie."

I stood proud like, "Yep, that's me."

"You say what you mean and mean what you say, Yummie. What they don't know, Yummie, is that you really putting dope in ya city." He chuckled.

I looked at him, but I ain't say shit, trying to figure out what the fuck was wrong with him.

"Huh, Yummie?" He turned around to unzip a bag as he sang words to my song. *"I'm putting dope in my city. I'm too shitty to be confused with an . . ."*

"Winky, what you doing, and why the fuck you keep saying my name?"

He turned around with one brown-wrapped kilo brick of pure cocaine in his hand and more where that came from. "What you talking about, Yummie?" Like he had no clue whatsoever.

"What is you doing?"

He looked at the brick. "I'm bringing your stuff."

"Huh?"

"Your dope."

Maybe it was the beads of sweat on his forehead in a well air-conditioned room, or the bricks of cocaine in my dressing room, or the repetition of my name . . . but something made me come to the conclusion that something wasn't right. People think when you high it hinders your judgment, but a scientist who probably never smoked a day in his life came up with that theory. From a weed junkie's point of view, you think better.

I looked around for hidden cameras but I couldn't see shit but a bunch of damn roses. He noticed me looking around and he started looking like, "Is this a setup?"

"Winky, I don't know what you talking about, Winky. And what you doing with that dope, Winky?" I was calling his name as many times as he called mine. Saying it loud enough for the hidden cameras if there were any to hear me and set the record straight.

"Yummie, me and Chanae got into it," Winky explained. "She went on one 'cause she found out me and Catrina still messing around. You know they stay beefing. So I packed all my shit and I couldn't keep this there."

I knew both of them broads and knew it had to be only money 'cause no dick in this world was that good to make you fight over Winky's ugly ass. To each his own and there is somebody for everybody. Regardless of the foolishness he had going on, he still was out of order for bringing work up there. I mean, how was I going to take a big black duffel bag of coke along with my bag of clothes out of there? I'm a celebrity with fans, and some of them stayed around afterward with high hopes and expectations just to see me.

I took a deep breath, exhaled, and walked to the bag counting each kilo to myself. *1, 2, 3, 4, 5* . . . "Gimmie my shit," I said as I snatched the one out of his hand. "Twenty."

I zipped up the bag and started to put it under my vanity set when the door flew off the hinges. The noise scared me more than anything. I love my fans, Lord knows I do, but sometimes they could be so persistent. They seemed to be everywhere. You couldn't eat or shit. That was the price you paid for being famous.

But it wasn't my fans this time. FBI, baby. They handcuffed me and stinking-ass Winky.

The newspapers, TV, and magazines had a field day with me. They painted a picture of this greedy female drug dealer/rap star who had it all yet wanted more. What did they know? Since I had been with Hym8nenz (High Maintenance) Records, I had not received one royalty check. I had signed a fucked-up contract. How was I supposed to know the videos and studio time and limo rides came out of my money? I thought the record company got it like that. Why not cater to your stars? Contract? All I remember is the pen and the million dollars. The money I did receive seemed like a fortune at first but it slipped through my hands just like water. I only sold drugs to maintain my rich and famous lifestyle. What sense did it make to be pushing a Continental GTC Bentley and you pulling up in a McDonald's drive-thru scraping up change for a number ten? *Humph!* Sound like a damn fool.

Yet, I thanked God every day for allowing me the opportunity to get my music heard nationwide. So I really couldn't complain, and even if I did, who cared? Everybody goes through the struggle and everybody gets pimped. It's a part of life. Sheet! Not for long. Not my life. And that's a promise.

Hym8nenz be bullshitting but they did come through with a mad lawyer. He wasted no time and I was out in less than forty-eight hours on pretrial since I had no priors. Only familiar face in the courthouse was Kai, which was no surprise to me. Bone had seen the inside of a courthouse enough to last him a lifetime, and I respected that.

Kai had this worried look on her face like she was straining to take a dump. You would think I was facing double life with no parole. Kai was beautiful inside and out. Sometimes she could be a little dramatic and we would clash. How can I play my role if she playing hers? But that's a woman for you, so what should I expect?

Kai was just as feminine as me. I didn't want a stud. Never saw the point. Why have an imitation of a man when you can have the real deal? And I had one of them, too. They knew about each other and they hated loving me the way they did.

"You want your cake and eat it, too," is all they would say. Does that make sense? You damn right I'm gonna eat my cake. It's mine. What else am I supposed to do? What I loved about the both of them is they would try so hard to make me see that their gender is where I belonged.

Bone would eat my pussy trying to prove a point each time and he did; he proved that he could never eat me better than Kai.

As for Kai, no matter how wet that mouth of hers got she still didn't have shit to stick in me when I would holler "just stick it in" in the heat of the moment. A few times I saw the bitch looking around the room with my pussy still in her mouth for anything to penetrate this hot pussy of mine. I erased those thoughts quickly by pulling that bitch by the hair as hard as I could. "Bitch, I wish you would." She wasted her money on dildos and strap-ons that I would never use. I kept telling her I got a sensitive pussy. Only thing going in me is dick and tongue . . . She got hot every time. It is what it is.

As soon as I got home all I wanted to do was scrub the jail smell off of me. Kai jumped in the shower with me. I really didn't want her there. She hadn't done anything wrong, but I had been around females for two days and I didn't want to see no more ass and titties. I wanted to be in the presence of a good, cologne-smelling, dick rock-hard nigga. I usually don't bite my tongue; my first thoughts roll out my mouth. Maybe the two days had me feeling a little soft 'cause I let her mess her freshly done hairdo up by keeping her mouth on my pussy while the water poured on her head. I felt like I was going to faint and drop to my knees where she was. She ate me like she loved me, which she do. She ate me like she missed me, which she did. She ate me like I'm going to spend the rest of the night with her, which (oh my goodness!) I'm not!

After she finally left I drove straight to Bone's house. As soon as I walked in I wanted dick on my breath. I wanted to suck his dick and swallow it like a raw oyster. *Gulp.* He had plans of his own. He held me in his arms like I had been in Iraq. Welcome home. He pushed me on the couch—that's what I'm talking about. He pulled my dress up. Oooh! He ripped my panties off. Whooo! He peeled off his wifebeater. Umm! Umm! Umm! He dropped his boxers. Look at him. He got on top of me and started to eat me. Uh-uh! I pulled his head up. He looked disappointed. Shiiit, so was I. People know your role.

He got off me and walked his naked ass to the bedroom. I laid there for a hot second before following him. He lay back staring at TV . . . His dick was playing sleep, shriveled up like a newborn baby. I wanted to be mad like, "Don't start this shit," but instead I smiled. He let me have my way so much, but at some point he had to man up. Um! My pussy getting wetter. I looked at the time. It read six forty-five. I looked at his dick and waited for the time to read six forty-six so I could time myself like I'm in a race. It would take less than thirty seconds for his dick to wake up in my mouth. Twenty seconds for it to reach its full potential and two minutes and ten seconds for me to quench my thirst. On your mark . . . get set . . . go!

He pulled my hair, and luckily for me I'm not tender-headed. I stroked his dick just like he jacked it. I sucked his dick like I had a passion for it. I never took my eyes off him until I knew he was about to shoot babies all down my throat. Within seconds the time came and I looked over not once taking that big black dick out my mouth and just like I said it was six forty-eight, I mean six forty-nine. I climbed on top of him to kiss him and he always kissed me afterward in the past, but this time he turned his head to avoid my mouth. I kept trying. He kept resisting. It should have pissed me off but it was turning me on like he thought I was a nothing-ass bitch who wasn't worthy of his kisses. *Humph!* I'm crazy. Listen to the shit I say.

I was going wild trying to make him kiss me. We were like two untamed animals in Africa. Finally, he pulled my hair down, damn near breaking my neck, and gave me a hard, nasty, wet-ass kiss. He pulled back.

"Is this what you wanted? Huh?"

I just kept kissing him.

"Answer me, bitch!"

I looked at him. This man right here did something to me. I loved when he talked shit to me and called me a bitch, but only in bed—otherwise, we got a problem. He then stuck that dick in me farther than any tongue can go. He knocked on every wall to see if anybody would come to the door and answer. Within seconds I let him know he didn't have to knock no more and hollered, "I'm cummin!" I kept my eyes on his 'cause there ain't no looking at the clock with me. I can only do that shit.

From day one Bone made me forget I was this big-time celebrity who's not making a dime. Just like now, this nigga made me forget I just got busted with twenty bricks. He made me forget my only connect ratted me out. I'm telling you, dick is a mu'fucka. Now that I've caught a nut, reality sunk in and all the shit I didn't want to think about resurfaced. I used to think there was no comparison to dick but there is: weed.

"Bone, I'm gonna need you to get that money for me." From time to time I would let him hold my money if I couldn't get to my stash spot.

Bone replied, "I'm already knowing."

I trusted Bone. I trusted that if you put him in a room full of at least fifty women he was gonna fuck at least two before the night was over. Five more before the week was out and fifteen before the first of the month. You can trust me on that one. When it comes to money, I can trust he'll never touch it. He love me and I know this, and his excuse for being a fuckup is I'm not right either 'cause I got Kai.

I must've waited three weeks for some dope to flood our city. Nobody had dope. Drought season. My loyal customers were calling me like they were junkies. With each call, it had me on one like I got to have it. A want turned into a need then all of a sudden it became a must.

Bone constantly tried to spit knowledge to me. "Yummie, you really ought to sit down."

"Sit down and do what?"

He continued talking but I never heard the words coming out of his mouth besides "sit down" and "I got you," which I thought were interesting. I looked at him and wondered if he heard the words coming out of his mouth and did he actually believe them? Surely not. If he had me why did I pick up a pack in the first place?

"Anything you need just call me, and like I said I got you. I'm not gonna let you be out here messed up with nothing."

"What am I supposed to do, Bone? Come over here and ask for this, then come back and ask for that? Do I look like a puppy? Do I?"

"What you mean by that?"

I grabbed my keys and put my purse over my shoulder. "Right now we not seeing eye-to-eye 'cause you got me fucked up if you think you getting ready to kibble-and-bit me like some puppy. *Humph!*"

"You so hardheaded, can't nobody tell you shit," he said, raising his voice.

I pulled out of his driveway with a disgusted look. Who taught this nigga how to hustle? He wanted me to throw in the towel. Maybe go to Michael's and buy some yarn, crochet me a damn sweater to wear back and forth to court 'cause it's gonna be cold? Is that what he want me to do? How about I park my Bentley and get a Dodge Neon and let's just get low with it? I rode in disbelief. Fuck what he talking about. I gotta get me some dope.

My fans were holding me down. I performed in my city and the flyer promoting the performance said the money was to go toward my lawyer. The city showed me love. Now that's a support system. I put on for my city!

My promoter got in some ears and had *Hippity Hop* magazine there for a one-on-one interview with me. They were going to share with the world how a case don't stop nothing, and if one comes along the way, go out with a bang. Leave a trademark out here. I inhaled more dope than I usually smoke. (I stay calling weed dope to get a response out of people.) I consumed more alcoholic beverages than normal. I felt the love and it just had me on one. This was all for me, therefore let me show my appreciation.

Ziggy, at the end of the bar, kept hollering my name. I didn't realize it was him because who wasn't, though? It wasn't until I heard him holla "Ah, bitch," that I knew it was someone who was close to me. I laughed. That nigga stay trying to keep me humble if I wanted to get on a high horse. I nodded my head to let him know he had my undivided attention 'cause I wasn't going to try to out talk the music. A no-win situation. I needed my voice and was not going to make myself hoarse messing with Ziggy.

He pulled his pockets inside-out to let me know he broke. Ziggy's tight ass comes out with forty dollars a day and that's got to get it. If not, he got homies like me who will make it work. He got it, that's what makes it wild. I hate to call his pockets, but I'm willing to bet he at least got two hundred grand put up. He had a few bitches by his side and I knew their thirsty asses wanted a drink. I wasn't going to be an upset by asking him how much. I reached in my black leather Burberry and tossed him a thousand dollars still in the rubber band. Straight dope money. Straight slow motion. It went in the air; everybody looked at it in awe as if Venus and Serena were center court at Wimbledon. He caught it and I looked around for any other homies who needed a stack. I just wanted to toss another stack for the hell of it 'cause I could.

A table full of girls were popping bottles like they had that work. Let me find out. I chuckled when I saw my sister was among them. Cubby wasn't really my sister but we grew up together, so you know how that goes. We shared everything but the same umbilical cord. Although we busy doing what we do, it never mattered how much time passed since we last talked, when we did see each other it was just like we saw each other yesterday.

She don't sell a lick of dope. Credit cards were her hustle. She popping and they scanning that card like it's a platinum with no limit. I knew she was working them, though, and switching cards like the hoes switching their ass in here.

I peeped her going big by sending some dude a bottle. His table looked like he didn't need another one. When he smiled and tapped his homie to tell him, I knew she had a victim. If only he knew that one bottle was bait. My sister going to work you. Ole boy wasn't from around here, country-ass Murfreesboro, Tennessee, and it was obvious. Everybody who's somebody knows you, and I'm that somebody, and never seen him a day in my life. A big boogly bear fucker. Only thing worth discussing on him was his ice. His ice outweighed the bad.

Cubby threw her hands in the air so that I would come to her table. She stood up and hugged me. She introduced me to the nobodies. I wouldn't remember a damn name. Who are you? She motioned for the waiter to come our way while her other arm never left my neck. She started pointing the hand around my neck down on me like the man right chea.

She grabbed her bottle of Moët rosé and hit it and then put it to my mouth. I tilted my head back. We never stopped swaying to the music. The waitress approached us and instead of her stopping what we had going on she just held up her bottle. She knew what it was.

The victim had hoodrats who flooded his table shaking their asses, ready to give up the bootie hole, meaning anything goes. However, how could he pay them attention when we shaking it? They say the economy down. You couldn't tell looking at the atmosphere in here. Fuck what Bush was talking about!

Cubby and the victim, Wes, exchanged numbers and I knew it was just the beginning of something beautiful, especially if he had that work. Everybody claiming it's a drought. Now that the song was gone off I looked around at the familiar faces. Yeah they down!

All of these non-voting drug dealers that couldn't find no dope all of a sudden were into politics real heavy. "It's an election year. There's a war in Mexico," was the excuse for the drought. They had all the inside information like they had a chair in the Senate. The price had skyrocketed to twenty-four thousand a key. That's high to someone who buys weight. Listen to me when I tell you ain't nobody got no dope here for no damn ten a key! I'm used to paying nineteen or twenty thousand a key. The more bricks you purchase the more love is shown. It's somewhat like a wholesale market. With the ticket being as high as it was, the others that were not into politics sat back on the porch and complained like a hot sunny day: "I ain't never seen it like this." Meanwhile they steady spending and not making nothing. Do the math.

I called myself a different breed, a real hustler. Due to my circumstances (on bond), I had ballz bigger than some of these niggas round here. I will raise the price just a little so they will feel where I'm coming from. I will cut the dope to make up the difference and retrieve the same profit cause it's worthless if the profit and risk don't add up. They will feel like they are getting a deal from me and we all on some come-up shit. That's all people wanted: self-satisfaction.

I had a bad habit of counting my chickens before they hatched. I had plans for those twenty that I got busted with. Even with my dope being in some evidence room with exhibit tape on it waiting just like me to show up in a courtroom, I still couldn't stop thinking about it. I couldn't get it back, but you best believe I was gonna make it up.

Unlike a baby daddy, Cubby didn't let me down. She had showed Wes everything a pussy could do and if he wanted to pop a pill—Viagra and ecstasy, which was his gig—she would bring females to the bed with them. She was on some "It ain't no fun if the homies can't have none." She let them take that dick however they wanted it, but that money was only coming to her. She knew he was spoiling her but she kept up the demeanor of that's what a man was supposed to do. She reported to me everything, even shit that I didn't want to hear. I pretended to be interested but all I cared about was did he have some work and what was the ticket. During pillow talk, Cubby gives it up for the home team. Go Yummie! After a couple of weeks, he slipped and let the number twenty-two go over the airwaves. That pussy had to be good to make you get that comfortable. WOW!

Wes wasn't fooling me, though. He needed me just like I needed him. But I'm sure my need was more urgent. Why else would he be in Tennessee?

He invited us to go to Miami for his homie's birthday. Cubby was to round up as many pretty girls as she could. He paid for everybody's tickets. I jumped on the bandwagon 'cause not only did he have me on first class, recognizing the bitch that I am, but I was teaming up with Da Bar Spitter to do a track. Da Bar Spitter hangs tight with Wes. I've wanted to do a collaboration with him for a long time now. Anything he spit is hot, and me and him together was going to be bananas. I couldn't wait. I only charge twenty stacks to jump on a track. So do know this trip was going to be beneficial in more ways than one.

The weekend was filled with so much to do. The first night the party was aboard the Majestic yacht. It was filled with nothing but bosses so I fit right in. It was the boss of the boss's birthday. Happy birthday to you, too! These men were from all fifty states and everybody was representing their city to the fullest. They all brought women and if their mammy's pussy still got wet she could come, too! Fuck a birthday, this was a dope man's convention. I was in the right spot. Now tell me these muthafuckas didn't have no dope.

Their clique was so deep they really needed a name for themselves. They was shaking it. This clique definitely couldn't be overlooked. I was going to call them Fam from here on, 'cause after tonight they were my new family.

The yacht docked and we went to club BED in South Beach. Beds were throughout the club as part of the décor. There was no line for VIP, and as far as they were concerned we all were very important. They even shut down the club to the public. It was just the Fam. Everybody was good and drunk. One of Cubby's girls kept shifting from one leg to the other. Her pussy could smell money. Sit. Sit. Good girl. She was on some groupie shit, I felt. She was all right. I wouldn't have her as a showpiece but I damn sure would let her nibble on this pussy to show me what a fan she was to me. I wouldn't kiss her, though. She talked too much for me and acted like she know everything. A bitch with a bunch of degrees and don't know what to do with them. Just shut up!

"I want to make me some money," Danessa said.

Cubby motioned for Wes to come our way, and then she leaned and whispered in his ear. He looked at Cubby's girl and nodded slowly in approval. He walked over to the birthday boy and gave him a heads-up on what's going on. He looked our way and hesitated but the alcohol made him say: "What the hell. You only live once, gotdamn it." Wes came back and handed ole girl a bankroll. "Hold this, Cubby." A prime example of she know too much. She never bothered counting it.

Ms. Big Mouth Degree stood up and straightened her skirt like she had some class to her ass. She walked like your average broad across the room. She whispered in the birthday boy's ear and took him to the middle of the dance floor like they were some teenage sweethearts. Ain't that sweet! They going to dance. Maybe the DJ will play a slow song. Awwwww!

She started backing that ass on him. I said your average broad. She twirled around him like he was the stripper pole. He had two bottles in his hands with his eyes shut, bobbing one when he wasn't drinking out of the other, not paying her no attention. She unbuttoned her shirt showing off her bra. Oh hell! Now she a stripper. She got low with it and her skirt was hiked up. There went the class and all you saw was ass. She unbuckled his pants. Let me find out this made man is a stripper! He pulled out his dick and oh my goodness! This nigga wasn't even circumcised. His dick had to be shy and hiding from us. Come out, come out wherever you are! That boy needed to be ashamed of himself. All that money he got and he still got all that skin from birth. I blame his mama, though. That would have been a good birthday gift. That's money when you like, fuck it. She licked that dick. What? The loungers even stood up, including me. This undercover ho saw all these beds in the club and wanted everyone to see what went on in the bedroom. You got to be kidding me.

She stuck that dick in her mouth like an Almond Joy candy bar; now you see it now you don't. Everybody went wild. Bottles and glasses were in the air. Everybody wanted that nut. Even the DJ came out the woodwork for that nut playing "That Nasty Bitch" by Bust Down. He hit her character on point. He know her. It don't take a degree to know that. She sucked it like she wanted that nut more. You definitely know that! He took one bottle and jacked it on her head and face just like nut. I didn't know her name, but I wanted to know, "Who is that ho?"

"Danessa," Cubby answered.

> I throw rubber band stacks, keep rosé on deck
> These niggaz seein' my status, I'm getting exec respect
> Nothing less 'cause I'm the best invest in Mitchell 'n' Ness
> Gimme CEO status for the street whose next
> I contest any competitor but it's by my rules
> If Forbes came to the streets, I'll be leaving these fools.

In the studio, I ripped it with a point to prove. We had a hit on our hands. Every subject you could possibly think of rolled off our tongues outside the booth. Then Wes asked the question that was music to my ears: "How much you getting that work for?"

With a straight poker face I said, "Twenty-two. Why? What's up?" It's my birthday!

I was told I didn't need any money down. My down payment was my word. Not only was Wes connected but he ran deep. Who would think of crossing him? Him is them. Them is him.

My adrenaline pumped like I was going to jump out of my skin. You would think I just hit some dope, and I mean dope literally this time. I imagined what the streets were gonna say about me, saying aloud, "Man, we can't keep work the way that bitch running through it . . . Is that the bitch that be rapping like she moving that weight? . . . That's real."

"Man, I ain't never met a bitch like that . . . They don't make 'em like that. She one of us. What part don't you understand? . . . I wish I had a bitch like that. You can't tell me nothing."

As I rode down Broad Street solo with no regards to the law, I felt the same way; you can't tell me nothing.

I felt like the Feds had created a monster. I was on a straight mission. Shit don't stop.

Pitching a bitch and living life in these streets
Mad at the world 'cause certain muthafuckas don't want me to eat
But I'ma get mine a long time before you get yours
Hate me if you want, but hate me when I'm away on tours
Exploring the world, seeing life from a different view
Shit don't stop till I say that I'm through

Being the only one in the city with dope had me feeling like I had an *s* on my chest. I was dropping off work like I was saving the day. Look at what I do for my country. Can't? Don't tell me you can't find no dope. Can't is nowhere in my vocabulary.

After my first shipment, I received fifty keys and made a $150,000 profit. I went out and bought a laundromat for one of my cousins who was straight legit. I had to have somewhere for all those 120 loads of Tide boxes filled with bricks to be delivered. I studied the boxes like a mad scientist trying to figure out how they sealed it back up. I finally gave up and reached the conclusion the Fam was so connected they got Mr. Duds and Suds himself involved. He one of us.

Everybody around me played a part because after my misfortune I felt a little wiser. Some might say a little too late, but you never too old to learn. The shit that happened to me with the Feds was a learning experience. For example: I had no business picking up my work from Winky. I didn't need to be around the shit. I could make shit happen. What was I thinking? I was all on the front line. If anything went down, the front was going down first. Aiight!

Ziggy would make it happen for me. Even Scarface had Danny. Nino had G Money. I had Ziggy. They weren't the best examples, though. What started off good always ended up all fucked up and shit. I was gonna have to kill my nigga in the end. Fuck that shit! I'd been watching too many movies.

I dismissed myself early because I had a meeting with my lawyer. When I arrived at his office, there were two white guys dressed like the men in black waiting for me. What could they want?

My lawyer took me in a conference room with the men in black. We sat around the big table like some big shit was bound to pop off in this meeting. The secretary greeted us all with a bottle of Voss water. She shut the door to give us privacy. My lawyer talked. They discussed their proposition. Then I talked. It's going down!

I met back up with Ziggy at Kleer Vu, the best soul food spot in Tennessee, to make sure everything was everything with moving the weight. I am my brother's keeper. Afterward I walked him to his car. As always, he had a bitch in the car. There was something familiar about her so I kept staring like I was on some choose-up shit from a pimp's point of view. Ziggy thought that I was inter-

ested since I go both ways, he had a dime on his hands, and we
had the same tastes. Yeah right! I hate I'm not good at names.

"I know she look good. Quit looking at my bitch!" Ziggy said.
Then it hit me.

"Ain't nobody looking at yo bitch!" I couldn't get my words out
quick enough. I continued, "Hehehe she the one from the party."
I laughed in between my words. It was Danessa, the dicksucker in
the flesh.

"Yeah, I was there," she said, nodding her head.

"You were there?" I asked. She said it as if she attended a func-
tion or helped coordinate it. "Girl you wild," I added.

She had to know that. I popped my tongue from the roof of my
mouth making a noise a horse makes when it walks, hoping Ziggy
would catch the hint. Whoa, Kemo Sabe! I know I told him about
this ho and what went down at the party. They rode off and I
couldn't wait to see this nigga tomorrow cause she ain't nuthin.
I'm gonna eat his ass alive.

The next day ready to burn him up, she pulled up with him
again. Last night was cool 'cause it was nighttime. It's hard to see
in the dark. Today it is all sunny and bright. Spotlight. Is that what
he wants? Is he serious? What is he doing? He's got to be out of his
mind. Nah, he must not remember. He couldn't have. No way
possible. I knew my boy way better than that. He got out to holla at
me, then backtracked to the car. He must've forgot something. He
better not kiss her. He better not. Ooooweeeeee! He handed her
his stash of weed and pills to hold. As soon as he caught up with
me, I asked, "What you doing with her?"

"That's my bitch!"

"She ain't nuthin."

"You crazy," he said, sticking up for his bitch. I love Ziggy to
death, but he's a sucker-for-love-ass nigga. I hate that shit. He actually be loving these hoes. "Man, that's that bitch that ate Gumby up."

He looked at me like, *And your point is?* "Who ain't sucking
dick? I bet yo mama got a dick in her mouth right now."

"I'm sure she do, but yo ho gonna eat any and everybody. Fuck everything!"

"You gotdamn right. She fucking me right now, though."

"Whatever nigga." If he like it then I love it.

I got ambitions to climb from the bottom
You can get 'em 'cause I got 'em, stack my cash then knot 'em
By the bundles, never struggle 'cause I'm keeping my hustle
So watch this bitch as I pull tricks and keep on flexin' my muscles
So understand that I got plans when it comes to my grand
I'm not a man but I got potential to do all I can
Just to stand on these two feet, don't give a damn if they hurt
Doing dirt for what it's worth, yeah I'm passing out work.

I was on the road doing show after show for six months. Each performance was sold out. Everybody has their time to shine and right then I was the hottest thing going. I got used to my weekends being booked up. What I couldn't get used to was all the shootings and fights that would occur at my shows. I grew up in the hood and I used to be that one who shut the club down 'cause I wanted to fight. This was normal for someone like me. What wasn't normal was when the media tries to make you responsible for the actions of the next drunk muthafucka. How they going to blame me? All I did was jump on stage and do what I do best. Not once did the media or the protesters say anything about the bartender that made that drink for Mr. Act-An-Ass. Those little clubs in those little towns really show their asses. They always want to show out and let it be known they on the map, too. Bumfuck-Egypt we see you!

My love life was shot to hell 'cause of my work. I didn't care 'cause it's not work when you doing something you love. Kai was on some "You-never-got-time-for-me" mess. I quit explaining and arguing and just said, "You right." Well she was, and she didn't like that, either. I gave up.

Bone thinks I had went BIG, but I was still the same person that I was. He wasn't fooling me, he was just mad 'cause he expected me to show him a certain kind of love. He wanted the same love shown to me on the price of the dope for him. How? Now I am changing. So I put that song on my ringtone by B.o.B. *They say that I'm changing 'cause I'm getting famous.* He hate that, too. When he started acting like that I just separated myself. He'll come back around. He always do. Right now I got too much going on to be having sex.

"You need to get over here."

The urgency in Ziggy's voice told me something wasn't right.

"You just got here. Now where you going?"

"Are you for real, Kai?" Asking me some crazy shit like that. She went mute. She knew better. That question might cost her. I'm subject not to come home.

I got to the laundromat and the back room was filled with boxes of Tide. A regular day on the job. Five boxes were emptied on the floor. A pile of laundry detergent. Why the mess?

"What's up, Ziggy?"

"I opened up five boxes and they're empty."

"Huh?"

"Nothing ain't in these. I didn't want to open any more."

I picked the other ones up and they didn't feel like nothing was in them. I shook up a few and opened up two just to see for myself. I examined the other ones just like I did the first time to see if it's a shuck. No shuck. A simple mistake. One phone call will fix all of this.

I reached in my black Gucci backpack and looked on the back of the phones until I found the one with the letter *W* for Wes. I had so many phones and the prepaid ones all looked the same. This line was just for me and him. I dialed him.

"Yeah?"

"You sent the wrong boxes."

"Huh?"

Humph! He sounds like me. "These are all empty."

"Empty?" His tone changed. "Look, homegirl. I don't know what kind of game you playing, but me and my peeps don't play like that. That truck that delivered your shit came all the way from Florida. It didn't just stop at you. How everybody else shit that made it is good? You the only one calling with some 'it's empty.' You got sixty bricks. That's what it is."

Basically he was telling me I had to pay for something I never received. He sounded like a fool. It wasn't April so squash the April Fool's joke. Ashton Kutcher plays all the time, but this is too Mafia for TV . . .

"I ain't paying for something I didn't get."

"I know what we sent."

"I only touched seven. The others still sitting here. Come up here and see."

"I ain't getting on no plane to come there and look at some Tide boxes they sell at the store. Silly-ass broad."

"Let me call you back." I didn't know what else to do. I thought about what he said. "Tide boxes they sell at the store." Somebody switched them. It was that simple. I looked at Ziggy, who I had known since we were in the third grade. I hated to even consider that. There was nothing sheisty about us. We didn't believe in that; besides, he was with me. He wouldn't do no shit like that. He eating too good to bite the hand that feeds him. He wouldn't jeopardize our connect. Besides, he know these boys were not playing.

I had him take me step-by-step through what happened when he came inside. Me and Ziggy. My army. How we gonna go to war? It's not us playing and it's not them. Who was it then? I got back on the phone.

"How well do you know the driver?"

"What?" Wes was not being reasonable.

"Is there a possibility the driver could have switched it?"

"No."

"Are you one-hundred-percent sure?"

"Yeah."

"How you know that?"

"It's my uncle. That's how I know."

"Oh." I hung up but I didn't think that meant anything. I got an uncle who smokes much dope and will steal from you in a minute.

The only ones with a key to this place are Ziggy, my cousin who knows nothing about my drug business, and me. Ziggy's whereabouts were accounted for 'cause when he wasn't with me he was doing something for me. There was no way. It was on their end. What was I going to do?

You can't trust nobody. Somebody did this and now I am responsible for the bill. I wanted to catch a flight to Miami since Wes wouldn't come here but I felt that if I did there was a strong possibility I wouldn't be coming back. I had to think of something to make this right.

I wasted two days trying to think of what could have happened. I called Wes with all my theories and he didn't want to hear none of them. I didn't want to get out of bed. I thought if I slept the bad dream would go away 'cause you control your dreams. I knew I had to do something. I didn't know what these muthafuckas would do and when.

Ziggy was banging on my door. I got up to let him in.

"Get up, bitch!"

"For what?"

He handed me a lit blunt for breakfast.

"I don't know if I want that stank breath to touch my blunt. Your breath smell like it fertilized this dodie we smoking."

I hit the blunt, stank breath and all.

"How much you got?" he asked.

That is not nothing you tell. From the attire to the rides to the crib, the picture may look one way, but it's always another. He shook off his question since he knew he wasn't going to get an answer.

"Yummie, I got three hundred thousand. I don't know what our bill is and I know that my little three is not going to get it, but do you got something to donate to the pot to pay these niggas so we can keep this shit going? Yeah, they wiping me out but it's a bigger picture. Shit don't stop. Somebody got that shit and we gonna get cut off trying to solve a case where the pieces are not adding up."

"But we—"

He cut me off in midsentence. "Look, man. This is what I do. You rap. You got a life ahead of you. This all I know. This like Dr. Dre coming to you and willing to back you up all the way. You can't go wrong. How you gonna go wrong? This how I feel about this shit. Gimme my blunt and go take a bath, bitch!"

The water rejuvenated my spirit and mind. I felt like a new person. Or was it the blunt? Regardless, I had a plan. I was stuck between giving Wes everything we had or flipping what we had. I had to do something.

As I was drying off, Ziggy stuck his head in the bathroom. "You know your boy got some work."

"Who?"

"Bone."

Bone kept work but he couldn't serve us, but whatever he got I was going to get it. Something is better than nothing. I got ready to call Bone but had to think of what I was going to say. Our last episode wasn't nice. I smiled thinking of his last comment. "You gonna need me before I need you." What can I say other than he was right?

"You want your props?" I said to him on the phone.

"Who is this?" Now he don't know my voice. "What you want, man? My props for what?" he asked.

"You were right. I need you, baby."

"You don't need me, remember?"

"Yes I do. I miss me some Bone."

"What you miss?"

"I miss how you stick that dick in me and pull it out and stick it back in my mouth. That's what I miss. Can I come home? Hold on." I put the phone by my pussy and stuck my finger inside of me. *Umph!* Her slurping noise told him she missed him, too. "You hear her?"

"Yeah I hear her."

"Can I come get me some D?"

"Huh?" If you can huh, you can hear. Yeah my pussy was wet but did I mean dope or dick? Both. I miss fucking that nigga. He know it. "Can I come get me some dick?"

"Yeah."

The baddest bitch getting it, I've been getting mine
I fuck him for his pack then flip it 'bout ten times
I'm really in these streets like these niggas say they is
Did my time in the pen like these niggas say they did
So before this rap shit I was on that trap shit
First bitch in the hood that they know that had bricks.

I felt like I had done all that sucking and fucking for nothing. This nigga wouldn't go down on the price for nothing.

"You wouldn't go down on your ticket," he reminded me.

"You wanted me to give them to you for what I am getting them for. That don't make sense, Bone."

"That's what I'm trying to tell you."

"You wasn't buying as many as I'm going to buy. I can't make nothing off what you trying to give them to me for. That's what I sell them for."

I wanted to throw up the nut that I just swallowed. Muthafucka. He had thirty I was trying to take off his hands.

"Suck this dick one more time and I'll go down one stack."

A thousand dollars off. Wow! Thank you but no thank you.

He noticed I didn't comprehend. "A stack off each of 'em."

He didn't have to tell me twice. I know it sounds real hoeish of me. I was his ho so I didn't care what nobody thought. I nutted sucking that dick. That time I didn't swallow it. I let that dick squirt all over my face. I rubbed it all over my mouth like a messy eater. A bitch with no manners. That's me. I made sixty profit and was calling him for more. More D. Please baby baby baby please.

I pulled up at Bone's. Dick is a form of reconciliation. Nobody ever asks "Will you be my man?" Dick seals that. I pulled up in his driveway like I had called his black ass and gave him a heads-up. He looked surprised. "Damn. You don't call?"

"Nope. I'm home. What I'm gonna call for?"

I had interrupted his shower time. I followed him to his bedroom. I small-talked over the running water. His phone vibrated. I had no idea I was sitting on it. Ooh! That shit felt good. I'm such a freak. I pulled the phone from my ass. The screen read Danessa. I only knew one of them. I looked toward the shower. He fucking with her, too? Damn!

Instead of answering it, I pushed in his code. I flipped to the text and the majority were from her. *I love you. None of these niggas don't mean nothing to me. I loved you since I was little.* How old is this bitch? *What we going to do for our five year anniversary?* Five years? How they going on five and we going on nine years? I skipped all the bullshit and went to the sent. Time is everything.

"You miss me, Yummie? 'Cause I really miss you," he said from the shower.

"You know I miss you, Bone."

He texted her, *I only love you. These niggas don't have a clue. Yummie swear she a down bitch but she don't have shit on you. You the truth. I raised you. You my bitch and don't you ever forget it.*

The water stopped. I closed the message and locked it back. If you not careful you can tell somebody been on your phone. Not me! My stomach turned. I knew he was not using a rubber on her. She freaking. He freaking. Whatever they got, I got it. Sharing is caring. I know he mess with other women but I thought this nigga only loved me. I keep it one hundred. How come he can't? Disgust had me ready to leave.

"You know my folks got some more dope," he said, standing in the doorway choking the life out his dick.

Die Dick Die!

"What he got?" I asked.

"He got thirty more."

"How much?"

"What you gonna do for it?"

"Quit playing, Bone."

"I'm for real."

I knew he was serious and I would have been, too, had I not read the texts. "I'm on my period." Everybody else lying, why not me?

"Your mouth not bleeding."

"You know I like to take my clothes off and play with this pussy while I suck that dick."

His dick was getting harder. Say something. I touched my imaginary pad. "Did I leave any of those overnight thick pads 'cause I'm bleeding big clots? I think something wrong."

He let go of his dick. Not only did Bone give up, but his dick did, too. Good.

"I got to go to the studio. I hate when they just show up and expect me to be there. That's crazy." Another lie.

"You lucky you on your period 'cause I was gonna punish you."

I bet. "Can you have that for me in the morning?" I asked.

"I'll tell him to hold them for you."

It's so true when you look for something you find it. I had to tell somebody. I wanted to go straight over to Ziggy's but that would be like answering the phone because he can't hold water when it comes to his women. She'll know I know, then they will have one up on me. I went to Cubby's. She still messing with Wes and he did a wonderful job upgrading her. I told her about her homegirl messing with Bone.

"That's not my homegirl. She my homegirl's girl. I'll call her now to see what she will tell me. She tells everybody's business. Watch this." She quickly dialed a number. "Shiela, when I see you I'm smacking the dog shit out of you and your friend . . . You know what I'm talking about . . . Your homegirl messing with Wes and he bought her a car. As a matter of fact, you got a new X6, let me find out you screwing him, too . . . Nah! . . . As a matter of fact, I'm on my way now."

Cubby was calling her bluff and making up shit. Everybody knew Cubby loved to tote that pistol. She did time for shooting a girl. Ole girl on the other line started talking like she was trying to save her life.

"Umm, hmmm . . . Yeah . . . Ummm . . . Hummm . . . For real? . . . I don't care about that. All I care about is Wes . . . I know. Girl, I'm not like that . . . I'm not going to say nothing . . . Don't you say nothing . . . Wes don't care about nothing like that."

I was dying to know.

"Okay. Call me, girl." She hung up and looked at me.

"What? Tell me."

"Let me get that Patrón out first."

I paid my debt and waited for my work to come through. Wes claimed I don't know how to talk to people. It ain't me. Although I'm still bothered about the whole ordeal, I'm not tripping. I know I wasn't in the wrong.

"You hear that? Shhh . . ."

It was so dark in that damn laundromat of mine you couldn't see anything. The light turned on. Her eyes got big when she saw me but they got bigger when she saw two other men with me. They were dressed in black and wore gloves. They only weighed 185 pounds, if that. Little-bitty-ass niggas that didn't play. She had locked the door behind her. There was no going anywhere. She did that.

"It was you. You stole all my dope and was going to steal it again. Ha! Well, all their dope." I looked at them.

"Don't do nothing to me. Bone told me to do it. Please. I'm sorry . . ." She started crying.

"Bone said you were more down than me, but I wouldn't be crying right now. You all begging and shit," I said calmly.

"What you gonna do? You gonna kill me?"

"Girl, no."

She took a deep breath, relieved and ready to handle her consequences like a big girl.

"You remember how I met you? At the club you were sucking good dick. I had never seen that done in my life. You are amazing! That's how I want to always remember you. I'm gonna tell you how we gonna do this. You taking us to Bone's house like you just stole from us again with your scandalous ass. One slip up and they," I said, gesturing to the two guys, "gonna do you."

"Okay. Okay. I'll do whatever you want me to do," she said, still pleading.

I kicked that ho in her ass while we were going out the door. "Yeah, bitch. I know your kind."

She escorted us into the house. Bone had left the door unlocked. Just ready. He walked into the room wearing nothing but a towel and holding a bottle of champagne.

"For me?" I asked.

He dropped the bottle, causing it to shatter.

"I didn't get to see what kind. We celebrating. You didn't even tell me. Awww!" I smacked my face with both hands. "Do you know what today is? *It's our anniversary,*" I sang. "That's that jam. Ain't it, Bone?"

He stood speechless.

"How you going to do me like that? Bone, this me. You raised me, too. You were my first. I've been with you since I was sixteen. I had my first threesome with you. You played a part in who I am today. I'm hurt." I pounded my heart.

He still said nothing.

I picked up a candleholder and swung it at him, hitting him upside his head. "Say something, muthafucka. She suck better dick than me, Bone? Do she?" He rubbed his head, looking like a mu'fucka suppose to feel sorry for his ass.

"Nah, man."

"I don't believe shit you say. Let me judge for myself if she is a better dicksucker than me." I laid back and crossed my legs.

"Nah."

The guys pulled out their guns with silencers and for the first time spoke. "You don't have a choice, playboy. Go to your bitch and drop the towel."

He did just that.

She looked at me.

"Don't look at me. Look at the nigga who raised you."

She was crying.

He looked like he had to shit. His dick would not get hard. They both were not cooperating. Danessa kept acting like she was going to choke on his dick even though she could easily deep-throat it. I got up 'cause I had seen enough. The guys took one step toward them.

"You said you wasn't going to kill me." She was talking to me with that dick in her mouth. I had to look at her before going out the door. "That's my girl right there. You know I'm not going to kill you."

Their bodies hitting the floor was the only noise I heard.

I went back to the laundromat to make sure business was being handled. As I approached the back, I could hear Ziggy opening up boxes.

"Man, you don't even know how I feel."

"How you feel?" I asked.

"Just glad we got some work." I tossed a pillow at him as hard as I could.

"Why you throw that at me?"

"Since you doing all that pillowtalking I thought you would tell me everything I needed to know."

He stood up.

"Or do I have to have your dick in my mouth for you to breach our trust? Fuck the shit out of you, and while you sleep, go get a copy of the key to the laundromat. Silly mu'fucka! How could you tell her our business?"

"It wasn't even like that, Yummie."

"Then how was it?"

He shook his head no. "She kept talking about what the next man saying about me, how they got this and that. I just got tired of hearing it. So I cut it short by talking big-boy shit. I told her if I cut their water they'll die of thirst."

"So you told her you supplying them?"

"In so many words, yeah."

"You told her how we getting our shit? Ziggy, what's big-boy about that? That wasn't cool. I didn't like it and neither did Wes."

"He ain't shit! What he got to do with it?"

"I got a lot to do with it, Mr. Lover Boy. Did you forget to tell her that?" Wes entered the room with It Number One and It Number Two.

"Man, I don't want no problem."

"Oh, we got a problem."

"You going to do me like that, Yummie? That's your get down?"

"You need to be asking yourself that. Is that how you get down? I'm a bitch and I don't even get down like that."

It Number One and It Number Two started putting on their gloves. "That's fucked up, Yummie!" Ziggy screamed.

"No! You fucked up! You can't turn this on me. I'm so fucked up, but because of me you just gonna get your ass whipped instead of killed. Fucked up would be me sitting here watching you get your ass whipped. I can't 'cause I'm gonna want to help you."

I got up and shut the door. I wanted to cry. No matter how hard I tried to hold back, a tear fell from my eye. "Where my sunglasses at?"

The streets were calling. I had five soldiers remaining. I had to get my hands dirty whether I liked it or not. Ziggy was supposed to be right here with his mouth wired up so we could keep this shit pushing. They promised they wouldn't kill him. How you beat someone to death?

"He didn't serve a purpose," is all Wes would say.

This nigga think he God? *How are you the one to determine that?* "He was too valuable to be off the team." No matter how strongly I felt about it, I didn't bother going into a debate with Wes.

"Yummie, if it makes you feel any better, he didn't want to be here on this Earth."

"He told you that?" I asked, sounding naïve.

"He didn't fight for his life. He's gone on home."

Home?

I went to the studio to take my mind off everything that was going on. I just wanted to release it all.

Imagine getting some head from a bitch that is so vicious
Deep throat'n, don't choke, said the dick's delicious
Get malicious in conversation and forget about
Where u at and all da shit that came outta your mouth
Pillow talks a mu'fucka it turns niggas to bitches
Never knowing that how you do it is far worse than the
  open snitches.

While the producer mixed down the track, it sounded like all my phones were going off at the same time.

"You can't put them on vibrate?"

"Nah." I felt like an operator for a shopping network. It wasn't the same person yet they had the same story. They were all complaining that the work was bad.

"Bad? Is something coming back when you cook it?"

The producer looked at me. I had forgotten my whereabouts. I'm so used to being in here by myself. Bad habit. I went into the other room.

"Yeah. But I'm losing a zip off each nine-uh."

He's losing an ounce off each quarter bird. Nine ounces in a quarter bird. Nevermind. "Just let me know your losses and call me back."

I called Wes and informed him of what was going on. "That shit wasn't bad. I got some of the same shit right here. Nobody else not calling."

How did I know he was going to say that? He was really getting on my nerves. I didn't get back half of what Bone took from me. I'm down and now he want me to come out my profit to make up the difference. Man, this shit is crazy! "So what you want me to tell them?"

"Tell them to find somebody who know how to cook. That oil base you got to cook slow. Besides, how they going to complain when there is no work in the city and they are getting it on consignment? They were not going to do anything but cut it anyway. Tell them don't cut it."

How I look telling them that? That's bad business. Him not trying to straighten this out was bad business. I was beginning to feel Wes was like the record contract I couldn't get out of. I couldn't win for losing. That's why I ain't got nothing!

My lawyer called me first. "Thank you Jesus." My case had been dropped. I paid him enough. They say them Jews know what they doing. He made a believer out of me. Handle your business. I see you!

I turned on the television and that fast it had leaked to the press. Damn! Did they know before me? I thought my fans would be happy for me. The press, the world, people's fucked-up way of thinking had turned something positive for me into something negative. They even had a number you could call to vote whether I was snitching or not. What? Why couldn't they accept the fact that I paid seventy-five thousand dollars to my lawyer and would have given him more to get me off?

I had a meeting with my record label. Every time something popped off or caused controversy, I thought they finally were going to let me go. I couldn't be that lucky. My album was supposed to drop in two months and the following Tuesday I was scheduled to drop my first single. I had the full layout of my first video. I was trying to get them to let Quanie Cash direct my first video. These meetings made me sick though. They sat around and sniffed a bunch of cocaine and thought about how they were going to screw me around.

"Well we think 'cause of the bad publicity that we should just put your project on the shelf for a minute."

"What's a minute?" I asked all frantic. I knew it was going to be some shit in the game. When I think of a shelf I think of it being dusty. Is my album going to collect dust?

"We are in the same city. We'll call you. Let's just see if everything that is going on in the media blows over. Nobody loves a snitch in the music industry."

"I ain't no muthafuckin snitch!"

"Calm down. I'm not saying you are. It just doesn't look good. That's all."

I called Wes to vent and let him know what they were saying about his number one hustler. I had already sent that money. I only owed him like one hundred thousand. I knew he was going to trip. A nickel bag sold in the park, he wants in on it. I was doing my best to round it up. It's hard when your clientele is short-handed.

"So, is it true?"

"Is what true?" I asked. All I could think about at the moment was what they were saying about me. I didn't know whether he was going to call the number and cast a vote.

"Did your case get dropped?"

"Yeah." I didn't sound like someone who was grateful or blessed. The case being dropped seemed more of a curse. Maybe it was just my punishment for all the wrongdoings that I had done in my life. Karma. My music was doing so well when I caught the charge. Now the case was gone, I'm not doing good at all. They want me to become a Ja Rule.

Wes sat on the other end of the line quiet as a church mouse. Mouse. Rat. Wrong metaphor.

"I'm going to have that money for you in the next few days."

"Forget about it."

"For real?" 'Bout time he showed me some slack. Now he was being business-minded. Then I paused. Was he quoting the movie *The Godfather*? What was he going to say next? Just leave the gun, take the cannoli? I wanted to ask, "Are you done fucking with me?" But I couldn't bring myself to say it.

I called back an hour later, and my assumption was correct. The number had been changed.

Somebody told somebody some story about what I did
What did I do 'cause what I did affects the way I live
They said I said something (huh), so what I say
I told what to who, to the cops, that ain't no way to play
Miss me with your misery history's gonna prove it
Dat snitching ain't in my blood but yours we can't remove it.

I had isolated myself in the studio, making hit after hit to prepare myself if I got locked up. I didn't want the fans that I still had left to forget me. *I can't be forgotten.* I put on my headphones to block out any sound. The headphones also prevented negative thoughts from coming to the surface. I wanted so bad to write, but the pen wouldn't write shit that made sense. Words turned into scribbles.

I held my head to prevent the migraine from coming. In a short amount of time, BET had pulled every video I had. I had mad publicity but the wrong message; no snitching. How that sound? I worked too hard my twenty-four years on this earth for this to be where I am. Where am I?

I despise a snitch. I never understood how a snitch could do what they do and walk the same streets and breathe the same air as the person they told on like it's nothing. That's unbelievable to me. I can't sell one brick 'cause a mu'fucka scared of me. Most of them locked up and the ones that are not act like they're done with the game. Yeah right! I don't blame them though. I wouldn't mess with me.

Kai strolled into the studio dressed like she was ready to go to a major event. She seldom goes out. She probably just shit, shaved, and bathed to come here. This is her happening spot. Her perfume cleared my sinuses. My mind was so gone I couldn't think of that smell to save my life even though I had the same perfume. She dressed like she ready to do something in that little skirt. I'm willing to bet she wasn't wearing any panties. She probably contemplated sex all the way up here. I hate to be the one to disappoint her 'cause I'm not thinking about her ass.

The engineer had left so it was just the two of us in the studio. She started rubbing my shoulders to ease the tension. She felt it. My mind went elsewhere. *Snitch.* I couldn't think of one person in my family that sold out. *Snitch.* Me. Never. *Humph!* The shit they say. I tell you they will say anything out here.

Kai had eased in between my legs and I never noticed her. Shows how much I was paying attention. She squatted down and began kissing my inner thigh. I looked at her. I couldn't be turned on tonight even if my life depended on it.

"No, Kai."

She pretended like she didn't hear me. I didn't want to have to repeat myself since she probably thought I was playing hard to get. Instead I rolled my chair back, away from her.

"Kai, I said no. What part of no don't you understand?"

"You sometimes say no and we still do it."

"Man, I can't do this."

She stood up and came toward me. "What you mean you can't do this?"

I didn't know what I meant. Was I actually speaking of the moment or of us in the present. Everything around me didn't make sense no more.

"Exactly what I said. Look, man, I don't need this right now."

Not able to leave well enough alone, she had to go and say, "It's always what you need. What about what I need? It's not always about you although that may seem hard for you to believe. I sit around and let you do you."

"You let me?"

"I never say nothing."

"You let me?" I couldn't get past that. How she going to let me do anything? I am a grown-ass woman. She's like the rest of these mu'fuckas, just say anything. I took the same hand that was holding this big head of mine and wiped down my face real slowly as if to change my expression. Here comes the drama. I swear this girl needed her own reality show.

"When you gon' realize it's me that loves you? Everybody else don't mean you no good. Bone didn't do half the shit I do. Now he dead and I thought he was always the problem, but it wasn't him. It's you."

I didn't want to be reminded of that. That's why I hate telling people shit. I got up 'cause I had heard enough. Meeting adjourned. She stood in front of the door because she didn't want me to leave.

"Move."

Tears flooded her face like someone in her family just died.

I was exhausted and it read all over my face. I exhaled. Here we go again. I turned my head to the right because I didn't want to see nor hear this shit. Out of all the shit going on with me, look at this. Does it ever stop?

Somebody, anybody, blow my gotdamn brains out! *It can't be that easy, huh Lord? You only gonna put on me no more than I can bear?*

I looked at her. She was still talking. Did this girl ever stop? Obviously not. I could hear her, but the words were not registering. She repeated herself so much that I could say it for her if she decided to take a break. I couldn't forget that if I wanted to. How? She's the type who goes on and on about everything that she had ever done for you. All the ripping and running, the penitentiary chances, the meals she cooked, to the gas she put in my car. A car she drives. How that sound? How I never paid her for the penitentiary chances. Yeah right! I felt I did so much for her that that was her obligation. I took good care of her. She my bitch, why wouldn't I? Anything she asked for she got and this bitch mouth stayed on ask. Her next victim got problems for real. She better have money.

So in reality, we even. Fair exchange, no robbery. I could try to bogart my way through the door, but she likes to scratch. I didn't have time for that. She the only female I know that don't go to the nail shop. A natural bitch. Her nails were not long but they were strong. They chipped in the right places to give them the sharpness they needed to draw blood. I think she kept them that way so that she could use them as a weapon.

Because of her tears and on some prove my love shit, there was no doubt in my mind she wouldn't fight me today. I walked back to the console and pushed record because a song played in my head and maybe I could get Kai on a skit. Since she wouldn't realize it, she'd be spilling her heart out and it'd be genuine. I chuckled within. You got to laugh to keep from crying.

"I love you, Mayam."

She said my government name as if that made a difference. Only white people called me that.

"I've done everything that I could possibly do, and it's not enough."

Don't tell me Kai going to throw in the towel, too. I never expected that. I thought she would be the last one standing. Just goes to show nothing last forever.

"What have you done? What makes you so different than anyone else?" I had all day to wait on an answer. After all, what else did I have to do? Nothing. I didn't have a nigga, no friends, no work, no money, no fans, and now my bitch was getting ready to leave me. I still didn't give a damn. I sat down.

"You don't love me like I love you."

"How you know? You don't know that." She was pissing me off. "Kai, you stay with your hand out. You don't do shit for me. Everything you do for me I do for you in return. You don't pay a damn bill. Say you do! You think you look that good? I got a bitch that's killing you." I didn't. She will never tell the next muthafucka she left me.

She got ready to charge me. I looked at my gun at my side. *Come on, you don't want to do that.* I wasn't fighting her today. I wouldn't kill her, but I would do some *Harlem Nights* shit and shoot her in her pinky toe. See if she love me enough not to press charges. Add that to the list of sacrifices. Let's test our love. I mean, how much time could I do for a pinkie toe? I bet I would've done more time for the coke than the toe. It's the law.

Her eyes followed mine.

"I promise, you don't want to do that today. I promise, you don't."

Her Keith Sweat face disappeared. Her tears were going nowhere with me so she tried another approach. Lil Jon in the house. I could tell she was getting ready to get nasty by her mean mug. She was moving her head like I had just conjured a major beat and had a hit on my hands and she was one of many that was feeling it. We all know Lil Jon will get a muthafucka whipped in the club. All I can say is don't do it!

"You use to talk about Bone like he that nigga. That's not the same nigga that didn't go to court with you, is it? Is that the same nigga that swore up and down it wasn't his baby, as if me and you could make one? *Tah!*" She let out a nasty laugh. "He didn't contribute toward the abortion, nor was he there. Oh! Don't tell me he was there. Was he, Yummie? I didn't see him, but he was right there." The bitch touched my heart.

"What you said!" What else was I going to say? I bobbed my head to the imaginary beat we all were vibing to. Don't stop now.

"It hurt when he did you the way he did, didn't it, Yummie? You so smart, yet you so stupid."

"Yo mama." I knew her mama was dead. She didn't give a damn, neither did I.

"He didn't do half the shit I do!"

I didn't want to hear all that shit again. "Get your ass outta here, Kai. I'm done with yo ass, too."

"How you think yo charge got dropped, muthafucka?"

"What?"

"How you think your charge got dropped? Fed cases don't get dropped, you stupid muthafucka. You thought it was God, huh? You thanked him, didn't you? Just like you. You thanked everybody but me."

She lost me. Confusion was all over my face.

"I'm the one that sat in an abortion clinic while you killed a baby I didn't make. I can't even have kids and here you are just killing 'em. Your form of birth control. I'm the one that was in court with you. I'm the one that cried my eyes to sleep 'cause of the time you faced."

"I didn't cry, so why you crying?"

"You so fucking hard. You should've had a dick, you ungrateful bitch. Yo ass wouldn't have been so hard if they would've gave you all that time they was talking. But, see, I know you under all that armor you wear, Mayam. Youse a bitch. Youse a me."

I never heard Kai talk like that. I guess R. Kelly hit it on the nose; When a Woman's Fed Up.

"I love you so much I didn't want you to do a day. I'm the one that went to the Feds and made their job easy. I'm the one that cut the deal with them."

"The Feds can't do that. You don't even have a charge."

"The Feds can do what they want to do." She not only worked for them she cosigned for them also. Where was this bitch's badge at? It wasn't around her neck on a long necklace. It wasn't on her side belt, nor in her wallet. Perhaps her purse? Nah! I couldn't see it. It was right there. I pointed at her heart. This bitch got snitch in her blood. Yeah, it was over.

Having no idea what I was thinking, she said, "Yeah, that's love."

"So, what deal you cut, Kai?"

"Every drop off I told 'em."

"You what?"

"I told them every time and every person you dropped work off to."

"Man-Man?"

"Yeah Man-Man. You or Man-Man?" She held up her hands—Man-Man in one hand and me in the other. My hand was higher than Man-Man. Lucky me.

"Man-Man is my cousin, you stupid bitch!"

"See, I knew you wouldn't understand; that's why I never told you."

"Bush?" I had to know.

"Bush, K.D., and Rachid."

"I grew up with all of them."

I had tears in my eyes. What had she done? She misinterpreted my tears and leaned in and kissed me with those same lips that she ran her mouth with.

"See? That's love, Yummie. Nobody loves you like I do."

"I don't want you loving me."

She backed away.

"That's that scary love. See, you thought you knew me, but you don't have a clue who I am. You don't listen to my music. My fans—well the fans I had before you did what you did—knew me better than you. I say what I mean and I mean what I say. I don't give a damn about going to jail. This is my first charge, bitch! I meet the safety valve."

"What's that?"

"You work for them and you don't know what that is? Less time for first offenders. You so fucking smart. I'm hot at you for not doing your homework. All I give a fuck about is my music and these streets. The streets would be waiting on me. My music was gonna be heard while I laid down. Why you think I've been in the studio doing a Tupac? I've been meeting with my entertainment lawyer and Jimmy Iovine at Interscope Records, and I was getting out of this contract and branching off to start my own label. Thanks to you, Miss Federale"—I let my tongue roll like a Mexican—"I lost that. I lost my fans. I lost my plug. I lost my soldiers."

"You got me."

I looked at her. She was beautiful inside and out. She meant well, but not what I stand for. Not representing me and what I'm trying to do. A tear fell from my eye. I thought of all the shit she did without her throwing it up in my face this time. Damn! I was gonna miss her.

"Naw, Kai. I'M GOOD."

She looked at me. A tear fell from her eye, too. She knew it was officially over. I picked up the nine. The red button was shining, meaning everything we said, and were still saying, was being recorded. A smile crept onto my face. I thought of my fans coming back to me 'cause my music was gonna live. I put the nine to my head. Nobody would ever believe Kai did that shit on her own. "I'd rather be dead than labeled a snitch. Here go your payment for fucking off mine."

BOOM!

Now that's a muthafuckin song for you.

To the Beat and You Don't Stop . . . Ya Don't Quit . . .
One for the Money . . . Two for the Show . . .
Come on Harold Turley . . . Rock This Show

CHASING THE RING

by Harold L. Turley II

Chapter 1

The clock on the scoreboard read zero, showing proof the game was over. Trey, filled with exhaustion, was jumping for joy knowing he was only one step away from fulfilling his dream. The championship ring he craved was finally within his grasp. He could taste it. This would finally validate his career and silence his critics.

Trey headed back to the locker room, where a team of reporters stood at his locker waiting for him.

"Trey! Trey! What a game tonight. Tonight you played like you had a purpose, were you trying to send the league a message? Thirty-seven points and thirteen assists—what inspired you tonight?" a reporter asked.

"No, it wasn't about trying to send a message. I just felt real good tonight. I wanted to come out tonight and be aggressive hoping it would put us in a good position to get a win. Thankfully,

I was able to get into a groove and the shots just kept falling and we were able to come away with the victory."

"You've won Rookie of the Year, you are a seven-time All Star, and have been MVP of the league three times, yet you haven't been able to win a championship. What do you say to the critics who say you don't have what it takes to win a championship?"

Trey couldn't help but laugh. Here he was one win away from achieving his ultimate dream and still, somehow, a reporter would try to find a way to diminish that light.

"Susan, you ask what do I say to them? My reply is nothing. I don't have anything to say to them. I allow my play on the court to do my talking. All I can do is give every ounce of me and play as hard as I can. Thankfully, tonight that was enough for a win. Right now we know that we are close and we can finally see that light over the mountaintop. But we still have a lot of work to do. If we lose the next three games all this talk is for nothing. We still have a task at hand and we don't want to lose sight of that. That is what happened last year. Last year we put ourselves in a good position to win yet lost in Game seven, so we know this year to take things one game at a time and not to take Dallas lightly."

"But with that said, up three games to one some might say you are the odds on favorites to win Game five on your home floor."

"Some might, but we aren't one of them. You won't catch me making any predictions, Susan. I'm not about to give Dallas any bulletin-board material. The only thing that I will predict is that both teams will come out and play hard on Saturday and try to get a win. Hopefully, with God willing, that will be us," Trey said, then winked.

The reporters started to laugh, all but Susan, who kept probing.

"Trey, surely with the next game being at home, you have to have some extra motivation."

"I'd be lying if I said we didn't. I love the city of D.C. Nothing would make me happier than to bring this city a championship. Of course, we want to do it on our home floor and that is what we are going to try to do. So if you'll excuse me, ladies and gentlemen, I need to take a shower. I'm sure you'll have more questions during my press conference. Until then, would you please excuse me?"

The crowd started to disperse, all except Susan.

"I hope you don't think I'm going to let you off that easy?" she asked.

"Actually, I was hoping you'd follow me to the shower and finish the interview there," Trey replied with a devilish grin.

"Boy, you know you aren't ready for that!"

"I'll race you there if it's like that. You and I both know it's not me. You are the one who is holding out," Trey replied.

"And you know exactly why there will be none of that so don't go there! This is your doing, not mine!"

"Okay, let's not go there. You are right!"

"Excuse me, Mr. Winfield, I'm sorry to interrupt, but there is a gentleman here to see you," one of the team managers said.

"It's no problem, Billy. Did he say who he is or what it's about? I haven't taken my shower yet."

Nervous, he replied, "I'm sorry, Mr. Winfield. He said his name is Slim and he is a friend of yours. He said you would know who he is."

Out of all the names to say and in front of all the people. Luck wasn't one of Trey's strong points. He could see the anger on Susan's face the minute she heard Slim was here. Trey knew he'd have to find a way to explain.

"Billy, do me a favor and escort him back to the lounge. Tell him I'll be out once I take my shower."

"No problem, Mr. Winfield."

The second Billy turned to leave, Susan jumped right in with her rant. "What is Slim doing here? Please tell me you are not still dealing with him?"

Trey didn't respond.

"I can't believe you are still dealing with Slim!"

"Susan, please don't start. I just played a hell of a game and finally can smell the championship I've been chasing my whole career. Please don't ruin this moment for me right now talking about Slim. I really don't want to argue with you."

The look on her face said she didn't care. "Just tell me this then, are you still using?"

Trey grabbed her by the arm and pulled her into the trainer's room where they would have more privacy.

"No, I'm not! I swear! I told you I stopped and I meant it."

"Then what is he doing here, Trey?"

"Susan, whether you like it or not he is my friend. What do you want me to do, just turn my back on him?"

"Friend? You have to be kidding me. You call that man a friend?"

"Yes, I do."

"That man is not your friend and you are too blind to see it . . . You know what, you are right. I'm out of here because I see where this is going and I don't want to ruin your mood. Great game tonight," Susan said as she began to walk away.

"Susan, please don't be like that. You know I miss you. Can we please just put this behind us? Let's hang out tonight and celebrate. Let's do something, anything, it doesn't matter to me. Whatever you want to do is fine. I just want to spend some time with you and try to work this thing out. You know how I feel about you," Trey pleaded.

"I'm sorry, I'm busy. I have to meet a friend," Susan said and then turned and walked out of the training room leaving Trey behind. Trey clasped his head in his arms. He knew that regardless of what he said, if he wasn't telling her that he no longer associated with Slim, it would cause an argument. And that was a battle that he wasn't going to be able to win. Regardless of their troubled past, he would never turn his back on a friend, and Slim was one of his best friends in his eyes.

Trey walked out of the training room and quickly threw on a team sweatsuit. It made no sense to take a shower now. He might as well go to the lounge to see what Slim wanted and get it out of the way. That way he could use the rest of his time trying to figure out a way to get Susan back.

"There is my man," Slim greeted Trey when he walked into the room. Slim walked over and gave him a brotherly hug.

"I have someone I want you to meet. This is my new artist, Candi," Slim said. She quickly caught every bit of Trey's attention. She was gorgeous and had a body to die for. She stood five foot seven, light skin, and weighed no more than 135 pounds.

"Hello, it's nice to meet you. Slim talks about you all the time," Candi said. She walked over to him and gave Trey a kiss on the cheek. Trey, amazed, stared at Candi. It was as if he was hypnotized by her beauty.

"You okay, homie?"

Slim's question broke Trey out of his brief dazed state.

"Huh, naw, I'm cool, champ. Susan was in the locker room and we were rappin'," Trey replied.

Slim broke out in laughter.

"You love playing with fire, don't you? I thought that was dead and over?"

"It might be now for sure. She knows you were here."

"Gotdamn! That woman still doesn't fuck with me? Shit!"

"She is past just not fucking with you, I think she flat-out hates your ass, nigga," Trey said laughing.

"Whatever, well I have just the cure. I'm having something at the club tonight to celebrate Candi's welcome to the label and I want you to swing by."

"Nigga, you must be out of your mind. I'm in the middle of a championship run. I can't be out partying it up. This is the Finals, I don't need any distractions. I don't care if it's Susan or you! That is the last thing I need."

"I'm hurt! All I'm saying is, swing back for an hour or two and then bounce. No one is telling you to get blasted or anything. Plus I want to rap to you about something business related."

"What's up?"

Slim looked at Candi. "Not here. Tonight! Just meet me at the club. You don't have to stay long. Just give me a moment to pull your coattail to a couple things and then you can bounce."

Hesitant, Trey agreed. "Okay, but I'm not staying long."

"Cool!"

"Now, can I please take a shower? I'll meet you there in about an hour or so. I have to do this press conference. You know how the league is."

"That's what's up. I'll see you later tonight," Slim replied.

Chapter 2

It had been awhile since Trey had been in Club Nikki. He looked around and noticed how much things had changed. It had started out as a pool hall, but now was upgraded to a club. Trey walked around searching for Slim. He wanted to be in and out as quickly as possible. He had a long day ahead of him tomorrow and the sooner he could get some rest, the better.

"What's going on, Trey, great game today," someone said.

"Hey, what's going on, Ricky? Thanks! I see y'all have got the place looking nice now."

"It has been a minute since you've been here. I forgot."

"Yeah, I don't get out much during the season, trying to stay as focused as possible."

"I can respect that. What brings you out tonight then?"

"I need to get up with Slim about something. Have you seen him?"

"Yeah, he's in the back," Ricky replied.

"Thanks. Let me get back there so I can get out of here and get home and get some sleep. I have practice in the A.M. I'll get up with you after the season though."

"That's what's up!"

The two of them shook hands and then parted ways. Trey continued to walk through the crowd, trying to get to the back when someone grabbed his arm. He quickly turned to see who it was.

"Hello, stranger," Candi said.

"Well, hello to you. Is your man still in the back?"

She moved in closer. "Slim is not my man. He is only a friend and my business partner. I don't have a man but if you want to apply for the job, I'll be glad to set you up an interview."

"Is that right? Well what does the interview process require?"

She gently kissed him. Her sensual touch was enough to make him fully aroused.

"I'll tell you what, meet me on the dance floor before you leave and we can discuss it further in detail. I know you have business to attend to with your boy."

Right on cue, the DJ started to play Snoop Dogg's hit song "Sexual Eruption" as if he heard their whole brief conversation.

"I'm a firm believer in why wait until later for something we can handle right now? Slim isn't going anywhere."

The two of them headed out to the dance floor. Candi didn't waste any time gyrating her body against Trey. It wasn't long before the two of them were passionately kissing. It was as if the two of them were having sex on the dance floor. Trey broke away. He couldn't take it anymore. He barely knew her but knew one thing, he wanted her and at that moment he couldn't have her. He had other things that needed his attention. Plus, it wasn't right. His heart belonged to Susan and having sex with Candi wouldn't be the way to prove he had changed his ways and grown to become the right man for her.

"What's wrong?" Candi questioned.

"Nothing, I have to catch up with Slim. I'll find you before I get out of here."

"Make sure you do," Candi replied.

Trey headed to the back. Slim was sitting down at the table playing poker.

"If it isn't the superstar, what's up, baby?" Larry said as he got up to greet Trey.

"What's happening, fellas," Trey said.

"You were on fire tonight. It looks like you are finally going to get that ring, homie. You can finally get that monkey off your back."

"That's the plan."

"I know that's right! What are you doing out? Shouldn't you be getting some rest?" Larry questioned. "Game five is right around the corner."

"I'm not staying out late. I needed to get out for a few so I figured I'd come down here and check out the spot. I figured why not celebrate a little bit. Plus, I needed to rap to Slim for a quick few."

"I know that's right!"

"Look here, fellas, y'all are going to have to excuse me for a minute while I rap to my man about a few things," Slim said.

"What about the game?" Larry asked.

"Nigga, your money isn't going anywhere. I have all night to take it. I'll be back," Slim replied as he started to get up from the table.

"Come on, Trey, we can talk in my office."

"Office? What the fuck are you talking about?"

Slim started laughing. "A lot has changed since you were last around. You got to remember you've been out of the loop for a while. I bought this place a couple months ago."

"What, you've gone totally legit?" Trey probed.

"Yes, I told you I was. I'm done with all that street shit. The record label is starting to take off and now I'm going to get the club the same way. It won't be long before I'm bringing in some serious money the right way."

"I'm shocked!" Trey replied.

"Come on, Trey, can you give me some credit? I'm not asking for a lot, but damn at least give me a little bit."

"My bad, my bad! It's just all a little shocking, you know?" Trey extended his hand out to Slim. "I'm proud of you."

Slim slapped him five.

"Well to your office we go. Show me the way, champ," Trey replied.

Slim turned and headed out the room with Trey following closely behind him. Once they reached Slim's office, he closed the door behind him. Trey surveyed the office. He started to really take Slim seriously. Maybe he had turned his life around.

"I'm impressed! I must say, I really am," Trey said.

"Thanks, that means a lot to me. Yeah, Candi set up the deal for me. She is my partner in this little venture."

"Oh, really? I thought you said you just signed her."

"I did, to the label. I never knew she could sing at first. We met on a personal level in the beginning and our friendship grew."

"Your friendship, huh? Is that all she is? I mean, is there something else going on with the two of you?"

Slim easily saw through the bush Trey was trying to run around and knew exactly what he was getting at. "It's cool, homie, do you!"

"What are you talking about?" Trey questioned.

"I know you like the back of my hand. And your eyes are wide and bright. I could see that at the arena. It's cool. We are only friends and business partners, Trey. Who she fucks, is who she fucks. That has nothing to do with me. As long as she keeps this place packed and people buy her album, that money will pour in and that is all that matters to me is the bread. Now, if you come between that, then I'll have a problem," Slim said and started laughing.

"Cool!"

Slim laughed harder.

"What's so funny?" Trey asked.

"Nothing!"

"Tell me," Trey shot back at him.

"I just find it funny how you were bitching about possibly losing Susan for good not too long ago and now you are in here asking about Candi. My how quickly things change; Susan seems like a distant memory if you ask me."

"Nigga, Susan and I aren't together. She left me, remember? I'm free to go at whoever I want to."

"You don't have to front for me. I've known you all my life. So I know better than to believe that bullshit. I know Susan has you wrapped around her finger. Your ass just doesn't know how to tell new pussy no. That has always been your problem. That's the reason why y'all aren't together now."

"Yeah, whatever! We aren't going to go there because it was more to it than just that. Don't forget, I know your ass, too, and I know you want something so let's cut the bullshit. What's up?"

"First, hear me out before you say anything."

"Okay, what's up?"

"I need you to throw the game on Saturday," Slim said.

Trey started to laugh. "No, seriously, what's up?"

"I'm serious. I need you to throw the game. Right now, every one knows you are on fire so y'all are a heavy favorite to win. If y'all were to lose the game think of how much money the person who bet on you to lose would win. Like the Super Bowl last year, one guy bet one thousand dollars on the Giants and when they upset New England he was paid well over a mil. This is easy money. I'm not saying lose the series, just the next game."

Trey stood up.

"You have to be out of your fucking mind. This is my life you are talking about. I can't believe you even have the balls to ask me something like this."

"Let's be serious, you have what, a year or two left tops? And you know it. There are no more big paydays coming your way. Who do you think you are kidding? We can make ten to fifteen million tax-free dollars easily off one damn game. I'm not asking you to lose the championship. It's one game. You'll still have two more games after that to win a championship and get your ring. It actually will probably make the odds even better and we can bet on that game also and make more money. But for us to do it, you'd have to throw the game Saturday."

"Fuck you, Slim! For real, F-U-C-K you! I can't believe you are asking me to do this shit. Here it is I get into an argument with Susan over whether you are my friend or not and you ask me to do this. I mean, my dumb ass was just going to bat for you and you prove me wrong and validate her point by asking me to risk my livelihood over a couple dollars. I have money. I have enough money to last me a lifetime. And you might be right, maybe I do only have a year or two left. Who the fuck cares? That is what I got a degree for, life after basketball. But ALL of that goes down the drain the minute I agree to do this bullshit. Again I say, FUCK YOU!"

"Did I say that when your ass needed me? When you nearly broke my door down for some fucking pain pills because you couldn't take the pain and the team doctors wouldn't give you any more? Did I turn my back on you? No, I found a way to make it happen because I knew you needed me and you always had my back. We go back how long, over twenty years, and I ask you to do me a solid and you can't. How dare you question my friendship? I've always shown and proved it."

Slim paused. "But your ass is going to sit there ready to bitch up. You didn't give a shit about your career then but now all of a sudden you do. It's funny how then all you cared about was playing and I made that happen. I kept your ass on the court. I found the pills, got you a supply, and then made a way for you to beat their damn piss test, too, so they'd think you were clean. I did that. I did all that for you and you tell me fuck you. Nigga, that bullshit career you have. You owe all that to me. Even that bullshit-ass degree, I'm the one who bought your professors to make sure you stayed on the court. I'm the one who made that rape charge disappear in college when that bitch tried to set you up. I've always had your back. Go run and tell Susan's ass that! She doesn't know half the shit I've done for you so I didn't prove that bitch right in any way!"

Slim calmed himself down then continued. "Don't you think I've thought this plan all the way through? Every fucking angle, every possible snag, all of it. I've thought it through to make sure there is no possible way we can get caught, just paid."

"Damn, you went there. It's cool. I see where we are at with things. I know the mistakes I've made in my past, Slim. I accept them, but I'll be damned if I continue to make the same fucking mistakes over and over again. Have you ever wondered why I haven't been around you that much lately? Why I've stayed away from you? This is the exact reason why. But I thought, maybe, just maybe you possibly grew up and changed. I guess I was wrong. I guess you are the same selfish nigga you have always been and probably always will be. Oh, and FYI, you didn't do all that shit for me. You did all that shit for you. That's the way you do business. You help folks out so they forever stay in debt to your ass. Well guess what, I don't owe you a damn thing. So again I'll say for the final time, fuck you!"

Trey turned and walked out of the office slamming the door behind him. As he was making his way through the crowd, Candi spotted him. She tried to catch up with him, but Trey was on a mission to get out of the club as fast as possible.

Chapter 3

Trey walked into the house and threw his keys down on his coffee table. He was pissed. He never would have imagined Slim would ever cross that line. Anyone who knew Trey knew that nothing would come between him and his love of the game. Basketball was all he'd known since he was a child. Trey took his suit jacket off and threw it down on the couch, then loosened up his tie and went into the kitchen to pour himself a drink just as his doorbell rang. Trey made his way to the door to see who it was. Surprise filled his eyes once he looked through the peephole.

"What are you doing here? How do you know where I live?" he asked after he opened the door.

"You sound as if you aren't happy to see me," Candi replied.

"I didn't say that, but I mean it is a little strange that you show up at my door. Especially since you shouldn't even know where I live. It's not like you've been over here before or anything."

"Well are you going to invite me in or are we going to continue to have a conversation in the hallway?"

"Please come in," Trey said, moving out of the way so she could enter.

Candi entered Trey's penthouse condo and sat down on the sofa.

"Well to answer your question, I liked our initial interview so much I thought we'd have a private affair. I tried to catch you before you left but you were in a hurry so I just followed you."

"Is that a habit of yours? I mean, do you always follow men out of the club to their homes? I don't know about that. That sounds kind of stalkerish if you ask me," Trey said, laughing.

"Oh, you find that funny. You wish I was stalking you. I don't have to stalk any man. You should feel lucky, better yet privileged, that I was concerned about you."

"Concerned, huh? Why would you be concerned?" Trey questioned.

"I told you I saw you rush out of the club. It was obvious something was bothering you. I take it things didn't go too well between you and Slim."

"Is that why you are over here? Did he send you?"

"Huh? Slow down. Slim doesn't know I'm over here. I told you I followed you because I was concerned. Whatever you and Slim have going on, I have nothing to do with that. That is between you and him, not me!"

"I apologize. I just have a lot on my mind right now."

"Well that is what I'm here for," Candi replied.

"Is that right? You think you can cheer me up and put my mind in a better place. That's wishful thinking, don't you think?"

"What I think is you ask too many questions. Better yet, I don't think, I know you do," Candi said with a smirk on her face.

"Okay, okay, I'll take that. But I only ask questions to make sure there are no misunderstandings on my part."

"Well sorry, babe, but some things you just have to let happen especially when you are dealing with me because I'm a spur-of-the-moment type girl."

"Okay, so with that said I'm following your lead," Trey replied.

"Good, now let's loosen you up because I don't want whatever happened at the club carrying over to now. What do you have to drink?"

"Actually, that is what I was in the kitchen fixing before you knocked on the door."

"Good, then I'm right on time," Candi said, then got up and headed into the kitchen to finish the task.

"Hennessy, huh? I guess that will do the trick," she replied.

"Oh really, did you need something stronger? Damn, how up-tight do you think I am?"

Before Candi could reply, Trey quickly said, "Don't answer that!"

They both shared a laugh. Candi came out of the kitchen with two shots of Hennessy. She handed Trey his glass.

"To tonight," Candi said.

"I'll drink to that, to tonight!"

They both raised their glasses, then threw back their shots. Trey was impressed at how Candi handled her liquor. She started to move in closer and kiss on Trey's neck.

"Is this all a part of your plan to relax me?"

"Shhhh, quiet, remember? You are following my lead."

Candi continued to softly kiss on Trey's neck. He began to give in to the temptation of her soft, sensual lips. Candi continued to kiss and suck on Trey's neck while she began to massage his dick with her hand. Trey couldn't explain what it was, but he was hornier than he could ever imagine. Candi stopped and started to unbutton his shirt. She removed his shirt leaving his tie still half on and worked her tongue down his chest. Trey could feel himself about to explode. The anticipation was killing him. He'd never felt like this before. His mind was past trying to reason. Something was wrong, but what, he didn't care.

Trey picked Candi up before she could continue to seduce him and started to deeply kiss her. Their tongues were locked in a dead heat. Trey laid her down on the couch and pulled up her dress. To his delight she had no panties on and her perfect V-shaped box was awaiting him. Trey began to suck on her clit intensely as Candi started to squirm. Trey moved at a feverish pace. Candi tried to crawl up the couch to get away from him for a slight reprieve.

Trey wouldn't let up though. He'd switch from her clit to fucking her with his tongue. He'd slide it in and out of her, tasting her sweet juices and savoring them. Candi knew she couldn't escape him. She bit down on her lip and just continued to repeatedly cum over and over again. Trey finally started to let up and flipped her over. Then without warning, he slid his tongue into her ass and kept going. Candi didn't know what to do. She enjoyed every minute of it but the intensity of it all was driving her up the wall.

"Please, baby, please stop. Oh my God! I can't take it no more. Please I want to feel you inside of me," Candi begged.

Trey pulled his pants down and put a condom on before placing himself inside of her. He softly stroked her from the back while sucking on her neck. Candi began to moan and threw her ass back at him so he'd thrust harder inside of her. Trey caught on to her hint and began to pick up his pace. Harder and harder he thrust into her, having no regard for Candi's insides. She wanted to be fucked and he was gladly going to oblige her.

Trey picked up Candi's waist so that her head and upper body still rested on the couch but her legs were wrapped around him in the air, and continued to fuck her from behind. Each stroke he'd get deeper and deeper in her. He could feel himself about to cum, but didn't care. He continued to stroke her harder and harder. Her screams of passion were mute and then he finally came. The room became black. Everything stopped. Trey clasped onto the couch under Candi. Candi, exhausted from her repeated orgasms, didn't object. Her body was still trembling. Once she was able to regain her composure, she fell into a deep sleep along with Trey.

Trey woke up the next morning with cottonmouth. His body ached and he had a screaming headache. He went into the kitchen and poured himself a glass of water. He tried to remember the events of the night before, but everything was a blur. From what he remembered, he'd only had that one shot. He didn't have the best tolerance for alcohol because he only had an occasional drink, but never had he felt like this the morning after one shot. He knew his tolerance wasn't that low.

Trey walked over toward the couch to wake up Candi. He wasn't sure what time it was, but knew he'd have to get to the training complex soon for practice. Trey noticed used condoms scattered about the living room. Nothing was making sense to him.

"Hey, sweetie, you have to get up. You can take a shower if you want to, but I need to get ready to get out of here and head to practice."

Candi didn't budge.

Trey nudged her again, and this time she woke up.

"What time is it?" Candi asked groggily.

Unsure, Trey went into the kitchen to look at the clock on the microwave.

"It's a little after eight," he replied.

Candi got up and looked for the dress she had worn. It was thrown behind the couch. She quickly put it on and straightened her clothes.

"You don't want to take a shower?" Trey asked.

"No, that's okay. I actually stayed longer than I wanted to. I'm sorry, it's just something about your own bed, ya know but you made it hard for me to leave last night. I can't lie, you wore me out." Candi walked over and gave Trey a kiss.

"Thanks, I just wish I could remember it."

Candi didn't respond.

"I'm sorry. I hope that wasn't insensitive of me. I apologize. It has nothing to do with you. What I do remember was great but there are a lot of blanks from last night."

Candi started laughing, "It's okay, sweetie. You are not hurting my feelings. That is all a part of the ex."

"I'm sorry, the what?" Trey asked, puzzled.

"The ex, you know, ecstasy."

"Yeah, I know what ex is but what are you talking about?"

"I wanted you to loosen up last night and relax so I put some ex in your drink. It makes the sex intense but I didn't know you had all that in you or I wouldn't have even used it because you damn sure didn't need it."

"What the fuck do you mean you put ex in my drink? Have you lost your fucking mind? Please tell me this is a joke? Please! Do you know I can be suspended for that shit? They test us before every fucking playoff game. I can't believe this shit!"

"I'm sorry, I didn't know. I'm so sorry!" Candi pleaded.

Trey was at a loss for words. He didn't know what to say or what to do. How could he even allow himself to be put in this type of situation? How was he going to get out of it? He couldn't be suspended. Not now! Everything he worked for seemed as if it was going down the drain.

"Maybe I should go," Candi suggested.

"There isn't no maybe about it, you need to bounce," Trey shot back.

Candi could tell her presence wasn't wanted.

"I'm sorry, I didn't mean for this to happen."

"Whatever!" Trey said as he walked over to the door and opened it. Candi didn't offer any resistance. She left as Trey slammed the door behind her.

Candi walked out of the building and took out her cellphone and dialed a number.

"It's done!" she said, then hung up the phone.

Chapter 4

There was no other choice. There was only one person who could fix things. By the life of him, Trey didn't want to ask but he knew he needed help. Trey walked into the studio. Slim was in a session with one of his artists.

"What, you back for more? You don't have to come up in here preaching. I got the message last night," Slim said before Trey could close the door.

"Look, I'm not here about that. I need your help with something else."

Slim broke out in laughter.

"You've got to be kidding me, right? Please, tell me this is a fucking joke. I know your ass isn't here for my help, not after last night. You have to be joking. Is this a joke?" Slim asked sarcastically.

By Trey's facial expression, Slim could tell he wasn't joking one bit.

"Wow, you have some balls, I will say that," Slim said.

"Slim, look, I didn't come down here to argue or fight with you. I don't have anyone else who I can turn to. You know me, you know after last night I wouldn't be down here unless I really needed your help."

"We'll be awhile finishing this track. Why don't you go grab us a quick bite to eat and let me rap to my man for a sec," Slim asked his artist. He didn't object.

"Close the door behind you," Slim said as the guy left the studio.

"So what's so urgent?"

"Long story short, Candi followed me home last night. I didn't think anything of it. I'm just thinking she is aggressive. Anyway, I invite her in, we have idle chitchat, and then she goes to make me a drink."

Slim cut Trey off. "Is there a point to this story? I mean damn!"

"That bitch put fucking ecstasy in my drink!"

"She did what?" Slim asked.

"You heard me . . . she put fucking ex in my drink thinking it would relax me."

"So how do I factor into this?"

"The league is going to piss test me tomorrow before the game. They do it before every game. If I test positive for a banned substance, there goes the play-offs and any chance at us winning a championship. Shit, probably my career. I can see the headlines now. TREY WINFIELD TESTS POSITIVE FOR ECSTASY." Trey jumped out of his seat. "What a fucking headline!"

"Look, you need to calm down. I'm not going to let that happen. I'll take care of everything. You know I got you so just calm down. We can get that out of you with no problem," Slim reassured Trey.

Trey rushed over to hug Slim.

"My man! You don't know how much this means to me. I'm serious. Through it all, you've always had my back and I appreciate that," Trey said.

"Save all that mushy shit, plus you wasn't saying that last night! Don't matter, regardless we boys for life, you know that. But also know this comes at a cost, too, nigga. I've got your back on this and I need you to have my back also."

"Slim, please, don't do this. I can't!"

"Gotdamn, Trey! Are you that fucking selfish? I mean does everything always have to be about you? You come in here interrupting time in the studio I have to pay for, begging me for my help, and yet you can't even return the favor on something that is going to put money in both our pockets. I'm not talking chump change either. I'm talking substantial paper that will have our grandkids set if we play it right."

"Look at me, Slim! Does it look like I'm hurting for cash? Does it look like I need a quick come up?" Trey shot at him.

"Nigga, does it look like I'm sitting on fucking easy street? Shit! I don't like having to grind for every fucking dime. I don't like the fact that I have to be out in these streets hustling. Yeah, I finally have some legit business poppin with this club but I see a bigger picture. I see more legit businesses. I see better things in my future and all of that starts with this."

"Slim, you've got me in your corner. I'll back any legal venture you trying to start. I've got you. We don't have to go this route."

"You aren't hearing me, I have my own plans. I don't need your money nor do I want it. All I need you to do is make sure y'all lose tomorrow. That's all I need from you," Slim replied.

"I don't need this shit in my life right now, Slim. I don't! You say I'm selfish and it's always about me, but I think I have the right to be selfish when it comes to my fucking career and my life! Don't you?"

"You are absolutely right, you surely do. Just as I have the right to tell you to get the fuck out of the studio so I can finish my business and good luck with that piss test tomorrow. Shit, maybe I should just call *The Washington Post* now and leak the story to them. Just get it out of the way. How much do you think they'll pay for a story like that? I'm sure that's some short shit, but hey, I can't get that long money, why not benefit off this bullshit right here."

"So that's how we are going now? That is where we are at with things? You are just going to blackball me, nigga?"

"Nigga, fuck you! This is far from blackmail. Your ass has a choice. You can either go in there tomorrow with dirty piss, get suspended, and figure out a way to resurrect your career afterward or you can throw the game tomorrow, get paid, and keep your career. You might not like the choices you have, but regardless of that fact, the choice is yours!"

"I didn't choose this shit. I didn't ask that bitch to spike my damn drink. I didn't ask for none of this shit, yet I have to be the one who has to fucking suffer. Where is the justice in that?" Trey questioned.

"Tell me when did life all of a sudden become fair? Nigga, you play the cards your ass is dealt. You know the name of the game and this is nothing different. You didn't ask for this, so the fuck what. Are you getting the short end of the stick, yeah probably, but you have a choice. You can easily go to the team and tell them what happened last night. I'm sure you can even have Candi prosecuted and you won't have to face any charges, but I'm also pretty sure the league isn't going to allow your ass to play until they investigate the situation. That damn sure won't be in a day or two. And you and I both know that y'all don't have a chance in hell if your ass isn't on the court. So you can sit there and play the self-righteous role all you want, but the bottom line is at the end of the day you are in my office asking for the easy way out. And I'm here offering it to you, but it's at a price."

Trey had no choice. He was being backed into a corner. Trey wasn't willing to risk going to the league and possibly not being able to play the rest of the play-offs. That was not an option.

"What do I have to do?"

"All you have to do is make sure y'all lose by five or more. Miss a free throw here and there, maybe a turnover from time to time. Nothing serious, we don't want you to overdo it and we get caught. Also, you can't let them blow y'all out either. That will be too obvious. I'll say maybe lose by like seven or so and we'll be straight."

"How the fuck do I make sure we lose? Does that even sound right?" Trey asked.

"I don't know, but you need to find a fucking way. I gave your ass some suggestions. Shit, you've had off nights before. Just make sure you have another one tomorrow night. You are smart, you can figure it out. Bottom line is that by the end of the day, Dallas has to get the win and we must cover the spread to get paid big."

"What about my situation?"

"Have you had practice yet?"

"No, I headed straight over here after that chick left."

"Okay, go to practice and do your daily routine, whatever it is that y'all do, and then when you get a free moment head over to the club. I'll have my man there ready for you."

"That's really telling me a lot, what is he going to do?"

"Have you ever seen the movie *The Program*? Well it's like that, we are going to remove that dirty piss out of you and put new clean piss in you. So when you take your test, you'll be fine. It's just like he said, call it an oil change," Slim said, then started laughing.

"I'm glad you getting a kick out of this shit. Understand this, after I do this for you we are through. I don't have shit else to say to you and you keep it the same way with me. We are nothing to each other after this."

Slim didn't know how to respond. Trey could tell his words cut Slim deeply.

"Hey, if that is how you feel, that's cool. I'll cut you your end of the action and be on my fucking way since that's how you want it."

"I don't want any part of that. I told you, I'm not struggling for money. Whatever you do, is what you do. All I want is to pass that test tomorrow and the rest I don't give a shit about."

"Even better for me," Slim replied.

Trey started to leave, then stopped. "And make sure that bitch isn't there when I get there later or none of this will matter because I will damn sure beat the shit out of her."

Slim started to laugh. "Yeah, okay! I hear you, tough guy. Now can I get back to my work please?"

Trey left the studio. Slim just looked at the recording booth. He never wanted to lose Trey as a friend. Together, they'd been through so much, but money had its way of being its own demon. Especially when you didn't have much of it and the other half did. In Slim's mind, this was something that had to be done in order for him to get to where he wanted to be.

A few moments passed and Candi walked into the studio. She walked behind him and started to massage his shoulders.

"It's going to be okay," Candi said.

"Maybe this wasn't such a smart idea. Maybe I did go too far," Slim suggested.

"So what do you want to do? Do you want to call it all off?" Candi asked.

"I don't know. I mean, I need this cash. We need this cash. We can finally take this club idea nationwide and open spots in Atlanta, Philly, New York, Chicago, and L.A. We will be able to stamp our names on something. How do I not go through with this?"

"Then don't stress. You know what you need to do. It's all going to work out. Everything will be fine! Trey just needs some time to cool off," Candi reassured him.

"I know, I know, at least I hope so." Slim paused. "Question, did you have to put ex in his drink? I mean that was a little drastic, even for you."

"That was all I could think of at the time. I knew he'd be in a jam and would ask you for help and you'd have him right where you needed him," Candi replied.

"Fuck it! It is what it is and there isn't anything we can do about it now."

Chapter 5

The game clock read two minutes and forty-seven seconds in the fourth quarter. It was turning out that Trey didn't even have to throw the game. He really was having an off night. Shots he was trying to make, he wasn't. Dallas was doing a good job of trying to contain him. The game was only close because his teammates were picking up his slack. As bad as Trey was playing, they were only down two points.

Trey continued to monitor the score. He knew how much they had to lose by. Hopefully he wouldn't be put in the position to play a role in that. Quickly his hope was diminishing and it was time for him to act.

Washington scored on its next possession then Dallas turned right around and turned the ball over for another quick Washington score. In a split second, the momentum of the game had changed. Washington went from being down two points to up two. Trey knew if he didn't do something, the game would slip away and they'd win. This was the moment he'd been waiting for all his life, but never did he imagine this would be how it would play out. Instead of ensuring his team's victory, he needed to do the opposite and make sure they lost.

Trey ran down the court to play defense. Once his man had the ball in his hands, he allowed him to go around him and left him open for an uncontested three-pointer. Dallas was now back up by one point. Washington quickly brought the ball up court and called time-out.

"Trey, you need to get up tight on him. You are giving him too much room," the coach yelled as Trey approached the bench.

Trey looked at the clock. There was now a minute and thirteen seconds left. He needed four more points. He had to make sure the ball would be in his hands. The coach started to draw up a play. As he expected, it was designed for him.

Trey got the ball at the top of the key. He allowed time to tick off the clock trying to set up his defender. He made a quick move to his left and created just enough separation to get off a shot. He rose to take the shot but missed badly. Dallas hustled to get the rebound. The frustration read all over Trey's face. He couldn't believe what he was doing.

Dallas knew how key this possession was so as they crossed half court and were about to call time out, Trey reached in trying to steal the ball, but fouled the opposing player with fifty-eight seconds left. The coach couldn't believe what Trey had just done. As the Dallas player approached the free-throw line, the coach called Trey over to him.

"Why would you foul him? We are only down one. This is no time to start panicking. We've been here before. Trey, you know better!"

"I'm sorry, coach. I thought I could catch him off-guard and get the steal. I didn't think the ref would make that call with the game on the line," Trey replied.

"Don't think, just do what you know how to do and win this damn game!" the coach yelled. He calmed himself, not wanting Trey to tense up. "Okay, regardless, if he makes both of these free throws or not we need a time-out. If he misses, make sure we get the rebound."

Trey nodded in agreement. He ran to the free-throw line. The Dallas player calmly sank both free throws. Trey did as the coach asked and called time-out. They were now down three points, however, there was still a lot of time left. Trey started to second guess fouling so early. This was turning out to be harder than he first thought.

"Trey," the coach called. "Are you paying attention?"

"Yes, coach, I'm with you."

"Good, I need you to knock this shot down. If you can get the three, good, if not, take the best shot available. It doesn't have to be a three," the coach stressed.

Every professional player wanted to be the hero, however most weren't afforded the opportunity. In this league, you had to be the marquee player for that privilege. Trey was that. He'd taken his share of clutch shots in the past. The pressure was what he thrived on. He knew how much time fifty-eight seconds was so if he couldn't get the quick three, he would go to the basket and get an easy two or put the referee in the position to call a foul. That knowledge only came with experience and on this team he was the only one with that experience. He knew if he allowed another player to get the ball, no matter how much the coach stressed a three wasn't needed, they would try to be the hero and take the three.

Trey made sure when they inbounded the ball, he wasn't open. He forced another player to take the inbound pass. As Trey predicted, he tried to be the hero and missed a three-point shot. Dallas got the rebound as the Washington players applied pressure, trying to force him into a turnover. Time was quickly ticking away. The coached yelled for them to retreat back to defense and get a stop. It was still a one-possession game.

Trey knew he needed Dallas to score, though. Washington played tough defense and forced Dallas to miss the next shot. As Washington got the rebound, Trey quickly got the ball. He had dodged a bullet the last time with his teammate missing the tying shot. However, he wasn't going to allow his fate to be in another player's hands again. He needed to make sure they didn't tie the game. As he crossed the half-court line he looked over to the coach to see if he wanted a time-out. The coach motioned for him to go. Trey looked at the clock, there were now less than twenty seconds left in the game. He took two hard dribbles toward the three-point line, then gave his defender a pump fake. The defender bit and jumped trying to block the shot. Trey slightly leaned in knowing the referees wouldn't call a foul and took the shot. It seemed as if it took forever for the ball to reach the rim. It *clanged* off the backboard and off the rim. The Washington players frantically tried to foul the Dallas player who got the rebound.

Trey ran over to the referee complaining, looking for a foul. He knew it really wasn't a foul but he had to sell the part. He was almost home. He'd done everything he could do to meet his end of the bargain. All he needed now was for the Dallas player to make these two free throws and he did. Washington was now down five with only seven seconds left on the clock. There was no way they could win. Trey took the inbound pass and walked the ball up the court as the time ticked down to zero. The Dallas players jumped for joy; they knew they had won the game. The deed was done. Trey walked off the court, leaving a piece of himself behind.

Chapter 6

Slim thought deep down inside, Trey would find a way to renege on their agreement. A part of him expected him to. He didn't actually think Trey would have the balls to go through with it, but he was wrong. He quickly picked up the phone to call Candi to make sure she knew everything was set and in place. Slim knew Trey would be suspected of point shaving if he placed the bet so he had Candi have one of her girlfriends whom she trusted place it for them instead.

"Hello," Candi answered.

"It's done! He came through."

"I know, I've been watching."

"I can't believe it, he fucking came through!"

"How much did we win?" Candi asked.

"A little over seven million total. As promised, you get a million of that. Can you believe it, baby?"

"Oh my God!"

"That is what I'm talking about! Okay, we have to be cool about this. Have you gone over everything with your girl?"

"Yes, Karen is cool. You don't have to worry about her. I knew you'd trip, that's why I flew out here with her."

"You're in Vegas?" Slim questioned.

"Yes, I knew you'd get all concerned and start worrying me to death. What can I do if I'm in D.C. with you? Nothing! So I flew to Vegas with her to make sure everything went smooth."

"Smart, very smart, that was good thinking! So this is what you do, have her pick up the money and once she does y'all get on a plane. Once y'all get here, I'll pay her her cut. Make sure she doesn't skim any money off the top."

"Okay, I told you I'm on it. You don't have to worry about it. She already knows the plan. I told her we'd pay her one hundred and thirty grand."

"Sweet, I was prepared to give her three but if she agreed to one thirty that sounds better to me."

"Yeah, I knew you'd overpay her, that's why I didn't even bother to wait. I got her to do it for one thirty and left it at that."

"You know I'm going to fuck the shit out of you when you get home! You are on fire right now."

"When am I not, and you better do more than just fuck me, I can get that any night."

Slim started laughing.

"What about Trey?"

"What about him?" Slim questioned.

"How much do we have to give him?"

"He already got his cut. All he wanted was clean piss, so that ship has sailed."

"So then maybe I should be getting a little more than a million, don't you think?"

"Baby, I can't even argue with you. Your ass has earned it. How about we add an extra million to that and make it an even two million?"

"That sounds good to me, baby!" Candi replied.

"Okay, so I'll see you tonight?"

"No, we'll be back tomorrow morning. That's the next flight out."

"Are you sure?" Slim questioned.

"Yes, I'm sure. Do you think I want to be here a minute more than I have to? I can feel Georgetown calling my name now. I have money to spend and things to buy."

"Calm it down now, you can't go crazy and start spending large too soon. You know I'm still watched, so all eyes will be on us. If you start spending big, they'll know something is up. You have to slow-walk it. Spend the money we make off the club and stack that paper, that way it doesn't draw any red flags. Trey really stuck his neck out on a line for us. I don't want this shit coming back to bite him or us."

"Fuck him!"

"All that right there . . ."

Candi cut Slim off. "I'm sorry, I know that's your man and all, but shit! Fuck him! Damn! What has he done for you? Here you tried to put money in his pocket and look how he acted."

"Again, you need to calm it down with all that. One, what I asked him to do wasn't fair to him, and two, he has been there for me more than you'll ever know. How is none of your business, which is why you don't know. Bottom line, I don't want this shit coming back on him. He doesn't deserve it. He actually was the innocent one in all this. Did you forget we are the ones who manipulated him to fucking do it?"

"Okay, okay, I'm sorry. I hear you. I'll make sure I'm careful. I'm sorry, baby, okay?" Candi said.

"I'll see you when you get here," Slim said, then hung up the phone.

Chapter 7

The phone kept ringing off the hook. Trey wasn't in the mood for anyone's judgment or opinions. He continued to ignore it. Even when the front desk attendant called up to let him know that Susan was there to see him, he wanted to tell him to tell her to turn around but he knew that would bring about questions. Which would make matters worse and Trey wasn't in the mood. The depression of costing his team a victory and possibly a championship had started to sink in.

Susan walked in the front door. Trey left it cracked open after he hung up with the front desk receptionist, so she would be able to get in.

"It's dark in here. You do know it's the middle of the day? You need to let some light in here," Susan said as she went over to the blinds to open them. Trey ignored her and went over to the couch to lie down. The TV was on and set to ESPN. Trey, of course, was the topic of conversation. Sportscasters talked about how Trey folded under pressure and wasn't able to get his team over the hump.

"Why are you in here watching this? Trey, you can't do this to yourself. You have had a great year, regardless. You can't let this get you down. It was only one game," Susan pleaded.

Trey smirked. "I wish it was that easy, Susan. I swear I do."

"You can't beat yourself up about one game. You are entitled to a bad game just like anyone else, aren't you? Don't pay any attention to the critics. This isn't like you. Usually, you let it motivate you for the next game."

"Not this time! This time is different. I don't even feel like playing. I feel like a disgrace and I let my teammates down. Shit, I let the city down."

"Trey, we wouldn't even be in this position if it wasn't for you."

Trey cut her off. "Exactly! We would have won the championship if it wasn't for me. I should have just not played! I don't know why I even went through with it. What was I thinking?"

Susan was puzzled. "Hold on, what are you talking about? Is something else going on that I don't know about?"

Trey got up from the couch and went into the kitchen. He started to pour himself another drink when Susan stopped him.

"Susan, I'm not in the fucking mood. Honestly, I just want to be left the fuck alone!"

"What has happened to you? I'm starting to not even know who you are anymore. You need to cut this shit out and you need to do it now! It's not like the series is over. You still have a game on Tuesday night. You are still up three games to two."

"It's not about that," Trey replied.

"Then what is going on? I can't help if you don't let me in. What is going on?"

Trey knew he needed to talk to someone about what happened. If he didn't, it would continue to eat him up. Susan was one of the few he could trust with anything. He knew whatever they talked about would stay between the two of them, but he also knew it would come at a price. How could he tell her everything?

Trey had been trying to reconcile with her for over a year now and rekindle their past relationship. Each time, Susan would turn a blind cheek to his attempt. When she caught him cheating on her, that tore her apart. She'd let him into a place within her heart that she'd never let any man in before, and for him to turn around and hurt her so much, she could never forget that. Forgiving him was the easy part, it was the forgetting that was holding them back. Trey knew the minute he told Susan everything, his chances of getting back with her would become slim to none.

"Okay, if I tell you, you have to promise one, not to get mad and two, not to hold it against me."

"Then I'll pass. I don't want to know."

"Huh?"

"Trey, if you want to tell me, cool, I'm here and ready to listen.

But I'm not going to sit here and make you a promise that I might not be able to keep. I don't know how I'm going to react to what you tell me. So if you don't want to tell me, fine."

"Why do you have to make things so difficult? Shit, why can't you just agree and let it be!"

Susan walked out of the kitchen.

"Where are you going?" Trey asked.

"If you aren't telling me, then there is no need for me to be here. Again, I don't know nor like this person you are right now. This isn't the man I know so I'd rather leave than be around you."

"Wow!" Trey said, speechless.

As Susan turned to head toward the door, Trey grabbed her arm to stop her.

"What, Trey?" Susan asked.

"I threw the game. We didn't lose, I threw the game. I made sure we lost."

Now Susan was speechless. She was at a loss for words. All she could do was stand there and stare back at him.

Trey continued. "You were right about Slim. My knee started to bother me again and the team doctor started talking about I might have to get it scoped. I didn't want that, we're in the middle of a championship run. That was all I needed was to find out that I might have torn something and I'm out for the play-offs. So I got scared and called Slim. That is why he was at the game."

Susan's facial expression clearly explained how she felt about the situation.

"And let me guess, Trey, Slim gave you something to take away the pain?"

"What other choice did I have? He only gave me enough for the play-offs, nothing serious. I didn't want to tell you and you get upset. I didn't know what to do, this was the only way."

"Fine, what does this have to do with you throwing the game?"

"Before I asked Slim for the valium he asked me to throw the game. He said we were favored to win since it was a home game. He could place a bet on the game and if Dallas won by five or more, he'd get a big payday. I was so pissed when he asked me. I couldn't believe it. Then I find out about my knee and I had no choice."

"No, you had a choice, but the one that you should have chosen you didn't. You chose the easy way out. Do you remember what those pain pills did to you? Because I damn sure do and do you remember how you almost lost your career over trying to get off them? What if management finds out you are back on them again? Have you thought of that? And you wonder why I get on you about him. He is the reason you almost lost your career and look, it's happening all over again. That man is no friend of yours but no, you keep wanting to associate with him."

"Susan, it is only for one, maybe two games, but now I don't want to even play. I can't even look at myself in the mirror after last night. You know, in the beginning, I wasn't even trying to lose the game. I really was off and having a bad game. I mean, I thought it was a sign from Christ. The day I'm asked to miss and not perform I actually couldn't hit a shot. But go figure, the night I'm off, the team is on fire. Irony is so funny."

Trey paused as his emotions started to get the best of him. "Then in the fourth I could see if I didn't do something either Slim wouldn't cover the spread or we'd actually win and that's when I did a couple things here and there to make sure we'd lose."

The light went on in Susan's head. "The foul with a minute left."

"Yeah, that and a few others. I played off Wilson when he hit the three and I made sure I didn't get the inbounds pass when we were down three."

"Do you know if you get caught, you'll be banned from the league? There goes your career and any front office or coaching position. Basketball is over!"

"I don't even care about all that, Susan. I mean I do but that's not what's bothering me. What bothers me the most is something I've worked my entire career for was finally right there within my grasp. I mean, after we lost in the finals last year, I was determined to never experience that feeling again. To be so close, and not win, it almost devastated me. And here I'm afforded another opportunity to seize the moment and I throw it."

Tears started to well up in Trey's eyes. Even though Susan was extremely disappointed in him, she knew what he needed most from her was her support. She could see the pain this was causing him. He needed to know someone was on his side and everything was going to be all right. She went over and hugged him.

"Look, everything is going to be okay. I know you can play better than you did last night and so do you. You had an off night, threw the game, and yet y'all still almost pulled it out and got the victory. I'm not worried and you shouldn't be, either. You've learned your lesson from this. So Tuesday night, Dallas just needs to be prepared to find a good vacation spot for the summer because you are going to play your ass off and bring that trophy back to D.C. where it belongs. They won't even know what hit them."

Trey couldn't help but smile. Susan was right. He needed to put that game behind him and take all his frustrations out on Dallas Tuesday night.

"You are right! You are absolutely right."

"I know I am," Susan replied.

Trey kissed her on her cheek and then her lips. Susan missed the softness of his lips. She started to kiss him back and they were soon locked in to their passion.

"No! Stop! Stop! We can't do this," Susan said, stopping herself from going too far.

"Susan, please! I miss you so much," Trey pleaded.

"No, I can't. I'll always be your friend, but I can't and won't put myself back into a position to allow myself to get hurt. I can't and I won't."

"Susan, please just trust me. Trust the fact that I'll never hurt you again. I promise. I just need you in my life."

"I'll always be your friend and a part of your life, but I can't do it, Trey. I'm sorry. I just can't!"

"You know faith and trust go a long way. I can't change the past and I wouldn't want to except to remove the hurt that I caused you, but the past made me a better man. And for that, I'm so grateful. I just want you to allow me to show you the man I've become, so you can forget the man I was. I'm not even asking you to commit to me right now, just give me the opportunity to show you. I just want you to look and watch my actions. Allow them to show you what I'm about and how serious I am."

"I don't know, Trey," Susan replied.

"Please, just give me that. Just give me that little bit of hope and I know Christ will do the rest."

"You sure sound awfully confident."

"That is because I am. It helps when you know the outcome."

"Is that right? Well at least you are starting to sound like the Trey I know. I'll tell you what, you promise me you'll go out there and win the championship on Tuesday, and stop taking those pain meds, and I'll think about it. I'm not promising we'll get back together, but I'll at least think about it. But if you hurt me or lie to me . . ."

Trey put his finger over Susan's mouth, hushing her.

"Say no more. Just leave it at that."

"Okay, do we have a deal?" Susan asked.

Trey grabbed Susan and pulled her in close. He just wanted to hold her.

"You damn right we do."

Chapter 8

Slim hadn't heard anything from Candi. She should have been back by now. It was now Monday. Slim had been past her house twice on Sunday and twice early that day. There was no sign of her. Every time he called her cellphone it would go straight to voice mail. That surely wasn't helping the situation. At first, Slim thought something happened to her. Maybe they were robbed. Even with that, someone would have been picking up that phone to let him know something. His thoughts then shifted to possibly being double-crossed. He didn't want to believe it, though, so he made every excuse imaginable to kill that notion. Maybe they decided to spend an extra day in Vegas and they were on the plane heading back now. Maybe she didn't have her charger and since they stayed the extra day she didn't have a way to call him. He thought of any and every possible thing, but he couldn't shake the idea that it was likely she was in the wind with his money.

Slim trusted Candi, but even still, in the back of his mind, he left room for the possibility that she would double-cross him. In his line of business, you couldn't trust anyone and the ones you did, only to a certain extent. Everyone was capable of anything when their backs were against the wall. Slim knew Candi could find seventeen million ways to change the script of their plan and just walk away with all the money. Especially if she actually counted the money to find out that Slim had lied to her about how much they really won.

Sitting around waiting to hear from Candi was driving Slim crazy, so he headed to the club. She'd know to come there once she got into town and he was just going to have to trust that. At least at the club there was always something to do and something to keep him occupied. Usually, talking to Trey would help calm things. Trey was always the other point of view Slim needed to balance himself out. He was the point of reason. But they hadn't spoken since Trey agreed to throw the game. Slim wanted to call him but his pride wouldn't let him. He finally decided to swallow it.

As Slim picked up the phone to dial Trey's number, Ricky and Larry rushed into his office.

"Slim, we've got a fucking problem," Ricky said.

"What's up?" Slim asked.

"I don't know how but somehow the entire shipment is in the fucking storage room."

"What do you mean the shipment is in the storage room? Why would it even be in the club?"

"Slim, how the hell would I know? I just found out my damn self."

"Okay, okay, we need to think this shit out. Who found it?"

"Larry did."

"Yeah, I went back there to get shit ready for tonight and I saw the duffel bags. I'm thinking what the fuck? It can't be. I must be lunchin, so I check and all the powder was in there. I'm talking every fucking key right there in the bags," Larry said.

"Okay, where is the shit now?"

"It's still in the storage room," Larry said.

"Why the fuck is it still in there? We are running a fucking legit business. I'm trying to leave that street shit alone. All I need is my cut of it, that's it. I've hooked y'all up with the connect and y'all were suppose to go from there. Why the fuck is that shit in my fucking club?" Slim asked as he pushed all the stuff on his desk to the floor.

"Slim, you know we would never disrespect you like that. I'm telling you, I don't know what the fuck is going on. The last shipment we got was on Thursday, you can ask Candi."

"Why would I ask her? What does she have to do with anything?"

"Candi went with us. She can vouch. I'm telling you I don't know how the shit got here but please believe when I find out, I'm going to handle it. That you don't have to worry about."

"Fuck all that right now, we need to get that shit out of here," Slim demanded.

"EVERYBODY GET DOWN ON THE GROUND! DON'T NO ONE MOVE!" someone yelled outside the door.

"Shit, this isn't happening. Shit!" Slim yelled.

As he was trying to go out the back door of his office, the police walked in with guns blazing.

"Don't fucking move!" one of the officers yelled.

Slim threw his hands up, showing he didn't have any weapons.

"Officers, if you wanted a good table, all you had to do is ask," Slim said jokingly, trying to lighten the mood.

The officer approached Slim and then punched him in his stomach, causing him to drop to his knees.

"We've finally got your smart ass and there is nothing that high-priced fancy lawyer can do about it."

"I didn't do anything," Slim said as he was trying to catch his breath.

As the officer started to laugh, his partner walked in with a duffel bag. The police knew exactly where it was. Slim knew this wasn't boding well for him.

"Is that right?" the officer asked. "Then what is this?" he asked as he opened the bag.

"That shit isn't mine. I run a respectable business now, I'm no longer in the drug game. I swear! That shit isn't mine! I'm being fucking set up."

"Come on, Slim, you can do better than that. Set up, huh? Okay explain it to me, who is setting you up? You are a respectable business man, why would anyone want to set you up?"

"Fuck if I know and I don't care."

"Exactly, and fuck if I care, too, because even if this isn't yours, it makes up for all the times when it was." The officer turned to his counterpart. "Someone please slap the cuffs on this piece of shit and get him out of here."

The officers cuffed Slim and took him away.

Chapter 9

The minute Trey took the court in Dallas, the fire burning in his eyes was proof this night's outcome would be a lot different than the last. He was determined to fix the wrong he committed. This was the only way he'd be at peace with himself and with what he did. No matter what Dallas tried to do, they couldn't stop him. Every time they would make a run to get in the game, Trey would take matters into his own hands and give his team a cushion. At the end of it all, Trey went off for forty-seven points, sixteen assists, and twelve rebounds, and captured the championship he'd been chasing his entire career. The triple-double was just the icing on the cake and made the victory all the more sweet. Trey was on top of the world.

As his teammates were in the locker room showering themselves with champagne, the reporters all tried to talk to the newly crowned MVP.

"Trey, Trey, how does it feel?" one of the reporters asked.

"Oh my God! I can't even explain it. We did it!" Trey said as he started shaking the champagne bottle; it exploded out. Trey broke away from the reporters and searched for Susan. She was the only one who believed in him. She was the one who he wanted to share this moment with the most.

The locker room was a madhouse. Every time Trey tried to make his way through, someone would either stop him to celebrate with them or a reporter would try to stop him to get an interview. All he wanted was Susan. This was their moment to share together. Without her, he couldn't have done it. She was his inspiration and motivation. Trey continued to make his way through the locker room until finally he saw her colleague at *The Washington Post*.

"Hey, have you seen Susan?" Trey asked.

"She is on vacation. She had something urgent that came up and had to leave. I'm here in her place. Do you mind if I get an interview with you?" the reporter replied.

"Sure, but not right now, though. Let me just enjoy this moment for a while," Trey said with a smile, but now concern filled him.

The reporter agreed. Trey needed his phone. He made his way to his locker and got his phone, then went into the coach's office. Before he could call Susan, his phone rang.

"Hello."

"Yo, I know I'm probably the last person you want to talk to right now but I really need you."

"Slim?"

"Yeah, it's me."

"Look, I can't even be mad at you. At the end of the day, I made the choice to do it. If there was anyone I needed to be mad at, it was myself. Consider everything water under the bridge. We are cool. We've been through too much to end our friendship over this."

"You don't know how happy I am to hear you say that because I need you right now," Slim said.

Trey misheard him. "Yeah, I wish you were here to celebrate with me, too. I finally fucking did it!"

"Huh, what are you talking about?" Slim asked.

"I finally got my ring. I finally did it. I got the ring," Trey said.

"Oh shit!"

"What?" Trey questioned.

"Trey, I'm in jail. I think that bitch Candi set me up."

"What!"

"Yes, that is why I need your help. I need you to get me out of here."

"What happened?" Trey asked.

"You know how I turned all that street shit over to Ricky and

Larry? Well they had a shipment that came in last week. Anyway, long story short, the shit somehow ended up in my damn club."

"And you think Candi had something to do with that?"

"She went with them when they went to pick up the shipment and drop it off at the stash house. She knew the whole operation and had access to put this thing in motion. It had to be her. I know it was."

"Okay, but even so, it's still not making any sense. Why would she want to set you up?"

Slim started to chuckle. "The money."

"What are you talking about?"

"She has the money. Her ass is in the wind with all the money. I didn't want anything coming back to you, so I had her get one of her girlfriends to place the bet and bring the cash back. Candi went with her girlfriend Karen to Vegas. They never came back, now this bitch cellphone is disconnected and she's in the wind."

"Okay, okay, just sit tight. I'll get on the phone with my lawyer and see what he can do. I'm coming home tonight so I'll come see you then and we will get to the bottom of it."

"All right, what choice do I have?"

"I have to know, how much did she get away with?" Trey asked.

"A little over seventeen million."

"What!"

"Please don't rub it in," Slim replied.

"My bad, my bad! I didn't mean to but damn, seventeen million is a lot. Can you blame her?"

"Trey!"

"Shit, I did it again, huh? My bad. Look I'll be home tonight. Let me go before they start looking for me."

They both hung up the phone. Trey then dialed Susan's number.

"Hello," she answered.

"Baby, I fucking did it. I did."

"I know, I heard. Congratulations! I heard. I'm so proud of you."

"Why aren't you here with me? This doesn't seem right. What happened? It's not like you to miss work and you never miss one of my games. For you to miss this one out of all games, it must have been something important."

"I just needed to get away," she replied.

Trey could detect something was troubling Susan. "Is something wrong?"

"Nothing, I'm fine," Susan replied.

"Susan, come on. I know you better than that. What is going on?"

" 'I just want you to look and watch my actions. Allow them to show you what I'm about and how serious I am.' Do you remember saying that to me?"

"Yes and I meant every word of it."

Susan started to laugh. "You can't be serious."

"Susan, what is going on? What are you getting at?"

"Does the name Candi ring a bell? I'm a fucking reporter! Did you think I wouldn't find out? It's obvious you did because you damn sure left out the part about how you fucked her. Instead, you tell me some bullshit-ass story about Slim, knowing I'd be pissed, but also knowing it was small enough for me to forgive you, and you wiggle your way out of it."

Trey was speechless. He knew he was caught.

"What, you don't have anything to say? You don't want to defend yourself? No, instead all I hear now is fucking crickets, crickets. You can hear a damn pen drop, your ass is so quiet. 'I just want you to look and watch my actions. Allow them to show you what I'm about and how serious I am.' Yeah, I see exactly how serious you are. Your ass hasn't changed. You are still the same selfish bastard who only thinks about himself, only difference is I knew it. I knew you would be, so this time, I'm not the one hurt."

"Susan, please can we just talk about this?"

"What is there to talk about? I don't have shit to say to you, Trey. I'm glad you finally got your championship. I'm glad you finally got your ring because that is the only thing that ever mattered to you."

"How can you say that? You know how much you mean to me."

"Is that right? You were willing to lose your career and tarnish your name by point shaving all to avoid getting suspended for the play-offs chasing that ring. But yet, you couldn't even come clean and be honest with me. Again; and you say, 'I just want you to look and watch my actions. Allow them to show you what I'm about and how serious I am.' Well guess what, I watched and they showed me. It's cool though, no hard feelings. You got what you wanted and so did I."

"And what is that?" Trey asked.

"I got the proof I needed to get you out of my life and you fell for it. At least this time I got paid doing it."

Everything started to make sense to Trey now.

"It was you. You set this whole thing up. You set up Slim and me in the process."

"I damn sure did and just like the asses you are, the both of you fell for it. I knew Slim wouldn't be able to resist a quick score. So I had Candi plant the seed in his head. He would sell his mother for enough money. And you, I knew the minute she threw the pussy your way you'd jump. Both of you did exactly as I predicted."

"Now boarding flight three seventy-two to Costa Rica," Trey heard over the phone.

"Well that's my cue, 'bye, Trey," Susan said and hung up the phone.

Trey just sat back and stared at the wall. He didn't even have the capability to celebrate. He'd lost all the energy to.

STOLEN LEGACY

by Allah Adams

Chapter 1

he tour bus drove down a desolate Midwestern road. Platinum-selling rap artist Trapp was completing a thirty-city rap tour. Trapp had become a huge success in the rap game, and his first album went platinum in a week. He had the hottest rap album out, hands down. Trapp was riding a wave of success that many could only dream of. He was living the life.

"Pass that kush over here! I didn't pay all that money to watch you all get high," Trapp arrogantly demanded of one of his crew.

The man passed him a pregnant blunt of the finest marijuana on earth. Trapp took a deep pull of the potent substance and closed his eyes. He thought about his road to success and what he had to do to get to this point in his life. He thought about his former friends and his former lifestyle. Trapp wasn't the most popular guy in his Brentwood, Long Island, neighborhood. All his life he was treated like a stepchild. Trapp never knew his real parents, he was raised in foster homes all his life. Now he was the biggest rap star in the country.

Trapp's mind started to drift as he thought back to how it all got started.

Two Years Ago

The music blasted from the twelve-inch speakers in the back of the midnight-black Chevy Tahoe. The three young Black men in the vehicle nodded their heads to the melodic beat as if they were in a trance. You would think that the young men were deaf or would be compelled to turn the extremely loud music down, but instead, the loud rap music fueled their adrenaline and thoughts of getting paid.

The driver, Jamal Jenkins, aka JJ Gates, was the rap artist the men were listening to. JJ was also the biggest drug dealer in his Brentwood, Long Island, neighborhood. His right-hand man, Dee, was always in the passenger seat of JJ's Tahoe, he was second in command of JJ's drug operation. The youngest of the crew was Trapp; he sat in the back rolling up a blunt of the stickiest haze on earth.

JJ was feeling himself. He was only twenty-three and he managed to stack over $100,000 selling drugs in less than two years. He considered himself Hood Rich. "If you have $100,000 or more in the hood you are considered Hood Rich, my nig. I am officially a Hood Rich nigga, ya dig," JJ said to his underlings.

"That's what I'm talking about. I'm trying to get my paper up, too," Dee replied.

"Stick with me and you, too, can be Hood Rich. I'll show you how to get this paper, ya heard."

JJ's ego had become a monster over the past two years. Sometimes things happen in a person's life that seem to be a golden opportunity, but that's only on the surface.

Two years ago Jamal Jenkins was a twenty-one-year-old college student with dreams of becoming a rapper. He had never sold drugs, nor did any major crime besides stealing a shirt from Macy's when he was thirteen.

Jamal came from a good family. His parents paid for his college tuition, they also tried to give him the money to pursue his rap career. But like any other middle class family in these times, they could give their only son so much before they went broke.

"Dad, do you think I could borrow two hundred dollars for the studio?" JJ asked humbly.

"Son, I have to pay the mortgage this week so you have to wait."

"But, Dad, I have to get these songs done before next week so I can get on these mix tapes *Underdog Classics,* and *Street's Most Wanted.* I can get on both of them," JJ said in despair.

"Son, I'm sorry, but I can't help you this time. With your tuition and the mortgage, I can't afford to give you any extra money until next week."

He walked away feeling desperate to get the money for his studio session. "How am I going to get this money?" Jamal's mental wheels were turning a hundred miles a minute. "I could just ask my man OG Rosco to lend it to me."

OG Rosco was the biggest drug dealer in JJ's neighborhood at the time. Rosco was an older man in his early forties, thus the *O* in OG stood for Older. You wouldn't know it from the way he acted. He wore his pants hanging low like he was twenty-one, and he was the leader of the Bloods in his hood. He ran a group of teens and young men.

JJ went to Rosco's house to see if he could get a loan for the studio. When he arrived, there were four young Black men all wearing red T-shirts and red bandannas. They all looked at JJ like he was a stranger even though they all knew who JJ was. The tough looks were all a part of the act whenever they were around OG Rosco. They were all bent on impressing their general.

OG Rosco saw JJ walk up to his fence. "What's popping, fool?"

"Ain't nothing, OG Rosco. I need to holla at you for a minute."

Rosco ushered JJ into his house. "What can I do for you, young gangster?"

"Yo, OG Rosco, I need a loan to pay for my studio time. I promise to pay you back."

"How much money you talking about?"

JJ had to think about it. *I might as well ask for a little extra,* JJ thought. "How about a thousand dollars?"

"A thousand; let me think for a minute."

OG Rosco thought like an old wolf. He was always trying to get more soldiers for his drug empire. All his soldiers were younger men that he could control because they believed that he was a gangster. The truth was that young men were the only men that OG Rosco could deceive into believing that he was the toughest man alive. Older men already knew that was game.

"I tell you what, JJ. I'll give you a thousand for your studio time. But I want back twelve hundred. I will give you some drugs to get me my twelve hundred back and you can make extra for yourself." OG Rosco was scratching his chin as he spoke.

JJ had to think about the drug selling part of the deal. He was against selling drugs, but he was desperate right now. *Fuck it, if I sell drugs this one time, it won't hurt.*

"I'll do it."

Rosco reached into his pocket and pulled out about ten thousand dollars. He peeled off ten one-hundred-dollar bills. "JJ, I knew you all your life. You know not to play with OG Rosco's paper." Rosco squinted his eyes to give JJ a serious look.

"Believe me, OG, I would never play with your money."

OG Rosco walked to his kitchen and came back with an ounce of crack. "This is an ounce of crack. I want eight hundred for this ounce. You should be able to make about twenty-five hundred. You owe me two thousand all together."

"I got you, OG. I won't let you down."

JJ left that day feeling nervous and happy at the same time. He knew nothing about selling crack, but he knew someone that did. He called his best friend Dee.

"Yo, Dee, I need your help."

JJ explained the whole deal with OG Rosco.

"You are crazy for fucking with OG Rosco like that. If you don't have his money the whole Blood nation will try to kill you," Dee said. "But fuck it, I will help you get the crack off."

JJ recorded his songs, then him and Dee sold all the crack in three days. When the crack was done they had all OG's money and three hundred fifty left over for themselves.

"That was the fastest money I've ever made in my life," JJ said in amazement.

"I'm telling you, son, we can get rich. OG got the best product on Long Island. That's why it moved so fast. See if you can get more. My fiends love it," Dee said with enthusiasm.

"How much should I ask for?"

"Get another ounce for now."

JJ went back to OG Rosco and got another ounce after he paid him his money.

"You're a natural at selling crack. I tell you what, I'll give you two ounces, just give me back fifteen hundred this time."

"I got you, OG."

JJ and Dee knocked off the two ounces faster than the first one. They were blowing up faster than they imagined. They gave OG his money again and he gave them more crack to sell. And again, they got it all off faster the third time.

"Yo, JJ, we have to find out who OG's connect is. If we could get it for the same price he is getting it for, we can be rich," Dee advised JJ.

"How do we get his connect?" JJ asked.

"We can follow him when he goes to Washington Heights to re-up. I know that's where he goes to get it because one of his soldiers named Trapp is my man, he told me one day."

"Do you think Trapp will help us without telling OG we're trying to get his connect?" JJ asked.

"Let's find out."

Dee called Trapp on his cellphone.

"What's good Trapp? I got a business proposition for you."

"Tell me about it."

"I will give you a hundred dollars if you help me get OG Rosco's connect."

Dee knew he was taking a huge chance telling Trapp that, but he knew that Trapp was a grimy dude. Trapp would do anything for money.

"Hell yeah I'll do it. OG Rosco be on some bullshit. He got me hustling for nothing. He doesn't pay us right. That's how he's able to get money because we do all the selling and he doesn't pay us much," Trapp replied.

"How long do you think it will take you?"

"No more than a week." Trapp paused. "I'm going to need half of that hundred up front, a nigga fucked up right now."

"Here we go with the bullshit. I tell you what, if you don't have the info in one week, you give me sixty back instead of fifty."

"Bet."

JJ heard the whole conversation. "Now all we have to do is find out when he is going and follow him to see the connect's face and then just approach him."

"That's the plan," Dee replied.

Chapter 2

Trapp sank into the plush white leather of the sofa. He took a pull of the exotic weed and started choking. "Damn! This is some shit," Trapp said, coughing. He took a sip of the Hennessy and drifted off to Fantasy Island. "One day I will have it all, the money, fame—"

Trapp was brought back to reality by the sound of OG Rosco's raspy baritone. "Nigga, pass that muthafuckin exotic! That shit cost me almost eight hundred an ounce and you sitting there letting the shit burn into the air. You lucky your bum ass is even sitting on OG's couch." OG paused to look Trapp in his eyes to see if he didn't like what he said. "Now what the fuck is so urgent? You said you had to tell OG something important, so get to telling."

"I have somebody that wants to buy some weight from you." Trapp made up something fast.

"You can't be serious. That ain't fucking urgent."

"I know but they wanted—"

OG held up his hand as a sign for Trapp to stop talking because his cellphone rang.

"Petey what's poppin, my man?" OG quickly changed his tone to a pleasant one.

"I just got them new Jordans in that I was telling you about. They're cheaper, too. When you get a chance, come see them."

"I'll be there in an hour."

OG sprang up from the sofa so fast that he spilled the glass of Hennessy on his Gucci shirt. In the midst of all the chaos, OG didn't notice that he had dropped his cellphone on the floor.

"Dammit! Now look what you made OG do!" OG headed toward the bathroom. "This Gucci shirt cost me almost a thousand dollars."

Trapp saw the phone on the floor. As he stood, he scooped the phone off the floor in one motion.

"I'm out, OG. I'll get up with you later."

"I hope not, with your bad-luck ass."

Trapp ran out of OG's house, then down the block as fast as he could. He didn't want OG to notice the phone was missing before he was out of sight. When he got to his house he looked into the call history of OG's cellphone. The last call was Petey.

"Now I got the connect's number and OG's customers." Trapp had a sinister scowl on his face. "Just to think I was going to put OG on to Dee wanting his connect, for a small fee of course. But since my 'bum ass' is lucky to sit on your couch, fuck your old ass."

Trapp had another idea. He called Dee up.

"What's goody, my man? I got something better than what you asked for. I have the connect's number, and something else that might be of service to you. I got OG Rosco's cellphone with all his customers in it."

"Here we go with more bullshit. How much do you want for the phone?" Dee said in an annoyed tone.

"I was thinking around a G."

"A thousand dollars! My fucking iPhone didn't even cost that much. I will give you five hundred, no more no less."

"Since you're my dude, I will give it to you for five hundred but under one condition."

"Here we go with more bullshit. What is that one condition?"

"I want to get down with you and JJ. Fuck that old-ass nigga, OG."

"Okay, you can get money with me and JJ."

That was how the three-man drug team was born. JJ Gates and Dee became the new drug lords of their hood; Trapp was just a worker.

A month after JJ and Dee bought OG's customers, OG was set up by the Feds on a half-kilo sell. The Feds charged OG Rosco with the 848 kingpin statute. He faced life in prison without the possibility of parole. OG Rosco's career in crime was over.

With OG Rosco officially out of the picture, Dee and JJ quickly took his spot. Within no time they rose to the top of the food chain. The whole hood was buzzing about the new neighborhood superstars, JJ Gates and Dee Money.

Chapter 3

Petey took a liking to JJ Gates upon first meeting him. Petey was heavily into American rap music. He listened to all the top rappers. Even though he couldn't speak English that well, he understood the drug talk that he heard on most of the rap songs.

JJ gave Petey a copy of his new songs when they first met. Petey drove around in his new CL600 Benz listening to JJ Gates all day. Petey loved the songs so much that he became a fan of JJ's music.

"Why isn't your music on the radio? Your shit is better than half the stuff they're playing," Petey said with excitement.

"I don't have any money backing my album. If I had some money to invest in my career I could get it popping."

"How much money do you think you'll need?" Petey asked.

"A good fifty thousand will do the job."

"Say no more. I have that for you. All I want is twenty percent of everything you make from the music business. Just say I'm a silent partner." Petey smiled and stuck out his hand for a deal-sealing handshake.

"Good looking, my man. You won't regret it."

"I believe in you."

When Petey gave JJ the fifty thousand, JJ only put twenty thousand into his career. The other thirty thousand he invested in the drug game. That was how JJ ended up with more money than his mentor Dee.

JJ couldn't see it, but his activity in the drug game was changing him. Before he got involved with the drug game he wouldn't rap about drugs and violence. All his new songs were about drugs and violence. Now that he had become a big-time drug dealer, his ego was out of control. Because he had more money than Dee, he thought he was a bigger boss.

The truth was that Dee was the brains behind the operation. Without Dee at the wheel, JJ wouldn't be as successful on his own. But you couldn't tell JJ that. Let him tell it, his quick rise to the top was all because of his skill.

"I'm that dude," JJ said, gloating out loud as he drove his Tahoe. "Who else in the hood just came in the game and caked up like the kid?"

Dee never responded to JJ's narcissistic rants. However, lately JJ was starting to get on Dee's nerves.

Trapp noticed that Dee was getting tired of JJ's constant bragging. Every day he was reminding them that he had more money than them.

"My album is about to blow, my cash flow is crazy. My swag is up."

"My man, I'm tired of hearing that shit. All day that's all you talk about," Dee stated defiantly.

"You sound like a hater right now."

"You sound like a dickhead right now."

JJ pulled up to Lobo Studios. That's where he recorded all his new music. Lobo was the most advanced state-of-the-art music studio in New York.

When they entered the building, JJ went straight into the microphone booth. He took the 9mm from his waist and put it on a table. "This is for the haters," JJ said into the microphone. "It's your boy, no, it's that man, JJ Gates."

Whenever he was in the studio his egotistical bragging was turned up.

"That nigga JJ is fronting too much," Trapp said to Dee.

"I know. He was never like that until I put him on to hustling," Dee responded.

"I knew him as the dude that always rapped, not as no gangster or money getter."

JJ couldn't hear what they were saying because the microphone booth was soundproof. He was too busy spewing his raps into the mic.

"Son is acting like he can hold down this operation without you," Trapp said, planting seeds of deceit.

"We all know who the real boss of this operation is."

"I don't know, son, that nigga JJ got the brand-new Tahoe, mad ice. The hood thinks he is the boss, not you."

Trapp was deliberately pushing Dee to hate his best friend. Dee was steaming with angry thoughts about JJ. Trapp got a kick out of playing the puppet master.

"Next time JJ say some slick shit about him being the boss, I'm going to show him who the real fucking boss is," Dee said with venom in his tone.

"That's what I'm talking about." Trapp was amplifying Dee's anger.

JJ was in the booth finishing up his verse. "Yeah, that's a wrap," he said to the engineer.

JJ stepped out of the booth and headed toward the exit, Dee and Trapp followed him silently. Anyone could tell there was something on Dee's mind.

Just as they reached the Tahoe, JJ stopped short. "I forgot my rhyme book. You know I can't forget that, it's worth millions." JJ ran back into the studio.

"You heard what he just said. His rhyme book is worth millions," Dee said with envy.

Trapp didn't put any more fuel on Dee's fire. He didn't have to, Dee was literally fuming.

JJ ran back to the Tahoe, he noticed the mean stare that Dee was giving him. "I'm saying, what's good with the evil stares and shit? You got something you want to get off your chest, Dee?"

"Matter of fact, I do got something I want to get off my chest." Dee squared off with JJ before he continued to talk. "You've been saying some fly shit lately."

"What you mean fly shit?"

"Don't get it twisted, my man, I'm the boss of this operation."

"You're not the boss of shit. It was my product from the beginning. All you did was sell it for me."

"Oh word, all I did was sell for you; dog, I made you. You're my student," Dee stated arrogantly.

"It looks like you're the student, because I've been selling drugs for eighteen months and I'm already Hood Rich. You've been selling drugs all your life. You just mad because my stacks is up and you still a little nigga in the game," JJ replied with more arrogance.

Those words cut deep into Dee. He wanted to punch JJ in his mouth, but he knew JJ had the 9mm on his hip.

"What, you don't like something I said?" JJ was pushing more buttons.

"Check this out, you do your thing and I'll do mine. Then we'll see who the real hustler is."

"Everybody already see who the real hustler is." JJ held up his diamond pinkie ring that matched the diamonds in his Benny & Co. timepiece.

"We'll see. You've been fronting a lot since Petey gave you that fifty thousand. That's the only reason you got money."

"Whatever, Dee, tell your story walking, my man."

JJ jumped in his Tahoe and sped off. "Fuck them bum-ass niggas. I'll show them who the hustler is."

Chapter 4

JJ was writing in his rhyme book while the youngster known as Cannon talked on and on like he was giving JJ a lecture.

"I got some shit, too, son. I did this one song over the Lil Wayne beat 'Mr. Carter.' I killed that shit, son," Cannon boasted.

Cannon was only eighteen years old, five years JJ's junior. He looked up to JJ because of his newfound hood status. JJ recruited Cannon to his team. Cannon rode on everything JJ said as if it was law.

That's what JJ liked about having Cannon around. He knew that Cannon looked up to him, so it fed JJ's ego. He needed his ego stroked more nowadays than ever.

After Trapp and Dee parted ways with JJ, his cash flow literally stopped. When Dee and Trapp left, they took the clientele with them. JJ didn't know how to get new fiends, so he had product with no customers.

JJ felt he had to keep up the front until he could get his

business popping again. His new ego wouldn't let him admit defeat.

"We're going to take this show on the road, baby. Down south you can make more money off this shit than up here," JJ said to young Cannon. "I'll show that nigga Dee who the real hustler is."

"Word, fuck that nigga Dee," Cannon said with animosity.

JJ noticed the hate in Cannon's tone. "Where do you know Dee from?"

Cannon paused and gave JJ a look of uneasiness. "I use to fuck with him back in the day." Cannon cleverly switched the topic. "I heard you can make like five thousand off an ounce down there," Cannon said with mock excitement.

"Yeah, something like that. That's if you break the ounces down."

JJ tried to sound like an expert. Cannon agreed with everything he said.

"Plus my album is about to be done. I'm about to pull a Jay-Z on the game. I'm about to drop an album on my own label."

JJ looked up to Jay-Z more than any other rapper. He liked the fact that Jay-Z owned the label he rapped on.

"That's how I'm going to make more money. I'm about to leave Dee and Trapp in the dust."

"Word, and I'm gonna be right there with you on top, son, like BAM! We here now!"

JJ just looked at Cannon with an annoyed smirk. He often did that whenever Cannon said something he didn't like.

"We're going to pack up the Tahoe tonight. We're going to Richmond, Virginia. I got family down there." JJ grabbed a stack of his CDs that were on the table. "I'm taking real crack down there, too." He held up his CDs.

They hid a whole kilo inside a secret compartment JJ had built into the Tahoe.

JJ went back into his apartment to see if he was forgetting anything. "I got my Guccis, my Louies, the Pradas . . . what am I missing?" He looked around the room. He saw his precious rhyme book laying on the table. He contemplated taking it with him. "No, I don't need my rhyme book. I'm not going down there to record, I'm going to get money." He looked around once more before bouncing out the door.

Trapp and Dee sat at the table in Dee's plush apartment smoking a blunt and bagging up crack. They were really getting money. Since they parted ways with JJ, they'd gotten more customers. They were still getting the product from Petey so it was dirt cheap.

"I'm about to show this lame who the fucking boss is. Dee is, that's who."

Trapp just nodded his head in agreement.

"I made three times more money since I stopped fucking with that nigga JJ."

"Word, we're moving a brick a week. That's crazy," Trapp added.

"I think I might cop a Benz next week, just to show this lame we getting it."

Dee was starting to carry on just like JJ. He was becoming more arrogant by the day. He was reminding Trapp every day that he was getting money in the same way that JJ used to do to him.

"I'm trying to cop a big-boy whip, too, son," Trapp said.

"If you got that big-boy whip money, do it my man. I got it."

Trapp was offended by Dee's statement. Dee knew that Trapp didn't have the money for a big car. Trapp felt like Dee was putting him down by saying that.

"I'll have it soon, watch."

"Of course you will, if you fuck with Dee Money. I'm the nigga that made JJ Gates rich. Stick with me and you will go places."

Trapp wanted to say something, but he knew it was best not to because he would show his true colors. Trapp was a chameleon, you never knew his real color.

"I heard JJ's new song on the radio the other day. It's hot," Trapp said, knowing it would push Dee's buttons.

"I heard that wack-ass shit. He might as well hang it up because he sounds too much like Jay-Z if you ask me."

"I'm going to keep it official, JJ Gate's music is hot. He might not be a good drug dealer but he is a good rapper."

"Damn, son, what are you, his number one fan or something? Stop riding the nigga's dick."

"I ain't riding nobody's dick, son, I call it how I see it. I'm going to keep it one hundred percent no matter what."

"Whatever, Trapp, I don't even want to talk about that nigga. Fuck it, if you like his music, you like his music. Let's finish bagging up this crack."

Trapp was playing mind games with Dee. He knew the outcome of his statement about JJ's music. He saw Dee becoming more like JJ. The more money they made, the more like JJ Dee became.

The drug game was consuming them all.

Chapter 5

It took JJ seven hours to get to Richmond, Virginia, from Long Island, New York. He drove the speed limit all the way there.

When they arrived, JJ's cousin Tim came out to greet them. "What's happening, cuz? It's been a long time," Tim said in a thick southern drawl.

"I know, but if things go well, I'll be here every week."

"That's what's up, cuz."

JJ wasted no time setting up shop in Richmond's infamous Jackson Ward projects on St. Paul Street. Drugs were sold there 24 hours a day, 7 days a week.

JJ let Cannon break down four and a half ounces all in twenty-dollar rocks. He bagged up twenty thousand dollars. On the first day he didn't make that much money; the fiends had to get familiar with him. Once they tried his product and it was good, the word spread. By the second day Cannon had ten thousand in cash.

Cannon had never experienced making this much money this fast. He kept counting the money over and over. Cannon's young mind became fascinated by the fast cash.

"Yo, I've never seen anything like this before in my life," Cannon stated to JJ with excitement. "By the time we're finished we both might be able to cop a Benz."

"I doubt it." JJ gave Cannon that look. "You're only getting twenty percent of whatever you make, my man. Don't get it twisted."

JJ didn't know it but he just crushed Cannon's hopes. Whenever you do that to a person, you create animosity. The way Dee felt when he was with JJ is the same way that Cannon was starting to feel.

I'm doing all the work and he's getting all the money, Cannon thought to himself. *I know how to get down here on my own. I'll come down here with my own work and put it in the same way I'm putting it in for this nigga JJ.*

JJ had a talent for rubbing people the wrong way lately. He wasn't even conscious of his actions. JJ went from a good dude that was in college living a normal life, to living the life of a big-time drug dealer overnight.

The drug game was ruining his morals and integrity. He was willing to risk doing years in prison for drug money, something that he was totally against two years ago.

The pace that JJ moved at in the drug game was like when LeBron James went straight to the league from high school. JJ went from an ounce to moving keys in a matter of months, something it takes most men years to achieve.

"Tim, where is the club where it be poppin? I'm trying to meet some honeys," JJ asked.

"Well, the Paradise Lounge is more your speed, cuz. Now, if

you want to go to a spot where them dope boys be, the Satellite Club is the spot."

"I think I'll do the Paradise Lounge. I'm trying to see some bad-ass VA chicks."

Just as he spoke, a beautiful caramel brown woman got out of her car and walked into the store. She caught JJ's eye immediately.

"Damn! Who the hell is that?" JJ asked so loud that she heard him.

"Why don't you just ask me?" the beautiful girl said.

"What's your name?" JJ asked in a shy tone.

"My name is Sasha. And what might your name be?" Sasha replied.

"My name is Jamal but my friends call me JJ."

"Nice to meet you, JJ."

"The pleasure is all mine." JJ paused to think of his next line. "You got to have a man as pretty as you are."

"No, because men don't act right."

"We don't act right maybe because you haven't met the right one yet."

"Let me guess, you're the right one."

"Maybe. There's only one way to find out." JJ smiled.

Sasha returned the smile. "Well, JJ, it was nice to meet you." She headed toward the store.

"Wait!" JJ shouted. "Can I get your number?"

She paused and looked him in his eyes. She saw something that she hadn't seen in a man's eyes before. She saw sincerity.

"Okay, Mr. JJ, I usually don't give my number out but—" She reached into her Coach pocketbook and gave him one of her business cards.

JJ read the card: Sasha Cohen, Attorney-at-Law.

"You're an attorney?"

"Yes. You said that like that's impossible."

"No, not at all, it's just that it's not every day that you meet a beautiful woman that is also intelligent."

Sasha smiled and continued to walk into the store.

"I'm definitely calling her."

JJ went home to get ready for the club. He put on his Gucci loafers, True Religion jeans, and a Gucci shirt that matched his loafers perfectly.

Even young Cannon got fly for the occasion. He put on a pair of aluminum-gray Prada shoes, gray Antik Denim jeans, and a gray Christian Audigier shirt.

When they entered the Paradise Lounge all eyes were on them. All the ladies were eyeing them.

JJ saw one woman in particular that caught his eye. She had a caramel-brown complexion, long black hair, hazel eyes, and the body of a goddess.

JJ couldn't resist walking over to her for a conversation. When he reached the woman he squinted his eyes because she looked familiar. He did a double take when he saw who the woman was.

"Sasha!"

"JJ. What are you doing here?"

"The same thing that you're doing, just having a good time before I go back to New York."

They sat in a corner ignoring everyone else in the club. Sasha was taken aback by JJ's smooth manner. JJ could tell that she was feeling him by the way she stared into his eyes.

They conversed for the better part of two hours. JJ felt that he knew enough to make a move on her. He leaned into her ear and whispered, "What you doing after this?"

"You tell me," she answered in a sexy tone.

JJ told Cannon that he was leaving with Sasha. "You're on your own, son."

"I'm good, shorty over there with the fatty told me I'm going home with her tonight," Cannon responded.

JJ looked over at the chocolate beauty with the roundest behind he'd ever seen. "Damn, son, she is stacked."

"It must be something in the water down here in Virginia, because all these chicks got fattys," Cannon stated playfully.

"I'll see you tomorrow. We're probably leaving then because we'll be done, most likely."

"I know." Cannon paused to choose his next words wisely. "Yo, JJ thanks for bringing me down here with you. You're like the older brother I never had. I will never betray you, JJ, my word is my bond."

JJ got a lump in his throat from the heartfelt speech. "No doubt, you already know what it is. Make sure you don't get in too late because we have a lot to do tomorrow."

"I always got your back."

With that said, JJ strolled away with one of the most beautiful women in the club.

Word spread fast about JJ and Cannon coming into town. Some of the locals weren't feeling the way JJ just came into town and tried to lock things down.

One of those locals was an OG like Rosco, he went by the name Chopper. Chopper got his name for shooting three men with an AK-47. In the hood they called AK-47s Choppers, because of their ability to chop limbs clean off.

Chopper controlled the whole Jackson Ward section that JJ was conquering. Chopper didn't take out-of-town cats selling in his area too lightly, especially cats from New York. In fact, the three men that he shot were all from New York.

"This muthafucka JJ must not know who the fuck he dealing with. They don't call me Chopper for nothing. Somebody better tell that boy," Chopper said to one of his cohorts. "I think we going to pay this JJ fellow a little visit."

Chopper cocked back the AK-47 and made sure the safety was off. He put the AK-47 in a duffel bag and walked toward his vehicle.

JJ and Cannon were both in the middle of the projects surrounded by fiends and dope boys trying to take all the orders. JJ's cousin Tim played lookout for the narcs.

"I need two ounces, pimping. I know you can trim some fat off the cost," said the local dealer known as Big, named for his striking resemblance to the late great icon Christopher "B.I.G." Wallace.

"I got you, my man, this is your fourth time seeing me so just give me fourteen hundred dollars this time." JJ reached into his pocket and handed Big a CD. "This is a couple of songs from my forthcoming album."

"I heard your songs were like that, dog. Good looking." Big gave JJ a pound and went on about his business.

JJ walked toward the building to get Big his order. He went into the apartment, weighed two ounces, and exited. Just as he walked out of the building, Chopper put the AK-47 to his temple.

"I know exactly what you're thinking, young blood. *How the fuck this nigga creep up on me like that?*"

Chopper had on dark glasses and a winter cap with a blue bandanna covering his mouth. There was no way for JJ to know who he was.

"I'm going to tell you how, because your bitch ass ain't from around here. You don't know my territory like I do. Now you're trapped."

JJ's heart was beating a hundred miles a minute. He was terrified. He'd never had an AK-47 held up against his temple.

"Now, slowly pass the muthafuckin bag over to me."

JJ passed Chopper the bag so slow you would've thought he was Neo from *The Matrix*.

Cannon knew that it wouldn't take JJ this long to get Big's order.

Something ain't right, Cannon thought as he grabbed the 40-caliber handgun they had stashed in case of emergency. "They don't call me Cannon for nothing."

Cannon slowly crept to the area where JJ had the weight stashed. He saw Chopper holding the AK up to JJ's temple.

Just as Chopper was about to grab the bag from JJ's hand, Cannon came from behind the building blasting the 40-caliber. He let off three ear-shattering shots right in Chopper's direction. One of the rounds hit Chopper in his shoulder, knocking him back.

Although Chopper was hit, he managed to hold on to the AK as if it were glued to his hands. Before Chopper hit the ground, he let off a barrage of automatic gunfire right in Cannon's direction. Two of the rounds hit young Cannon's body. One hit him in his chest, the other hit him in his throat. Both hits were fatal. Cannon was dead before he hit the ground.

The hole that was left in Cannon's chest was the size of a grapefruit. His head was hanging by a piece of muscle tissue to his neck. If it were not for the muscle tissue, Cannon would have been decapitated by the AK round.

Both men lay on the ground, except Chopper was still living. However, the 40-caliber did some major damage. Chopper's left arm was separated from his shoulder. It seems that AK-47's aren't the only guns that chop limbs clean off.

Chopper started to go into shock. "I can't feel my arm!" he shouted.

JJ was also in shock. He stood still, staring in the direction of young Cannon's cold body laying on the floor. He heard the sirens coming, but he couldn't run. All he could do was slowly walk in the direction of Cannon's body.

At the same time JJ reached Cannon's body and looked down, a red-haired police officer yelled, "FREEZE!"

Freeze was all JJ could do. The sight of what the AK did to his little homie traumatized him so much that he fainted before the officer could put cuffs on him.

The officer panicked; he thought JJ fell to the ground because he was hit. He quickly walked over with his 9mm held out in front of him. When he got close enough to see Cannon's body he shouted, "Oh shit!"

The police academy didn't prepare him for this. As much as they thought they'd seen it all, there is always something crazier than the last.

"This is Officer Putnam. We have three men down at the south entrance of the Jackson Ward Projects."

He mistakenly thought JJ was down because of a gun wound, until he noticed that JJ wasn't bleeding, and he was moving. Officer Putnam knew JJ was alive; that's when he grabbed JJ's hand. He let it go right before the ambulance got there.

When the ambulance got there, the medics noticed that JJ wasn't bleeding from anywhere. "He must be in shock," one of them said.

He put smelling salts under JJ's nose until he began to cough.

"Yeah, this one is okay."

JJ shook his head from side to side, scrunching his nose up from the effects of the powerful smelling salts. "What happened?" he asked, trying to move his left hand but it was chained to a metal rail.

Officer Putnam was sitting next to him. JJ recognized that police shield immediately, then the rest started slowly coming back like a bad dream.

"NO! What happened to Cannon?" The memory of what he saw was coming back and he was going back into shock.

"Sedate him!" the head medic ordered.

Before he could blink, there was a needle being injected into his arm. Within seconds he was back in la-la land.

"Don't worry, when he wakes up again, I'll be right here. Detective Hewes has some questions for you," said Officer Putnam, the same cop with the red hair who had ordered JJ to freeze. "You're facing some pretty big charges. Yeah, he's a big fish, all right. Attempted murder, and possession of narcotics," Officer Putnam said with pride.

This was the biggest catch of his mediocre career in law enforcement. He was ecstatic about arresting JJ, and was going to charge JJ with possession of the 40-caliber that shot Chopper's arm off.

JJ's good luck looked like it had just ran out.

Chapter 6

"This fucking drought is killing me!" Dee complained. "I haven't made a fucking dime in two weeks!"

Trapp just shook his head in silence. His pockets were hurting so bad, he didn't even have any more lint left in them. Whenever times got this bad, Trapp resorted to grimy measures. Trapp had devious thoughts running through his mind.

"Yo, we need to do a nice jux." Trapp spoke like a hungry wolf.

"Fuck it, right about now I'm ready to do whatever," Dee said in agreement with Trapp.

Trapp liked it when he was able to convince someone to do evil. It fueled a strange feeling of power in his mind that was becoming dangerous and uncontrollable.

"Anybody can fucking get it," Dee added.

"That's what the fuck I'm saying!" Trapp gave Dee a strong handshake to increase the negative energy.

Just then Trapp's cellphone rang. "What's poppin?"

"Yo, did you hear about what happened to JJ and Cannon?"

"No, what happened, son?" Trapp's diabolical mind was always looking to profit from anything, especially now.

"Little Cannon from C.I. by one-eleven and Sycamore went down South to VA with that nigga JJ and got murdered, and the nigga JJ locked up for a body and like a half a key or some crazy shit. He facing life in prison."

"Son, stop playing!" Trapp said with a hint of glee in his voice as if he was half happy about JJ's demise.

"Word bond, son. This bitch that fuck with his cousin aunt's cousin, or some shit like that, told me." The youngster on the phone paused to pull on a blunt.

The truth wasn't the truth once it traveled a block, let alone four hundred miles. The story was twisted at least a hundred times before it got to Trapp from his source.

"She said Cannon got his whole torso and head blown off, and this nigga JJ killed the nigga that killed Cannon. Then they found made drugs on JJ. He finished, son."

"Son, I'm going to call you later." Trapp was anxious to tell Dee about JJ's misfortune.

"Who was that, Trapp?"

"Some lame, but yo! This nigga just told me that JJ got locked up for a body and a half-key possession. He facing life in prison." He paused. "Oh yeah, some kid named Cannon from C.I. got murdered down there with him." Trapp spoke about Cannon as if he was nobody.

"Wait a minute, did you say a kid named Cannon from C.I. by one-eleven and Sycamore?" Dee's face became flushed.

"Yeah, he did say by one-eleven. I don't know that nigga, though." Trapp stopped talking because he saw the look on Dee's face. "Yo, Dee, you all right, man?" Trapp asked with concern.

"Noooo!" Dee screamed at the top of his lungs. Just then his cellphone rang. He saw the name on his caller ID and automatically knew what they were going to say. "Hello."

"Derrick, this is your Aunt Beverly." She spoke calmly, then came the storm. "They killed my baby! They killed my baby! He was only eighteen years old and his birthday was next week!" she shouted into the phone with a river of tears running down her smooth brown complexion. "They killed my baby!"

Dee hung up the phone and began to clutch his heart. Young Cannon was Dee's first cousin. A cousin that Dee used to be very close with. The thing that was hurting Dee the most was the fall-out they had the last time he saw Cannon.

"I don't want you to hustle, Li'l Cannon. I can pay for your studio time and pay for the video and everything. Just don't hustle because you can't rap from behind bars, let me take that risk."

"Fuck that, if you can hustle I can, too. I'm not little Cannon no more. From now on knock that little shit from in front of my handle. I'm getting money and can't nobody stop me."

"Yo, little nigga, don't get it fucked up! I will still put the beats on you!"

"You ain't going to do nothing to Cannon. Move out my way."

Dee punched Cannon in the face, then Cannon pulled out a .357 Magnum, hit Dee in the side of his head, and pointed the barrel between Dee's eyes.

"I should blow your fucking head off." Cannon saw the blood leaking from Dee's temple and was content with that. "Now your stupid ass is leaking for fucking with a G!"

Dee felt the side of his face and saw blood on his fingers. "Yo, from now on I don't give a fuck what happens to you. Don't call me, you're dead to me! You ain't shit to me."

"I don't need you any fucking way, lame."

Cannon stormed out of the house.

That was two years ago.

Dee was reminiscing on that last moment with the only male cousin he had in his whole family. Cannon was like Dee's little brother, in fact Cannon's short tenure in the drug game was due to Dee.

Cannon wanted to be just like his older cousin. Dee built a formidable reputation for himself on the local drug scene. Cannon used his cousin's reputation on many occasions to get connections in the game.

Dee knew that his cousin wanted to be like him, and although he was flattered, he wanted Cannon to be more than a drug dealer. He saw Cannon as a talented rap artist. He wanted him to be successful in something positive, because he had the talent.

Dee saw too many people from his hood with talent that did

nothing with it. He wanted Cannon to transcend mediocrity, to be the greatest. Now Cannon would never get that chance.

"It's all that nigga JJ's fault. If he wouldn't have taken the little nigga down there, he wouldn't have gotten murdered. You know how that nigga JJ is, he always want somebody to do shit his way. Well look what his way did, it got his dumb ass locked up for life, and he got your little cousin killed."

Trapp was using this situation to his evil advantage. He saw the vengeance building up in Dee's eyes. He looked as evil as Trapp did when he was in this mode, so Trapp knew the look.

"You right, son, it's all that nigga JJ's fault. Fuck that nigga JJ Gates, we going to run up in that nigga's apartment. I know where he keep his money and everything. That nigga still be keeping his bread in shoe boxes," Dee said deviously with tears for his cousin running down his face.

"Fuck it, son, let's get it poppin."

JJ's apartment was in the hood. He was still a novice in the game, so he hadn't learned the simple but complex rule, don't shit where you sleep. Although he had come up fast in the game, it was pure luck. He just happened to be at the right place around the right people that made it happen for him, but he took all the credit.

It didn't take Trapp any time to break into JJ's apartment. Once they were in, Dee led the way straight to a closet that had fifty Jordan sneaker boxes lined up against the back wall.

"Which one of these boxes has the money in it?" Trapp asked impatiently. "We don't have time to go through them all."

"I think he keeps it on the third row or some dumb shit."

Dee took the whole third row and quickly went through them. There was no money in none of the boxes on the third row.

"Fuck it, move over, son, let's both go through the boxes. We don't have time to bullshit." Trapp shoved Dee to the side and started going through the boxes with him.

Trapp opened a box. It was stacked to the top with hundreds. He didn't say a word. He moved that box to the side.

Just then there was a loud knock on the door.

"Oh shit!" Dee said in a shouting whisper. Dee headed straight for the window in JJ's room. It led to the backyard.

That was Trapp's chance to stash the money he found. He started stuffing as much of it as he could into all his pockets.

Boom! Boom! Boom! "Open up!" Then the door burst open. Two police officers slowly canvassed the area.

Someone saw Trapp break in and they called the cops.

Trapp headed for the window. He saw JJ's golden rhyme book laying on the nightstand. He snatched the rhyme book up and fled out the window.

As Trapp fled through the backyard, he thought to himself, *Why did I snatch this fucking notebook?* Then the words of JJ ran through his mind.

I can't forget my rhyme book, it's worth millions.

"I didn't get all the money. Fuck it, I got a lot."

Trapp separated from Dee and went to his house. He emptied all his pockets and counted the money. He had $12,360.

"It must have been at least eight thousand more left. Fuck it, twelve thousand is a come up."

Trapp looked at JJ's rhyme book. He picked it up and started reading some of JJ's raps out loud as if he was performing them.

"JJ gunplay / my chick on the runway / slang yay / all day / cook cake like soufflé / wrap 'em up / then ship 'em out of town / man your boy outta bounds / we don't ball with you clowns / we pop champagne until we spit it up / that new CL 600 / 'bout to pick it up/ the whole rap game / Trapp about to stick it up / 'cause ain't no clique on this planet / spit as sick as us / Trapp is a don / hundred g's on my arm / plus fifty on the charm / got your girl on my arm."

"I think I can do this rap shit," Trapp said after a quick session with JJ's rhymes.

That night Trapp spent eight hours smoking kush and spitting JJ's rhymes as if they were his. He started to envision himself on stage performing for hundreds of fly girls and thugs. He envisioned all the money and fame, something that Trapp always wanted.

Trapp was always the low man on the totem pole. He was never known for anything other than being broke, instigating beef, and being a soldier under someone. No girls wanted to get with him because he was only fly one day out of the week, the rest of the week he was wearing the same outfit. Then he would buy a new outfit every week because the one he wore all week couldn't be worn again.

People were always putting Trapp down whenever he spoke of doing something big. People treated him like a nobody so he acted like one. However, since he had been hanging with Dee and JJ, he got a taste of money, and the hunger for more settled in.

"Fuck that, Trapp is about to be that new nigga everybody talk about."

Trapp fell asleep with visions of being a rap star dancing through his head.

Chapter 7

"Twenty-three-year-old Jamal Jenkins is awaiting trial for attempted murder and possession of two ounces of crack cocaine." They showed JJ entering the courtroom in cuffs. "He is facing twenty-five years in prison if convicted. Next up is Sal with your five-day weather report," the newscaster reported.

"I know him!" Sasha shouted.

"You know who?" her best friend Mina asked.

"That's the guy from New York that I met that I was telling you about, JJ."

"Damn, he is in a messed up predicament."

"I think I can help him," Sasha said sincerely.

"How did I know you were going to say that?" Mina asked sarcastically.

"No, seriously, I'm going to take his case pro bono. The firm has been asking me to take on some major cases, so this will be my first one. Plus, the fact that homie put it on me!" Sasha and Mina gave each other a high five.

"I know that's right, because I heard your freaky ass."

"I'll be at the courtroom first thing tomorrow morning. Jamal Jenkins." Sasha scribbled the name on a legal notepad. "JJ, Jamal Jenkins, very clever."

Sasha couldn't get JJ off her mind. That night she had broken her golden rule for the first time; she gave up the goods on the first night. It may have been the way JJ spent a thousand dollars on drinks that had something to do with it. Nevertheless, she thought about JJ every day.

Sasha Cohen came from a privileged family. Her exotic features were due to a mixture of Jewish and Black heritage. Both of her parents were lawyers, so she was a second-generation lawyer in the family.

Sasha graduated with a law degree from the University of Colorado at the age of twenty-five by doubling up for four years. She landed a probationary job at a local law firm immediately, due to her father's influence. Whether she stayed at the firm would depend on her skills as a lawyer.

"I'm going to look extra special for JJ tomorrow at court." Sasha was going through her wardrobe in the closet. "This right here will do."

She picked out a sexy but conservative teal-green skirt and matching blouse that hugged every curve of her voluptuous body.

"He will like this." Sasha already had plans to save JJ from his plight, and to seduce him at the same time. "I can't wait to see him again."

Sasha dozed off thinking of JJ.

Incarceration quickly desensitized JJ; he was numb to his situation, and he accepted his current reality. JJ didn't know anything about the legal system, so he was confused in the courtroom. On his first court date the judge appointed him a legal aid.

"People recommend one million dollars bail," the DA quickly announced.

"Bail set at the sum of one million U.S. dollars!" The judge slammed her gavel down.

JJ was escorted to the bullpen to wait for a bus to return to the Richmond County jail. While he was in the bullpen, he met a cool old-timer named Solomon.

"Young blood, let me school you on something."

At first JJ was defensive, because in jail you have to be, but his instincts told him that Solomon meant no harm.

"Listen to me, get yourself a lawyer, because they are going to hang you."

"What do you mean they're going to hang me?" JJ was confused.

"When Black people were slaves, and afterward, White folk use to hang us from trees for their amusement. Now they found a different way to hang us, and that's in the courtroom, by taking so much time from you, that you may as well be dead."

Solomon's words were so powerful that they automatically sparked JJ's intuitive mind. He knew that Solomon was not like the rest of the old-timers he knew, like OG Rosco. Solomon displayed a genuine sense of caring and integrity that JJ respected.

"I can't get to my money in Long Island. I don't even know what the fuck these people are talking about. They're trying to say that I blew Chopper's arm off, and the drugs—" JJ stopped talking midsentence.

"Look, it don't matter what you did, all I know is that your case is a high-profile case because I saw you on the news. That means the DA is going to try to fry you because the media is involved."

"Damn, I didn't look at it like that," JJ said, bewildered by this epiphany.

"Don't worry, young blood, things sometimes have a way of

turning around when you least expect them to." Solomon rubbed his full beard as he spoke. "I'm Solomon." He stuck his hand out for a handshake. "What's your name, brother?"

"My name is Jamal, but everybody calls me JJ Gates or just JJ." JJ firmly shook Solomon's hand.

Solomon was facing life in prison for his third felony. His criminal history dated back to the seventies. The system was ready to lose him, but he was ready to save one young soul before they took him out.

"How old are you, JJ?"

"I'm twenty-three."

"Man, you are a baby. You have a lot of life left in you. You can come out of this smelling like a rose, my man."

The words of inspiration were working. JJ's spirits started rising instantly.

"Look at the bright side, JJ, you still have your health, you seem pretty smart, you're handsome. You have all the attributes to become something great in life. Don't waste your time on the streets, because you can end up like me. I'm forty-seven years old with nothing but years in jail and a bunch of war stories to show for it. You can be something great, JJ."

Their conversation was cut short by a CO. "Jamal Jenkins step up to the cage, your lawyer is here to see you," the CO said to JJ.

JJ found that strange because he just saw his lawyer earlier. He stepped up and the CO led him to a private chamber.

When JJ saw Sasha's beautiful smile it was like the sun shining in a dark universe.

"Sasha, what are you doing here?" JJ couldn't believe his eyes.

"I'm a lawyer, remember, or did you forget?" She gave JJ her sexiest smile with enticing eye contact.

"I was kind of drunk, but I remember your name."

She smiled, but then she quickly went into lawyer mode. This was no time for romance.

"First things first, I personally fired your legal aid for you and appointed myself as your new counsel. Second thing is that you have to tell me what happened no matter what you think. I'm your lawyer and I can not discuss anything you tell me with anyone. Understood?"

"I understand."

"If you didn't do what they accused you of, we're going to trial. If you did do it then I will get the lowest possible deal with the DA."

"I didn't shoot anyone, the drugs were mine but they didn't catch them on me. So I'm innocent."

"I can work with that," Sasha said with confidence. "If we are going to fight it, you're going to lay up in jail until we beat the case, unless you have the million-dollar bail they requested."

"No, I don't have a million." JJ thought about all the bragging he used to do about being Hood Rich.

"I didn't think you did. Well I can put in a motion for a bail reduction, but like I said, you will probably lay up for at least six months fighting this case."

"Fuck it, as long as I don't blow trial."

"Don't worry, I got you, JJ." Sasha gave JJ the most serious look she could. "There is no guarantee whenever you go to trial, but I can guarantee that I will fight for you with the best of my ability."

"I believe in you, Sasha. Just the simple fact that you're here gives me confidence." JJ gave her back a serious look.

It was obvious that Sasha was very interested in JJ. The fact that she came to his rescue made JJ like her more than he had ever liked a female before.

"I'm going to get you through this."

She exited the meeting feeling more intimately connected to JJ than any man in her young life.

"One way or another, I'm going to save him," she said to herself as she entered the judge's chamber to defend JJ.

Chapter 8

Trapp was in the same microphone booth that JJ was in not even a month ago, spitting JJ's rhymes. Trapp was a natural at saying JJ's rhymes, in fact Trapp's delivery was better than JJ's. Trapp had a smooth tone that held bass. The tone of his voice was almost hypnotizing.

The engineer was very impressed with the way Trapp sounded in the booth. "Yo, man, you sound awesome, dude. I think I can pass your music off to my friend that is an A&R at University Records. I'm sure they will sign you."

"Word, I appreciate that, Sammy. You already know if I get a deal I'm going to hit you off for hooking me up," Trapp said with excitement.

"Don't worry about me, all I want is a shout-out on the album."

"I got you, Sammy. Once again, thanks, man."

Trapp left the studio feeling like a million dollars. He'd begun to record JJ's songs two days after he stole his rhyme book; two weeks later he may have landed a record deal.

Trapp felt comfortable fronting because it was what he did best. It came natural for him to steal and lie, so this was something he was enjoying.

"If I get this record deal, it's on and poppin."

Trapp got a phone call; the caller ID revealed that it was Dee. Trapp pressed the ignore button, which directed Dee to Trapp's voice mail. Trapp hadn't answered any of Dee's calls since that day he stole JJ's rhyme book and the money.

Trapp also hadn't seen Dee since they ran up in JJ's apartment two weeks ago. Trapp started his own drug operation with the money he took from JJ. He didn't even have the decency to look out for Dee, after all Dee had done for him. Trapp left Dee for dead.

Dee went into a deep depression after his cousin Cannon got murdered. He stopped hustling and starting drinking and smoking weed all day. He started hanging with a bunch of broke cats that did what he was doing, smoking and drinking all day.

Things were looking up for Trapp. He was making money and recording songs. He was seeing more money than he ever saw in his life. He bought himself a brand-new wardrobe and some nice jewelry. He wanted everybody to know that he was getting money.

Trapp was feeling himself so hard, girls were noticing him now. Word in the hood was that Trapp was the new boss in town.

"I think I'm going to cop me a BMW 540i after this next flip." He looked at his iced-out Breitling watch. *Time to get with Shonda. I've been trying to get with her since fifth grade. Must be my watch, or maybe it's my chain,* Trapp thought with cockiness.

Dee and JJ's ego put together couldn't match Trapp's. Trapp would show up to a party in Gucci loafers with a matching shirt, then he would go home and come back in Dolce & Gabbana from head to toe.

Trapp never had anything his whole life, not even a family. All his life he had to fend for himself. Trapp grew up in the foster care system from the day he was born. He was one of the kids that never got chosen by a family. When he was eighteen he went out on his own and the gangs of the streets became his family.

Trapp was forced into a backstabbing and cutthroat way of life. He came up among hungry wolves that were just like him. There was no rules among wolves; that's where he learned to snake everyone in his circumference.

Trapp did every possible type of sneaky act imaginable. Trapp set up his man to get robbed, he snitched on drug dealers for the Feds. He instigated beefs that caused murders. He did these things to satisfy an innate beast-like hunger. Trapp is the epitome of a grimy dude.

Word in the hood was that Trapp snitched on OG Rosco. Rosco

was having his lawyer look into who signed statements on him. His lawyer said he would have the information in one week.

"Rosco, I have the DA working with me right now. Being that you copped out, we can't get a motion of discovery to find out exactly who signed statements on you. However, the DA owes me a favor."

"As soon as you find out who snitched on me I want to know right away, you understand me?" Rosco spoke sternly.

"I definitely will. You know this is going to add two thousand to your bill."

"I don't care if it's twenty thousand, I need to know who snitched on me. If it is who I think it is—" Rosco stopped speaking before he incriminated himself. Someone was always listening to inmates' conversations.

"I will see you in a week." Rosco's lawyer left the jail.

Rosco went back to his cell. He laid on his bed thinking about who he was going to get to do the job on whoever snitched on him.

"I won't rest until I get the rat that put me in this hellhole."

Rosco put his headphones on and went to sleep with visions of murder dancing in his head.

"Hey, Sammy, you were right, man, this guy Trapp is the truth. We want to sign him to a record deal immediately," said Ronald Schwartz, the head of University Records. "We want a single out before the summer is over."

"I'll call him right now. We can be in your office in an hour."

"That's even better. Make it happen for me, baby," Ronald said in an enthused tone before hanging up.

Sammy swiftly called Trapp, he answered on the third ring. "Come to the studio ASAP. Ronald Schwartz from University Records just told me that he wants to sign you immediately."

"Say no more, let's go." Trapp was excited.

"I'll see you at the studio."

Trapp and Sammy drove to 456 East Houston Street in lower

Manhattan to the University Records headquarters. Trapp could smell fresh money throughout the building.

"Trapp is here to see Ronald Schwartz," Sammy said in a professional tone on behalf of Trapp.

They must have known Trapp was coming because the red carpet rolled out as soon as he told the receptionist his name.

"Come right this way, Mr. Trapp. We've been waiting for you. Mr. Schwartz will see you in two minutes tops, he doesn't want to keep his new rap star waiting." The beautiful receptionist gave him a seductive smile. "Would you like something to drink; Hennessy maybe?"

Trapp was so mesmerized by her smile and round backside that he was at a loss for words. "Sure."

"If you need anything, I mean *anything*"—she put extra emphasis on "anything"—"ask for Cookie."

"No doubt, Cookie, you look like a sweet-ass cookie, too."

"Ha-ha-ha." Cookie let out a faint female laugh. "You are so funny, Trapp." She grabbed his arm and rubbed it. "Remember, *any thing,*" she whispered in his ear right before sticking her tongue into it.

Trapp gave Sammy a raised eyebrow look. "Damn, I never had a chick that bad jump on my dick like that."

"You're going to get a lot of that soon. Get ready for the ride of your lifetime," Sammy said with a smile.

"Mr. Schwartz will see you now," Cookie said, winking at Trapp as he passed by.

"Have a seat, Trapp," Ronald said after shaking Trapp's hand extra long. "Now before you say anything, we want to show you our gratitude for considering us as your label. A man with your talent can sign a deal with any major label in town." He paused and signed a check. "Here is a fifty-thousand-dollar check, and these are the keys to a beautiful loft apartment in SoHo. When you sign I will give you another hundred-thousand-dollar cash advance."

He didn't have to say anything else for Trapp to say "Where do I sign?"

"See, that's what I'm talking about. You're a man that doesn't waste time. You know a good thing when you see it. For that we won't waste time with you, either. I'll have my engineer master one of your songs, and by Friday your song will be in rotation on every major radio station in the world. Then we will have your video in rotation on every major video show in the world."

Trapp couldn't believe his ears, but he knew this bald White man wasn't faking. Trapp was in a daze, his head was spinning because everything was moving so fast.

"And on top of that, Cookie will take you down to the company garage. Pick out any one of the cars you want. I like the Maserati myself."

"How could I ever repay you, Mr. Schwartz?" Trapp asked with humility.

"Call me, Ron, that's what all my close friends call me. I got a feeling that we are going to be pretty close in the future. All I want you to do is to keep making that hot music, baby."

Trapp drove the aluminum-gray Maserati with care on the Long Island Expressway. "I can't believe it. Two weeks ago I was just regular old Trapp from the hood. Now I'm Big Trapp. I'm Hood Rich in one day."

When Trapp got to Brentwood, he drove the Maserati through every block that was popping. By the next day his whole hood was talking.

It didn't stop there. Ronald kept his promise and Trapp's new single "Trapp or Die" was in rotation on every major radio station in the world. "Trapp or Die" was a huge success early on. "Trapp or Die" reached number one on the hot singles charts in two weeks.

Trapp shot a video in his hood, and just as Ronald promised, the video premiered on every music TV station. Trapp was quickly catapulted into rap superstardom overnight.

Trapp couldn't go to the mall, or to the local bodega, because he was too famous. There was a riot at South Shore Mall because Trapp went to Foot Locker to cop a pair of Jordans. It would take Trapp twenty minutes to get a Dutch Master because he had to sign fifty autographs before he could leave. All this fame and he didn't even have an album out yet, just a single.

Trapp's whole lifestyle changed. He was becoming bourgeois because of his new associates. He was mingling with important New York socialites who accepted Trapp because of his newfound success. If it weren't for that, they wouldn't even let Trapp use their bathrooms.

"How's the rest of the album coming out?" Ronald asked.

"It's coming out hot as ever, Ron." Trapp was lying.

Trapp ran into a little problem. He was running out of new material to steal from the rhyme book. The only songs left were songs that JJ already recorded before he got locked up. Trapp knew that if he recorded them, people that had JJ's CD would automatically know that Trapp stole his lyrics straight from JJ Gates.

It was crunch time for Trapp. Either he used the songs or forfeit getting more money from the label.

"Fuck it, don't nobody know JJ Gates like that anyway, he was just a local cat," Tripp reassured himself. "Plus that nigga doing life, he can't do nothing with them."

Trapp went into the studio and began recording all of the songs in JJ's rhyme book. He completed his album and turned it in to Ronald. When Trapp's album was released, it reached the number one spot in the country, selling one million units in the first week.

Trapp was officially a rap star. He was leaving a legacy that would live on for years to come. A legacy that was stolen.

Chapter 9

JJ sat on his bunk reading *The Destruction of Black Civilization* by Chancellor Williams. Solomon was putting him on to Black scholars.

"These Black scholars are unsung heroes. They turned down big money and opportunities to teach African history in less fortunate, predominantly Black neighborhoods," Solomon said to JJ with the passion of a scholar himself. "These are the only true sources that we as Blacks can rely on to teach us our history. We cannot rely on the White man as a reliable source on Africa. They will always paint Africans in a negative light."

These type of talks were what made JJ begin to read more about his African history. Before he was arrested, he could care less about his African history, all he cared about was making drug money.

Getting locked up brought JJ back down to earth. He was stripped of all his jewelry, his money, and his street status. Anyone in jail could be whatever they wanted to be, but in reality, in jail he was just another number.

JJ was reflecting on his life more nowadays. He missed going to college, and his family. His short stint in the drug game taught him more than he expected to learn. He thought everything was peachy when he was making money riding around bragging about how Hood Rich he was. The image of young Cannon's body laying cold on the concrete showed him that the drug game is not a game at all, it's serious.

That could've been me shot up like that, JJ thought to himself. *It's not worth it.*

It didn't take much to turn JJ away from the drug game. He realized that he really wasn't built for it.

JJ worked out regularly with Solomon. When he wasn't working out, he was writing letters to his new lawyer and love interest, the beautiful and intelligent Sasha. Being locked up brought out the romantic side of JJ. All he thought about was Sasha, and his case, which wasn't looking good.

Apparently, the DA had a smoking 40-caliber handgun with JJ's fingerprints on it. Because of that, the DA was pushing for the maximum on the attempted murder charge, which was twenty years if JJ blew trial. The DA offered him ten years if he copped out in court, otherwise he was facing twenty years to life.

The letters and phone calls to Sasha, the working out and reading books helped him to cope with his situation. But mostly it was Sasha that kept him grounded.

Sasha spoke to JJ on the phone for two hours every day. Sasha had taken a minor in psychology, so she was good at comforting JJ in his time of need.

Sasha was also getting attached to JJ. She thought about him every day. She wondered what would happen if he did get acquitted of his charges.

Is he going to do all the things he mentions in his letters? Sasha thought to herself. *I think I love JJ, although it's too soon, I still do.* Then the thought occurred to her, *What if he blows trial?*

A million thoughts ran through Sasha's mind. She knew that his case wasn't looking good. The DA wasn't budging from her offer. Sasha had the evidence, and it would be almost impossible to beat this case.

No matter what, I'm going to fight to the end for my king, Sasha thought with determination.

Her phone rang. She knew exactly who it was. "Hi, JJ, how are you doing today?"

"I'm doing better now that I hear your voice. How is your day so far?" JJ asked.

"I'm okay, but I have bad news about your case."

JJ's stomach dropped. "Lay it on me."

"Well, the DA claims to have your fingerprints on the weapon.

I know you told me that Cannon shot the weapon, but the forensics test came back positive for your fingerprints."

"I'm telling you, Sasha, I didn't touch that weapon. I let Cannon handle that, there was no need for me to touch it."

"I don't know, JJ, it doesn't look good. You were at the scene with a weapon that had your fingerprints on it. As your lawyer I have to give you my expert opinion. I think you should cop out. I can see if I can get you five years instead of ten on the cop out. I don't think you can win at trial, their evidence is too strong."

JJ's hope fell off a cliff when she said that. He went silent, a thousand thoughts ran through his head.

"There has to be a way to prove my innocence," JJ said with desperation in his tone.

"It will take a miracle."

The TV was playing in the background. Music videos were playing loud, and all the young men were gathered around the TV bopping their heads. Something about the words to the song sounded so familiar to JJ. The more he listened, the more he was drawn to the screen.

"Sasha, let me call you back." JJ hung up the phone and strolled toward the TV.

When JJ got within eyesight of the screen, he couldn't believe what he saw. "That's Trapp!" Some of the guys heard him. JJ was ecstatic at first to see Trapp on TV, until he listened closer to the words of the song.

"Yo, that's my shit! That's my rhyme!" JJ suddenly got angry. "How the fuck is this nigga spitting my rhymes?"

He stood and listened to Trapp spit the verses right from his precious rhyme book. JJ couldn't believe what was happening. He was actually standing in jail watching his rival get the credit and the money from his work. JJ took pride in the songs he wrote.

Solomon saw JJ's expression while he watched TV. "What's happening? Why the long face?"

"He stole my rhymes." Tears of anger were welling up in JJ's eyes. "I use to get money with that dude, and now he is spitting my songs on national TV."

"Wow, that's serious, my man." Solomon always had something wise to say, but this time he didn't know what to say besides, "Don't let this situation get you down, there is still a chance for you to turn this around."

"Turn it around! First my lawyer tells me to cop out because my fingerprints are on the gun. Then I look at the TV and my enemy is spitting my songs. What's next?" JJ said in an angry tone.

"I hear you, my man, but one thing is for sure. As long as you have life, things can change for the better."

"Yeah, whatever. I'm going to my cell. I'll see you tomorrow." JJ moped his way to his cell. He was hurt beyond belief.

What else can go wrong? he asked himself.

Chapter 10

Big was laid back as he rode in his vintage 1989 Cadillac Deville. It was gold with spoked rims and a system that knocked like he was in a club. Ever since the day that JJ gave Big a copy of his CD, that was all Big played.

"I'm telling you man, JJ Gates is the truth. Cats ain't fucking with my boy," Big said to Vic, who was riding in the passenger seat.

"I don't know, Big, there's this new cat out named Trapp. Trapp's album is the hottest album out."

"I never heard of him."

"I got his CD in my pocket."

Vic took out the CD. Big ejected JJ's CD and inserted Trapp's CD. As Big listened to Trapp's lyrics, he unconsciously started singing along with him. He knew all the words to his song.

"Yo, that's my man JJ's shit! I know all his shit, that's all I been listening to."

Another song came on and Big sang along with the second song, and then the third song.

"Something isn't right, how the fuck is this cat Trapp spitting JJ's rhymes?" Big was baffled.

"You got a point, how the fuck is he spitting JJ's rhymes, unless JJ stole Trapp's rhymes."

"I doubt it because JJ's shit been out, and he's been in the county jail, I had his CD for like three months now."

Big was determined to get to the bottom of it. He had a feeling that JJ was the victim, not Trapp. Big knew that JJ was locked up, that he had no control over the situation. Big wanted to help JJ in any way he could.

"I'm going to blow this cat Trapp up at the radio station," Big decided.

Big's best friend was the top DJ at Power 91.5 in Richmond. "Let me give DJ Real a call." Big pulled out his cellphone and dialed DJ Real's number. "What's good, DJ Real?"

"Nothing, just working. What's good with you?"

"You heard of this new cat, Trapp?"

"Who hasn't, he's the hottest rapper out right now."

"He's a thief. All his songs are stolen from this rapper named JJ Gates. I have his CD. Trapp has the same lyrics on his album."

"How do you know that JJ didn't steal Trapp's lyrics?"

"I had JJ Gates's CD for months before Trapp came out. And I'm sure that JJ recorded the songs months before that."

"You might be onto something. Come up to the station and let me hear this JJ Gates."

Big made a U-turn and headed for the radio station. When he arrived, he heard Trapp's music playing on air. He saw his man DJ Real and he led him to an office.

"Now, let me hear this JJ Gates cat." DJ Real took the CD from

Big's hand and inserted it into a CD player. After a few listens, DJ Real noticed the same lyrics. "You're right, they do have the same lyrics. That's crazy. I think I'm going to talk about this on my show tonight, to see what the people think."

"I'm telling you, Real, my man JJ Gates is a gangster. He locked up right now for blasting Chopper's arm off and selling weight."

"Well, let's see what the people have to say."

DJ Real played JJ's songs and then played Trapp's music. "Anyone out there that has a comment, call two-two-two two-seven-seven-seven, and let me know who you think the originator is and who's the thief."

The phone lines lit up. People from all over Richmond called with their opinions.

"This Half Dead from Jackson Ward. I know that nigga JJ Gates. He gave me his CD, that's all I've been bumping. This cat Trapp is an imposter. JJ Gates is the truth," said one caller.

"I'm from Jackson Ward, too, I been playing JJ Gates's songs. He gave it to me one day, I think JJ is the truth."

Ten people from Jackson Ward called up to support JJ. He gave out a hundred CDs in the Jackson Ward projects for free. The whole Jackson Ward Projects was feeling JJ Gates.

"Wow, you was right, Big. This needs to be taken national. This was the highest ratings that my show has had in a month."

DJ Real sent out an email blast to all the major radio stations in America. They all requested a copy of DJ Real's "Real or Not" radio show that exposed Trapp as an imposter.

A week later the whole industry was talking about Trapp being an imposter. His quick rise to fame was falling even faster. His record sales began to decline. That's when Ronald from University Records requested a meeting with Trapp and his whole staff. He had to do some damage control.

"It doesn't matter at this point if you stole his rhymes or not, we have five hundred thousand records in stores that have to be bought. I'm scheduling a press conference for you today. You better convince them that those fucking rhymes are yours or everything I gave you will be back in my possession so fast you'll think it's magic."

Trapp knew Ronald was serious. "Yo, Ron, those are my fucking rhymes. I know how he recorded those songs, I left my rhyme book at his house and he went to the studio. I know him, he was never a rapper. He stole my shit!" Trapp was becoming a good actor. He knew he had to be to save his career.

"You don't have to convince me, go out there and convince the media. Like I said, I could care less who wrote the lyrics, as long as we sell records."

Trapp went to the press conference and did the best acting he ever did in his life. He convinced the press that he was a victim of plagiarism.

"I will prove that this JJ Gates character is an imposter. I will do a whole new album, then we'll see who the imposter really is."

That was a bold attempt to prove his point, and Trapp knew it. He couldn't write rhymes, Trapp could barely read and write. He just needed something to say to convince the world that he was telling the truth.

The middle-aged woman stared at the TV screen as Trapp spoke. She knew exactly who he was even though Trapp had no idea who she was. Tears welled up in the woman's eyes as she stared. She took a swig of the powerful 151-proof rum and wiped tears from her cheeks.

"I have to tell him," she said to herself. "He has to know."

JJ had become a celebrity in the county jail since DJ Real aired his show. Young men on his tier asked him questions about the whole situation. He would often have six men around him while he told his story.

"This dude Trapp worked for me and my man Dee. He was a bum before he got with us. I don't know how he got my rhyme book, but he did."

"Yo, JJ!" a young stocky kid yelled out. "Yo this guy Trapp is on TV talking about you."

The group of men all ran to the TV to see Trapp tell his side of the story. JJ hated to see Trapp, he was shining off of his hard work.

"I will do a whole new album, then we'll see who the imposter really is."

"This nigga is fronting! He can't even spell, how the fuck you going to write a whole album. I want to see this," JJ said in a hyped tone.

Everyone in the county jail was riding with JJ Gates. He was the star behind bars, but Trapp was traveling the world as an international star. JJ didn't show it, but inside he was hurt.

His case was still looking bad. Sasha was still working hard to get JJ off, but it still didn't look good for him.

Sasha kept having JJ's court dates adjourned so she could find something to acquit him. She was working around the clock trying to find some evidence.

I know there has to be some witness or something to prove JJ's innocence, Sasha thought to herself. *Let me go back to the scene of the crime one more time, I know there is something I overlooked.*

Sasha went back to Jackson Ward Projects to canvass the area for the thousandth time. She looked around at everything. She walked slowly around the area where the alleged victim was shot.

"I know there was someone watching."

She looked up at the windows that were facing the scene, and that's when she saw the savior of JJ's life. The one thing that could free her love from certain incarceration.

"That's it!" Sasha shouted. "I have to get that footage."

On every building at the top corners, there were surveillance cameras. There were at least three facing the exact circumference of the incident.

Sasha followed the signs that pointed to the security office. She quickly dashed toward the office.

"Excuse me, I'm Sasha Cohen, I'm a lawyer. I need to speak to someone in charge."

"Hold on one minute, Mr. Charles will be right with you."

The young man disappeared into an office. Two minutes later he came out.

"You can go in, Mr. Charles will see you now."

Sasha took a deep breath before entering the office.

"Let's see what we have."

Mr. Charles sat behind a desk. When he saw Sasha his eyes lit up and he stood to greet her. "How are you today Mrs.—"

"Hi, I'm Sasha Cohen, I'm a lawyer at Simpson & Simon. I'm representing a client that was falsely arrested in the south side of the projects. I saw security cameras pointing directly at the location where the alleged incident took place. Is it possible for me to view the footage from that day?"

"Sure, sweetheart, I'm always willing to help a damsel in distress." Mr. Charles showed her a snaggle-toothed smile.

Sasha smiled back. "Thank you, Mr. Charles."

"Just give me the date and time of the incident and I can type it into the computer. I love technology, back in the day they didn't have things like this."

Mr. Charles went on and on about technology, while Sasha stood nervously and impatiently. She couldn't wait to see the footage, she knew it was possible that it could free her new love interest.

"Okay, here we go." He turned the screen around so she could see it also.

The first image on the screen was JJ walking into a building, then Chopper creeping from behind an adjacent building. Then JJ coming out of the building and Chopper putting the AK-47 to JJ's temple. Then JJ slowly handing Chopper a brown paper bag, then Cannon comes from behind a building opposite JJ and Chopper and lets off three shots. Then Chopper's shoulder gets hit and as he is falling back from the impact, he lets off six rounds. Then the fatal blows to Cannon's chest and neck. "Damn!" Mr. Charles shouted. Sasha squeamishly turned her head to the side.

JJ slowly walked up to Cannon, looked down, then comes the officer with his weapon pointed at JJ, then JJ fainted.

Then something happens that both Sasha and Mr. Charles couldn't believe. The officer picks up the 40-caliber, takes JJ's hand while he's unconscious, and puts it around the gun's handle.

"Wow, now ain't that some shit?" Mr. Charles said in a comedic tone.

Sasha was at a loss for words. "He told me that he never touched the gun and he didn't."

Sasha couldn't believe what she just saw. "I have to get a copy of this footage, a man's life is at stake."

"You got it." Mr. Charles burned the footage onto a disc. "Here you go. Good luck."

"Thank you."

Sasha headed straight for the DA's office with the evidence that would get all JJ's charges dismissed.

"I'm coming to get you out, baby," Sasha said to herself as she stepped on the gas.

When Sasha arrived at the courthouse, she went directly to the DA's office with the footage. When the DA viewed the footage, she couldn't believe her eyes.

"Listen, I will release him today and drop all the charges, even though the tape shows him with the drugs in the bag, on one condition."

"What is it?"

"I want him to sign a waiver saying that he won't sue us for unlawful imprisonment, and this whole matter will disappear. But the officer will be arrested for his actions."

"I think my client will have no problem with that. I want the immediate release of Jamal Jenkins."

"He will be out in one hour."

Sasha couldn't believe that she got JJ off. She had butterflies in her stomach just thinking about being with her new man. They'd established a serious relationship in the past few months. Sasha knew that JJ was sincere about being with her, he would be especially now that she'd gotten his charges dropped.

"Jamal Jenkins!" the CO shouted. "Roll up. You're getting released in one hour!"

JJ couldn't believe what he just heard. "You're joking, right, CO?"

"Listen, you can stay here if you want to, I'm only telling you what they told me."

Solomon was standing next to JJ when he got the news. "I told you that things turn around. You're a good dude, JJ, stay focused when you're out there. And don't worry about that clown Trapp, he will get his in the end, trust me. Spend time with your family, get cool with your father again."

"You right, I let my family down and, oh yeah, I got something for Trapp, I'm going to do it the right way."

"That's what I like to hear." Solomon handed JJ a book. "I want you to have this book. It's called *Stolen Legacy,* by George G. M. James. This is an outline of how the Greeks plagiarized African philosophy and science. Study it, and teach those that need to know. Do that for me."

"No doubt, brother. It has been real building with you, I learnt a lot from you, Solomon. I will keep in touch with you."

"I already know." They gave each other a brotherly hug.

It didn't take JJ any time to get ready for release. He gave Solomon all of his property, and he headed for the front gate. When he got there he saw Sasha standing with open arms and tears of joy running down her cheeks.

"I did it, baby." She hugged him so tight that he let out a sigh. "I got your charges dropped. I will tell you all about it, but first we have to go to the DA's office so you can sign a waiver not to sue them. Is that okay with you?"

"I will sign whatever they want me to as long as this shit goes away. The nightmare is over."

"Yes, baby, it's over. Now we can start a life together."

"I love you, Sasha. If it wasn't for you I would be doing a lot of time. Thank you, baby." JJ kissed her lips passionately.

"Let's go before I jump on you out here." Sasha was aroused by JJ's kiss.

JJ walked hand-in-hand with his new queen to her car. They rode off with plans of being together for life.

Chapter 11

The press conference did excellent damage control for Trapp's career. The people accepted his version of the story. Now it was back to business for Trapp.

Trapp was at the end of his fourth thirty-city tour. He was not Hood Rich anymore, Trapp was a multimillionaire. Trapp made three hundred thousand off this tour, he made three hundred thousand off each of the three other tours, equaling one point two million dollars in tour money alone. When you add the money he gained from the endorsements he got from major clothing companies, and many other corporations bent on capitalizing from his image, he'd grossed ten million in six months.

Trapp bought a six-million-dollar mansion in East Hampton, Long Island, sitting on two acres of beachfront property. His garage held the Maserati that University gave him, plus a Range Rover Sport, a Lamborghini Murciélago, and a yacht sat on a dock in his backyard.

Trapp wore so much ice that people couldn't help but stare at him. Trapp stayed draped in the finest designer wear you could imagine. He walked around with thirty thousand cash in his pockets just to show off. He was living the life of his dreams.

"Fuck that bitch-ass nigga, JJ. He trying to come up off me like I'm some lame," he said to the beautiful Brazilian riding shotgun in his Lamborghini. "Everybody know that I'm nice with the mic device." He made an attempt to say a rhyme, but it was corny. Even Miss Brazil noticed it.

After Trapp did the press conference, he made efforts to rhyme, but even he knew he was wack. He didn't care as long as his bank account was packed with money.

"I'm taking you to Brazil with me next week, I know that's where you're from, but fuck it."

"You know I'm with whatever." She knew he was a trick so she agreed with everything he said as long as he set her out with money. "Baby, what happened to the diamond bracelet you were getting me, I want it for the trip to Brazil."

"We can go get it today."

"Thank you, baby." She leaned across the seat and began to un-button his True Religion jeans. She pulled out his penis and started to suck it while he drove.

"That's what I'm talking about."

Trapp was a sucker for a pretty face with breasts and a round behind. Miss Brazil was only one of the five different women that Trapp tricked on. Trapp spent almost ten thousand a week trick-ing on gorgeous women.

"You're going to go broke if you don't stop squandering your money," Trapp's accountant told him.

"It ain't tricking if you got it," was Trapp's reply.

"Okay, we'll see if you still have it in one year, the way that you spend money."

"I'm never going broke, I get too much money."

Trapp was an obnoxious and arrogant person. He rubbed everyone the wrong way. No one at University Records liked him, no one that he met liked him, only the fans liked him until they met him. The way he treated people created so much animosity that he had to hire a bodyguard when he was in public.

What Trapp didn't know was that things were about to change. He was about to get a visit from an old friend, a friend that he thought was finished.

Trapp drove down Islip Avenue with the top down on his Lamborghini, Miss Brazil was riding shotgun, talking on the phone, when JJ's truck pulled up alongside them at a stoplight.

"What's up, Trapp? Remember me?" JJ said with a smile on his face.

Trapp was at a loss for words; he just looked at JJ with confusion.

"What's wrong, cat got your tongue? I bet you thought I wasn't getting out. You think you're going to get away with stealing my songs, but you're not."

That's when Sasha handed Trapp court papers. "You've been formally served with this affidavit to appear in court for copyright infringement."

"Oh yeah, my money too long for y'all to think you can stop me," Trapp replied arrogantly.

"We'll see you in court."

JJ drove away with a victory smile on his face. What Trapp didn't know was that every song JJ recorded was copywritten with the Library of Congress, so he was protected. With the help of Sasha again, JJ was able to prove that Trapp stole his lyrics.

When they went to court the judge awarded JJ all the money that Trapp had in his bank account, which was a little under ten million. Trapp was sick.

"That ain't nothing because I can get money anywhere now. The people love me," Trapp said foolishly.

"We'll see. I'll make sure that everybody knows that you lost in court. You're finished," JJ replied.

When the news got out that Trapp really did steal all the lyrics on his album, his short career came to a screeching halt. No label wanted to sign him, the chances of him making a hit record again were slim to none.

Trapp pulled up to his estate. He was lucky that he paid cash for his mansion. He was also lucky that the judge left him with it.

When he pulled up to the front of the house he noticed that there was a slim dark-skinned lady sitting on his porch. His first thought was to curse her out and kick her off his property. There was something in her eyes; he felt a familiarity in them. He knew that he didn't know this lady personally, but there was something about her that made him connect with her on a deep level.

"Hi, Trent. I know you don't know me, but I know you."

"How do you know my government name?" Trapp had a perplexed look on his face.

"Because I'm your mother, Trent."

"You're my mother." Trapp gave her a deep look and he saw his own face. He knew she was telling the truth.

"What are you doing here now? You waiting for me to get rich to show your face."

"I didn't come here for a handout, Trent, I came to tell you who your father is."

Trapp's heart started beating fast when the woman spoke the words *your father*. He wasn't sure if he wanted to know, but he had a feeling that she was going to tell him anyway.

"What made you come forward now? I mean, I'm twenty-four years old. If you knew me why didn't you come forth when I was being mistreated in all those foster homes."

"I can't take back the past. I don't have long to live, I have terminal cancer. That's why I'm here, to tell you before I die."

Trapp had emotional lumps in his throat that he couldn't control. Tears started welling up in his eyes. The woman began to cry as well when she saw her son cry.

"Your father's name is Terell Swan."

"I don't know nobody by that name, so this was a waste of time."

"You do know him, just by another name."

"Who is my father, lady? I don't have time to play wit you," Trapp said in a loud tone.

"Your father's name is OG Rosco."

Trapp's face dropped. "OG Rosco is my father?" Trapp couldn't believe his ears. "Are you sure, I mean how are you sure?"

"I know for sure that he is your father. Terell was my childhood sweetheart. I gave you up for adoption because I was only fifteen years old when I had you. I was a baby myself, so was Terell. He never knew that I was pregnant because I hid it the whole time. Then he left me to be in the streets, so I never told him."

"I can't believe that OG Rosco is my father."

"I'm sorry for everything you been through. If I could take it back believe me I would. But I can't." She looked him deep in his eyes. She saw the pain mixed with something else she couldn't explain. Maybe it was guilt or confusion, but his whole vibe changed. "I don't want to waste any more of your time, I know you're a busy man."

The lady started walking away; that's when Trapp stopped her.

"Wait. If you like you can spend some time here with me. There is more than enough room."

"Thank you, but I have to go."

With those words the woman walked away from Trapp's sprawling mansion.

"Terell Swan, you have a lawyer's visit," The CO announced.

"This is what I've been waiting for."

OG Rosco strolled down to the attorney-inmate visiting room. When he got there his lawyer was seated. He stood and shook OG's hand when he walked in.

"How's everything, Mr. Swan?"

"As good as it's going to get. Now let's cut to the chase."

OG's lawyer handed him a piece of paper with a name and a few paragraphs written on it. The name read: Trent Sanford aka Trapp. OG read the statement. It basically was a detailed account of OG's drug operation.

"I knew Trapp was a rat!"

"Now, Mr. Swan, don't go killing him just yet."

"Don't worry, I got this." OG stood as a sign for him to be escorted back to his cell.

When he got to his cell block, he got on the phone.

"What's poppin, Shank? I want you to talk to Trapp for me."

"I'm going to see him tonight."

"Good." OG hung up the phone before he said anything else. "You're going to get yours, Trapp."

Trapp drove his Range Rover down his old block remembering the time when he was a nobody on these streets. The news that his mother gave him disturbed him deeply.

I snitched on my own father, he thought to himself. *It's not like I knew he was my father.*

He stopped at a traffic light and nervously pulled on a cigarette. He was in such a trance that he didn't notice Shank get out of the car behind his and creep up on his Range with a 45-caliber handgun in his palm.

By the time Trapp saw Shank, it was too late.

"This is for OG Rosco!" Shank emptied a full 16-shot clip into Trapp's door. "Rat Bastard!"

Trapp's forehead hit the steering wheel causing the horn to blast continuously. The last thought that Trapp had before he died was, *OG Rosco is my pops.*

JJ wrote a whole new album in a new rhyme book. His new album was hotter than the first. JJ had more to talk about nowadays because of his ordeal with the game.

JJ changed his subject matter up on his new album. The information that he learned from Solomon went into every song he wrote. JJ even wrote a song about the situation with Trapp, called "Stolen Legacy," named after the book that Solomon gave him.

"Stolen Legacy" became JJ's biggest single from his new album. Everyone knew about the whole Trapp fiasco, so it was easy for people to like the song.

JJ went through hell in order to come out right. He learned a lot of valuable lessons from the ordeal. The most valuable lesson he learned was to never take life for granted.

"You ready, baby?" Sasha asked JJ.

"Yes, ma'am."

She smiled at him before speaking. "Can I ask you a question, honey?"

"Sure." JJ was anxious to see where she was going with her question.

"When we first met, did you want to take me serious, or was you going to play me and never call me?"

"Actually, I was going to call you every day after that day because I couldn't get you off my mind." JJ paused and reached into his pocket and pulled out the biggest diamond ring Sasha ever saw. "In fact, I have a question for you."

When Sasha saw the ring, she knew what his question was.

"Oh my God!" she screamed with excitement.

"Will you marry me, Sasha?"

"Yes! Yes! Yes!" She hugged him around his neck and he squeezed her in his arms.

They stayed in a lover's embrace until they both were tired of hugging. They were happy and in love, their future was promising, all due to the past. Even though, all we really have is the moment.

The Roof . . . the Roof Is on Fire!
We Don't Need No Water . . .

LOSE TO WIN

By Lana Ave

Chapter 1 | I'll Watch

"Yeah, Daddy, give it to me."

Kessy's canary-yellow thong underwear were tossed on the mess of papers on the cherry oak desk as she bounced on the lap of Nicholas Michaels, the owner and president of Hustle Hard Records. Kessy humped Nicholas aggressively, and his smooth brown face and chestnut-brown eyes stayed calm as he let Kessy work him. He fondled her breasts, but mostly rested his head back on the black leather chair with his eyes closed.

I sat on the yellow suede couch near the window, bored. Kessy and Nicholas had only known each for about four hours. We saw him at a red light on Thirty-sixth Street in Manhattan.

There wasn't much space between Kessy's butt and the wood desk. She didn't care if her butt bumped the desk a time or two. She never felt the scratches the wood splinters left on her behind.

She was in a zone. There was hardly anyone left in the office of the small record label. It was after eight o'clock in the evening and only the janitor, the security guard, and Nicholas were here when we arrived an hour ago. Every now and again Nicholas would try to quiet Kessy down. As empty as the place was he still wanted to be quiet.

"But you're Nicholas Michaels. Ooh, you feel that? Oh my gosh I get wetter just saying your name!"

And with that she gave two more hard bounces. Then three slower, more careful ones. Her caramel C-cup breasts flopped against his bearded chin. Nicholas's ebony skin glowed with a hint of red in his cheeks. Was he blushing? Kessy was good! She always knew when it was time. A man didn't have to shake, tap her on the behind, or whisper. Kessy had power between those legs!

Seeing Nicholas close his eyes and grip Kessy's waist was my cue to leave. I got what I needed. As she slow-grinded to pull out whatever he had left, she held on to the top of his black leather chair firmly and pulled herself closer to his chiseled chest. I'm not sure if Nicholas even remembered I was in the room. Kessy was a twenty-three-year-old caramel beauty and my best friend. She was well stacked and had a waist perfect for a size four but a booty that took a size ten. She still had on her red pumps, and her long legs straddled Nicholas's lap to secure his position although he wasn't moving anyway.

I tried to be discreet when I got up to leave although there was no need. Nicholas looked like he was ready to take a nap, and Kessy would caress him until she knew I was gone. Nicholas's pale blue jeans were around his ankles. The janitor saw me trying to be quiet closing the office door. He wore big old school silver and black headphones that looked like they could keep anyone's ears warm on a cold winter night. My purple and gray Air Max sneakers kept my footsteps light. When I reached the glass double doors I saw the reflection of a twenty-four-year-old woman in dark blue jeans with a matching denim jacket. The grape color of my button-down shirt made my light skin look lighter. I saw a woman who was transitioning from being a girl. A woman who decided what she wanted to do with her life and how she was going to get there. My parents taught me I should own whatever business I work for. My mother taught me how to be dedicated. My father taught me how to cut to the chase and take what you want. The path lay ahead of me. I just had to lay the bricks down. The music business is where I belonged. It was a game, and I was great at playing games. Just like Monopoly. I always liked getting the small houses first then building up to the bigger ones. Hustle Hard Records would be my small house.

I looked to see if I could see the brightness of my green eyes in the glass. Instead I saw the janitor looking at me there standing still. He probably was curious as to why I was leaving alone.

Chapter Two | First Day

I showed up at the offices of Hustle Hard Records the morning of Monday, September 15th. I requested to see Mr. Nicholas Michaels. Just as the receptionist started to turn me away (since I didn't have an appointment), Mr. Michaels was getting off of the elevator. He recognized me although my pinstriped skirt and jacket were quite different from the attire he saw me in last. He stared curiously at the manila envelope in my hand.

That became my first day working at Hustle Hard Records. It was just an intern position, but I didn't care. It was a start. People in the office looked at me crazy when Nicholas introduced me. No one knew I was coming and it was obvious I wasn't a student. The other interns looked like they were about twelve and thirteen even though they claimed to be in college. I wasn't there to make friends, though. I was there to start my business. Yes, my business! You see, the music business is one of the best hustles there is. I mean, not if you're a singer or a rapper, but if you're the owner/money lender. You lend them the money to finance what they need to get them on top, and they owe you. Now, that's a business that makes money! It's like being a bank. All you have to do is find the right borrowers. You know, like the ones who want a house so bad they don't care the interest on it is damn near more than the loan? Yeah, you need some of them. My mama always said, "If I owe you, you'll never be broke!"

Of course, she said that as she was borrowing my allowance money to buy her and her boyfriend a case of Coronas. Whatever, it's still true. As long as you owe me, I'm not broke!

"Good morning, Cassandra. This is Sakia Sands. She'll be our new intern."

I hope Miss Cassandra didn't think she was hiding her thoughts. I saw right through that phony smile. When she heard my name she twisted her mouth a little. Not too much so that Mr. Michaels saw it. But just enough that I did. She thinks I'm some chick this dude is freaking off with. No, boo, that would be Kessy and Kessy ain't trying to work for anybody! Shoot! Kessy's parents got boocoo dough and all she wants to do is sex every and any man who thinks he's at the top of his game. She doesn't even need a whole hour to break 'em down. So even if I was Kessy, this chick right here wouldn't know the half and her little paycheck would be embarrassed to stand in my presence!

I had to keep a straight face while the hater acted like she was happy to show me around. Tossing her spiral-curled shoulder-length weave must've made her feel pretty. Her insecurity was obvious and unnecessary. Her dark skin and almond-shaped eyes were actually quite beautiful. Her doo-doo green pantsuit needed a little work, but she was still cute. Besides, I wasn't trying to compete with her. In a short time, I was going to be the head woman in charge. She'd be lucky if I let her work for me!

Let her keep thinking her stuff don't stink. She'll smell it in a minute!

Cassandra tried to keep me busy with refiling things that were already in order and refilling the coffeepot like I was part of a high school work program. I played cool because she had no clue of the deck I was working with. That's just who I am. My daddy taught me that. When he found my mother in bed with his best friend, Mr. Paul, my dad acted like it was okay. Hell, he even jumped in the bed to join them. Yes he did! He stripped down and he rammed himself into my mother's behind while she nervously gave Mr. Paul oral sex. Mr. Paul was probably dumb enough to think that whole situation turned out for the best. My mother, on the other hand, was basically getting raped up her behind while my father was "playing it cool." It's funny how my mom tells that story thinking it will make me hate my father. She wants me to think of him as a rapist, but I just think of her as a whore. Mr. Paul was broke and always coming by to borrow money. All she got out of that was a sore ass and Mr. Paul still owing her fifty dollars. I don't know if it was my father or the fifty dollars he borrowed from my mother that made him never come by again. Knowing Mr. Paul, it was the fifty dollars.

"Hey. My name's Brooke."

Her hair was brown and her frame petite. Her skin was white at one point but it was now orange from what seemed to be over-tanning. Her Malcolm X glasses made her look very professional even though she wore jeans and a T-shirt. Still, she was pleasant and the only one who reached their hand out to me. The other interns acted like I was trying to take their job. As if there was a ranking or something and their superior intern status was at risk.

"Hi, I'm Sakia. Nice to meet you, Brooke."

"Sakia? That's an interesting name. What does it mean?"

"I don't know. I think my mom just liked it. I don't care much about it. It's just my name."

"Just your name, girl? It's what everyone knows you by. Girl you can be a CEO with just a name. Think of whose company you're working for. Nicholas Michaels. That's his name. There's so many people who aren't really sure what he does or what his role is, but they know his name. If your name doesn't have a meaning, you better give it one."

I've been here for four hours and I finally learned something that might make a difference to me. When I start running this place, I will keep her on my team for sure.

"Okay, Brooke. I'll reintroduce myself. My name is Saks Sands."

"Nice to meet you, Saks. I love your name!"

"Thank you: I was named after Saks Fifth Avenue."

"Girl, that's one of the best places to shop! On the high end, huh? That's a cool name!"

Brooke schooled me about the people in the office. Rob was the office manager and gave up his job at Power 101.3 to work at Hustle Hard when they only had one artist, Breeze. Rob believed in Hustle Hard for all ten years it had been in existence and hustled the hardest to make sure the artists got heard. He oversaw everything from the street teams to the album covers. By the time it got to Nick, he just had to sign off on it. Everyone in the office was part of Rob's team. There were only like eight other people there I could count. That included the interns. Brooke had been his assistant for the past four years. That's the kind of loyalty I needed.

All I had was Kessy. Don't get me wrong, we were like sisters. She did any and everything I needed since the day I met her at my high school prom. Some basketball player who thought he was going to be a star brought Kessy as his date. She lived in New Jersey at the time. Kessy just looked like money. She wore round pink diamond studs in her ears. Her prom dress was a simple long, black gown with a pink ribbon curved in between her breasts. At the time, her black silky hair hung to her shoulders.

I wore a white halter suit. The skirt was formfitting, stopping right below my ankles, with a mid-thigh split. The top was a double-breasted jacket, which showed off the cleavage I had before everyone else in my school. I made the dress myself. Once my father was gone, so was the money. I was proud of it and Kessy liked it. She said I seemed so much more sophisticated and conservative than everyone else at my school. I told her that was because I was thinking about money. She told me she got money and thinks about sex. We laughed. At the time, I thought she was joking. She wasn't!

I ran out to the limo to catch a smoke and the principal's silver Camry was parked next to it. Everyone else was inside so at first I was scared to see the car moving. When I squinted my eyes and looked a little closer, I saw Kessy on her knees in the backseat with her face pressed against the window and Principal Allan's face nuzzled in her butt. As my eyes opened wide and I covered my mouth to stop the laughter, Kessy caught my eye. She winked, smiled, and mouthed, "Give me a minute."

Of all the people in the office Brooke told me about, I did find Cassandra to be the most interesting. Apparently everyone likened her to a dog. She was loyal to Nicholas, they said. She was Breeze's girlfriend when Nicholas met her. Breeze slept around a lot on her (what a surprise) and gave her something. No one knows what he gave her, but it was something. It was enough that when Breeze's contract was up about a year ago, Nicholas didn't re-sign him and Nicholas hired Cassandra as his assistant. Breeze started his own record label. She's been loyal to Nicholas ever since.

Nicholas had a dedicated team. I had to admit that. That's why he was so successful. I mean other than the two regular people in Marketing and the rotating door of A&R's, he had a close-knit team. A loyal and sturdy foundation. But what makes people loyal? Is it the money? The opportunity? Or is it really their belief in you? Do people who you think are loyal really believe in you or just believe you. Is it the same? Can you have one without the other?

"B, I can't talk right now. There's a new intern here."

If she couldn't talk she should have gotten off the phone. The fact that Cassandra mentioned me, the new intern, made me curious enough to find out who she was talking to. I got up to act like I was checking to see if Brooke had anything for me to do.

"B, I know he's hot. I don't know if Nick is planning on signing him. I don't think he's made him an offer. I'll let you know when he tells me. He didn't tell me anything yet. No, B, I don't know why he won't sign. Just wait and see what we're offering first. I'm not lying! Can we talk about this when I get home?"

B? Is she serious? Who is B? Breeze? She can't be talking to him. That wouldn't even make sense. But who else would be questioning her like that? It was obvious it was someone she shouldn't be talking to. From what Brooke told me, when Nick wouldn't renew Breeze's contract, he started his own label and has been in fierce competition with Hustle Hard.

"So, Cassandra, Brooke told me there's a party tonight for the singer Lakaya. Are you going?"

"No. My ex-boyfriend will probably be there and I don't want to see him."

"Well, I'd like to go. Do you mind if I go in your stead?"

"You know what, yeah. You should go to the party. Brooke and Rob are going, too. It'll be good for you to see who's who in this industry. If you stay here long enough, you'll need to know these people. Ask Brooke to tell you about everyone. She's good at that!"

"Do you think they'll let me bring my friend with me?"

As soon as I got the okay, I called Kessy. She would know who was who at the party. I didn't need Brooke for that.

Chapter 3 | That Was a Breeze

"Hey, I'm Kessy. And you are . . ."

Kessy could've been the only one in the room. She was a vision in her white slacks and white beaded corset. Her skin was soft and her jet-black hair was just long enough to cup the nape of her neck and it was neatly tucked behind her ears. Her white triangle diamond studs were just big enough to sparkle, yet they were small enough not to brag.

"Breeze. CEO of Breezy Records."

"Wow, I get a name and a résumé. Impressive!"

Breeze smiled. Kessy had this way about her. No man could shake her spell. Plus she exuded money, position, and sexiness. They knew she wasn't starstruck. She was too comfortable with herself. Her voice sounded like smooth honey. She cupped her glass with confidence and his eyes were drawn to her nails—short and neat. They weren't long like so many of the girls he came across. No acrylic, no colored polish, no weird designs, just natural. Her skin was brown but like the caramel taffy he used to buy from the corner store by his grandmother's house. She was new candy. He wondered what she tasted like.

"I'm sorry. I just figured . . ."

Kessy laughed at Breeze's clumsiness in trying to clean up his wack game.

"I know what you figured. It's okay. At least you told me who you are. That's why I came over."

They had barely been around each other for five minutes and from afar it looked as if they were old friends. He was a little clumsy with the bottle of champagne he clutched. It was obvious he'd had more than his share of champagne for the night. Her movements were precise. Whenever she laughed he seemed to be studying her. She did have a beautiful laugh.

"So, um, Kessy, are you here with anyone?"

"No. I'm a big girl. I'm allowed to go out by myself."

His smile showed he enjoyed the answer she gave. Within seconds they were headed over to the coatroom. Before exiting Kessy motioned for me to come outside.

I stood at Kessy's car smoking a cigarette. Breeze saw me waiting. He'd had quite a bit to drink so it didn't even look like he was focusing on me. He was just anticipating the situation that was about to jump off. His head was so stuck up his own behind he never asked my name.

"You bringing your friend with us?"

Caramel and Sugar! He was easy. I looked so different from Kessy. It was not about who was his type at all. She was five foot ten and I am five foot four. She's proportioned like a black Barbie doll. I have a more round-the-way shape. I'm a size fourteen. My stomach isn't fat and my butt is round and wide but firm. My breasts are a D-cup and full. My hair is silky straight thanks to the perm I got last week and it hangs around the middle of my back. My bangs swoop over my eyebrows. My skin is the color of a butter cookie and my emerald green eyes reveal my real focus: money. Breeze's eyes showed his focus, too, as they bounced from my breasts to Kessy's bubble of a behind.

Kessy and I followed behind his Phantom in her black Mercedes. He lived in Long Island so we were going to be a long way from Manhattan! During the ride we went over the plan.

"Okay, I just need you to get him to do something that will look wild in some pictures."

"Wild in pictures. Got it. Do I get to enjoy it?"

"Of course, but he can not enter you. It's important you remember that."

"Why?"

"Just don't let him do it. I'll tell you later. You have to promise."

"Okay, okay. I got it. What you gonna use the pictures for anyway?"

"I don't know yet. I'm sure I'll think of something."

Breeze's house was a five bedroom mini-mansion. His foyer was brown marble and there were ivory columns greeting you at the foot of a spiral staircase. He wasted no time leading us to his bedroom, which was big enough to fit my entire Brooklyn apartment. He had a sitting area on one side and a master bathroom off to the other side of his bed. His fur comforter was appropriate for the October chill that filled the Long Island night.

Kessy stood at the foot of the bed and removed her pants to reveal her bodysuit corset. She placed her hands on her hips and Breeze paused and stared. For a minute, I almost did, too, as it never ceased to amaze me how forward and to the point Kessy was. When Breeze snapped out of it, he turned to me as if he was waiting for me to undress. Kessy purred, "She's just going to watch. You don't mind, right? I just want you to myself this time."

How could he say no to that voice? He lay back propped up on his fur pillows wearing a wife-beater and his boxers.

Kessy climbed up on the bed as Breeze watched her. She faced him, looked him in the eye, and positioned herself on his face. She moved her hips around slow in a back-and-forth motion. He was in a trance. He moved the bottom of the bodysuit to the side and dove in. I was soon forgotten. Kessy took a white oval-shaped pill from the breast of her corset. She placed it in her mouth then she rose from Breeze's face. She positioned herself to be face-to-face with him and using her tongue, she dumped the pill onto his.

"Umm, that feels good, Daddy! Talk to me while you eat."

It was interesting to see this unfold. I watched this man go to pieces. She had him. He seemed so turned on by talking about himself. His words slurred a bit.

"Girl, I am the man."

"Yeah, baby, you are the man."

"I'm 'bout to sign the next big thing and make so much money."

"Yeah, baby? Damn, he can't be bigger than you."

"Nah, Fingers ain't bigger than me, girl. But he big."

"You're going to make a lot of money? Ooh, right there."

"Yeah, baby. A lot of money. Ain't nobody going to be bigger than me! I got somebody working on it right now as we speak."

"You gonna be big like Hustle Hard?"

"Girl, they ain't got nothing on me. That dude Nick over there is corny. Yeah, that's right, I feel you coming."

"Ooh, Daddy I like that! Yes, baby. Nick ain't like you, boo. No one is. Take 'em out."

"Oh I will. Damn, c'mon, girl, I feel you. You're ready."

"I'm 'bout to cum. I don't want to cum. Turn over."

He obliged easily. He poked his butt in the air. Kessy dug into her large pocketbook and took out a lavender-colored penis. She started off slowly then plunged it into him more aggressively. He moaned and begged for more.

"You turn over now. Let me slide in that."

"Um, sorry, boo. Not on the first date. I can't give up all the goodies!"

He tried to take it, but he was weak. When he realized he wasn't getting anything, he yelled for us to get out. It's not like I didn't expect it. We didn't come in his car so that wasn't a problem. Can you imagine all those women who must've hitched a ride with him after the club and had no ride home? That's the game right there! He damn near be guaranteeing himself some bootie. But I knew the rumors. No way was I going to let Kessy have sex with him. I still don't know what he gave Cassandra. He might not have given her anything. But still, I had to be safe. Cassandra could be stupid or in love or whatever she wanted to be, but Kessy's life wasn't worth it.

Chapter 4 | Bye-Bye Birdie

"Good morning, Nicholas."

"Good morning, Saks. How are you?"

"Hey, how'd you know to call me Saks?"

"You can't get Brooke all excited and the office not know about it. She loves the new name. It fits you, too."

"Thanks. Well, you know I went to the party last night."

"Right. How was it?"

"Oh, it's cool. I actually got to meet a lot of people. You know, I saw who was who. I also got to see who wasn't who."

"Hmm. What do you mean?"

He knew I had something to tell so he walked over to his office door and closed it. That was the sign to the rest of the office he didn't want to be disturbed. I'm sure everyone thought I was kissing butt or he was kissing mine for that matter. But this was better. It was like having your second chess move catch your opponent off guard. The first one is simple but the second one, that's where the strategy really begins.

"Do you have a way to listen to the phone lines?"

He looked a little perplexed.

"Why do you ask? I mean, I should know better than to ask the same person who has an envelope full of pictures of me, but I'll go for the bait."

"You still mad about that? Please! You wouldn't have given me a job any other way. We provided a service for each other. You had Kessy and I got a job. No biggie. But back to my question."

He smiled as if to say he liked my move. A dude who hustles loves to see a woman who does the same. He knows how he thinks, so when he thinks there's a possibility, I think the same way, it's enticing.

"I may have a way to listen."

"If I were you, I'd listen to Cassandra's line every now and again."

"And what would I find?"

"I don't know. It depends on what you consider a find. I'm just a friend looking out for a friend."

"Oh. Who is the friend you're looking out for?"

"You. You gave me a job, that makes you my friend!"

Me and my black Coach heels Kessy bought me for my birthday sashayed out of his office. I'm not sure if he ever saw a pair of black jeans look so good. I played with my pearls as I knew I won the first round. We weren't in competition but still, I was winning.

The day wore on and Cassandra still had her sneaky little phone calls. I still wasn't sure if she was talking to Breeze, but soon Nick would know.

I gathered the hundreds of demo CDs people sent to be heard by the great Nicholas Michaels. Each time I went past Cassandra's desk to go to the copy room to get a new batch, she'd start whispering. No one else seemed to notice. I mean, she was Nick's assistant. She was expected to be on the phone all day.

Then the silence broke. A glass vase shattered against the door to Nicholas's office. For two seconds the bustle on the other side of the door froze. No one knew what had Nick so upset.

"Cassandra, can you come into my office, please?"

I wanted badly to go into the office and watch the events unfold, but unfortunately, I wasn't invited. Within minutes Cassandra walked out to her desk and packed her things. She surveyed the room to see who was watching. Everyone pretended to look elsewhere. Almost everyone was in shock. No one looked up from their desks, except me. The girl who treated me as hired help was no longer helping the hired.

After a few minutes Nicholas came out of his office. He looked surprised to see Cassandra.

"You're still here? Girl, don't let me call security."

Cassandra tried to throw everything in the box Brooke put near her desk. She looked like she was moving fast but maybe to Nicholas not fast enough. I hadn't known Nicholas that long but I had never imagined that he would be so upset or aggressive. As he barrelled his way toward Cassandra, Rob positioned himself between them. Cassandra bowed her head, grabbed her pocketbook, and rushed out. Rob went to her computer and sat down. Brooke instantly went and got some discs for Rob to download what he viewed as necessary. No one knew what to say so everyone just kept their heads down and pretended to do work. So that was it. No more Cassandra.

"Sakia, come into my office please."

Brooke looked scared for me. How cute. She liked me, and she was all right with me. I wasn't worried though.

I entered Nicholas's office. I didn't want to look too confident, but I knew he needed me. We both knew he did.

"Well, I don't know how you did it."

"Did what? If you think I set her up . . ."

"Not saying that. Did you?"

I knew better than to answer.

"Well anyway, you did what no one else seemed to be able to do. Breeze has been outbidding me on fresh talent for a little while now. I could never figure out how he knew what I was going to offer. I'd make an offer and the artist would immediately reject it. Basically he countered before I offered."

He stared out the window as if he was deciding the world's next movements. His black velour zip-up sweater tried to cling to his chest but there was too much room. It didn't drape off him, but it didn't show off his slim muscular build I knew existed. He stroked his chin. That's where the beard was. It wasn't all over his face and all up his cheeks. It was only on the chin. Short, trimmed, maintained. The waves in his closely cropped hair showed he had curls when he let it grow. I noticed he was attractive.

"Mr. Michaels, I . . ."

"Don't be so formal now. If it wasn't for you, I might have continued to lose business and the company I worked so hard to build would eventually bankrupt me. So I thank you."

"Oh. Well, you're welcome."

"But now it seems I have an issue. I don't have an assistant."

"Yes, that would be the case."

"So of course, you're going to be my assistant."

"Of course."

He laughed a little to himself. My face stayed serious.

"You know, Saks, you're a hustler! It's okay, though. We need hustlers in this business. I think you'll do just fine. I'm actually glad you got me to give you that job."

Good news travels fast is what my father used to say. That's what he told the police when they showed up at our door arresting him for embezzlement. All those years of me going to private school and living in a Park Slope brownstone were over my junior year in high school. I always believe my mother snitched. It wasn't a secret how we got to take all those vacations to the Cayman Islands. After the incident with Mr. Paul, Daddy acted like nothing happened. He and Mr. Paul didn't hang out anymore but he went on with life as usual. My mother could've asked for a divorce but she wouldn't have been satisfied with child support. When he went to jail and the lawyer explained to her that the government held on to the money in his business bank accounts, she hit the roof. Somehow she expected to inherit all his assets like he'd died or something. My dad kept close to nothing in his personal bank account. For weeks all she would say was, "For nothing. I can't believe it was for nothing! Let him rot in jail."

Yeah, she called the police.

Nervously Brooke rushed over to me with a blank notebook and pen.

"Here, you're going to need this. Just write down everything they tell you and don't think. When you get to your desk you can rummage through it all and figure out what needs to be done. Oh, and Saks, good luck with your new position."

How in heaven's name did she know? I just came out of Nick's office. Was she listening from the other side of the door? She had to be. Maybe everyone was listening.

Chapter 5 | This Is Fingers

"How was your day at work?"

Sometimes it seemed like Kessy was my husband.

"You know I'm his new assistant."

"Of course. I never doubted that. Did you get the photos developed?"

"Kessy, you ever known me to slack on that?"

"You're right. Girl, you are lethal! I'm glad I'm your best friend, or else I'd be some rich whore running on a lost road somewhere."

"Shut up, what are you talking about?"

"No, I'm serious. When you want something, you go get it. Can't nobody get in your way. I'm just happy you let me be an accomplice on the winning team!"

"Please, let you? You are such a willing participant! You're the one who was in Principal Allan's car that night. You weren't even looking for the long-term benefit of that one!"

"Yeah, but you're the one who used that whole thing to make him pay for your college education."

We laughed.

"Girl, let me call you back. My mother's calling on the other line."

"Oh, goodness. Yes, see what Miss Melissa Sands has to say. I'm sure it'll be interesting."

"I'm sure."

My mother went on her usual tirade of how nobody ever wants to help her out. I went to college and all I could do was be somebody's intern. She thinks I think I'm hot stuff because I'm hanging out with some rich girl who just parties all the time. Blah blah blah. What it all boiled down to was she spent all her money on cigarettes and beer and now she can't pay her rent. We had this conversation once a month and it never occurred to her that my rich party friend might be paying the rent for us both. I let her talk her own head off. When she was finished, I let her know the check was already in the mail. I didn't think it necessary to let her know about my promotion. No need to have her rent mysteriously increase.

I called Kessy back.

"Yeah, I'm off."

"That was quick. Miss Sands didn't have a whole lot to say today?"

"Maybe. I don't know. I just listen for my cue to let her know when the money's coming. That's all she wants. The complaining about me and every other thing in the world is just her gear-up."

"Thank God for my mother and father."

"Yes, the sun rises and sets on Kessy Johnson. I'm just glad they love me, too."

"Who, Sakia Sands? Oh please. Love you? They adore you. They never say it, but I know they wish I went to college."

"Maybe, but they love you more than life anyway. They don't hide it. My mom is comfortable with getting a check and thankful to not have a son-in-law who could tell me I shouldn't be giving her money. Could you imagine if she paid enough attention to realize I don't have that kind of money and it must be coming from you?"

"Well actually it's coming from my father who insists on supporting his adopted child, but I get what you mean. Oh, and I forgot to tell you, I got some more info on that rapper Breeze was talking about."

"Girl, you are vital for opportunity. I love you!"

"Girl, I love you, too. Just listen. His name is Fingers, remember?"

"Yeah. Is he the kid on the mix tapes? He plays the piano, right?"

"Yes, girl and he is hot! He does all his beats himself and they are all mostly piano. Then he's not even a conscious rapper. He's like on some no-nonsense hard-core stuff."

"Cool. So now I just have to figure out how I can sign him to Hustle Hard."

"No problem, sweetie. Apparently he's in the studio tonight. We can go up there if you want to talk to him. I hear he likes y'all redbones."

The studio wasn't what I expected at all. I thought it was going to be some big elaborate place with wood panel walls and big glass mirrors. The place looked like it used to be someone's apartment. The carpet was a dingy blue that had very small hints of its former pale blue color. Marijuana smoke filled the air and it looked like a party was going on. There were at least ten people with no purpose in there.

Observing everything, I immediately knew who Fingers was. Five foot eight maybe, and skinny as I don't know what. He had on a belt and his black jeans still slid down, showing his black boxers with big white polka dots. His face was like cherrywood and his eyes were dark. There was yellow where the white part of his eyes should be. He barely looked up at me and Kessy while he was rolling some dirty green marijuana in his cigar. Clearly we didn't catch his attention and that was fine with me. My dad used to tell me observation was the first step in your attack.

Fingers blew out a pillow of smoke as he touched the white girl who stood between his legs while he sat on the arm of the brown pleather couch. After two more pulls, the white girl took a drag of the rolled cigar. I giggled to myself as I thought, *I guess Kessy was wrong. He doesn't like redbones. He likes white-bone. This is the guy everyone wants to sign so badly, huh? He had nothing and still he acted as though he had it all. If Kessy's parents knew she was in this run-down building with piss-infected hallways, they'd have her committed. Then they'd probably have me committed for being crazy enough to come here with her.*

The young lady Fingers flirted with was clearly a tease and he wasn't that good at game. I mean, the atmosphere itself wasn't sexy. The room smelled like someone poured beer all over the carpet. Not spilled, just poured it! The smell of marijuana seemed like it came from the cracks in the walls. Still he smiled the gold-tooth grin as the snowflake took a rubber band and put her blond strands into a ponytail. When she lifted her arms, her too-tight purple sweater showed her navel and the silver rod in it. He eyed her up and down. Then some overweight bald guy came out to tell Fingers it was time to record. Kessy went in the other room to watch Fingers record. I stayed with the girl.

"Hey. I'm Sakia. Love that sweater!"

"Oh, thank you. I'm Amber."

She sounded like straight bubble gum. I almost lost my cool with belly laughter as I thought of how stereotypical she seemed. It was like she studied what movies projected Ambers to be and decided to become it.

"So, Sakia. That's your name right? It's pretty lame here, huh?"

"Not really. That guy is kind of cute. Why didn't you want to give him any play?" Okay, shoot me for saying he was cute. Maybe he could have been halfway decent if his braids were fresh and not so fuzzy. Or if his eyes didn't look filled to the rim with liquor.

"I don't know. I mean who is he? Would you talk to him?"

"Girl, yes! He may not be anyone now but he's about to be that dude!"

I spent the next thirty minutes talking to Miss Amber. The

song Fingers was recording, "I'm a G," seemed more than appropriate background for the conversation. When he was finished Fingers came into the room where Amber and I were. Everyone else, including Kessy, stayed in the other room to hear the new recording over and over and over again. For the first time, Fingers saw me. He squinted a bit like he was trying to figure out who I was but then made a face like he decided it wasn't important.

"Hello, Fingers."

"What's up. I know you?"

"No, but don't worry about that. You know this young lady, Amber."

I could hear Kessy entertaining the other room. Everyone was high and drunk. All Kessy had to do was talk a little and laugh a lot. Amber's demeanor changed from a girl trying to be part of the scene to a straight kitten.

"So, um, about what you were saying before. I think I could show you some things."

Her voice was seductive and she pressed against him. Who was she kidding? Not me. She wasn't new to this. Only a pro could change up that quickly. All she needed was some motivation. She's probably blown more people in the past year than Kessy has her whole life. Amber heard about Fingers. She probably just got real disappointed when she came to this dingy old run-down place. She changed her mind quickly when she thought about what he might be in the future. Now everybody wants to get in on the ground level.

"Oh yeah? Let me see some things then."

Before she had a chance to hesitate, I went and closed the door making it obvious I was turning the lock. Amber barely looked my way. She was comfortable. He pulled on her arm hard enough to let her know he wanted her but not enough to scare her. She grabbed her purse and took something wrapped in tinfoil out. She opened it and sniffed it real hard. She grabbed the half-full bottle of Heineken on the lamp table and downed it. With the bottle still in her hand she began to tongue kiss Fingers. At first it was all sloppy and nasty and I was a bit disgusted. I got past it though. I wasn't there to enjoy myself. I was working.

Fingers took the bottle from her hand and placed it on the table beside the couch. He held on to her waist and she removed her sweater over her head. Her round perky breasts were relieved. He sucked the right one vigorously as she sucked the other. His fingers tugged the fly on her stonewashed jeans that hugged her behind. She grabbed the beer bottle and poured whatever was left down the middle of her breasts. He licked the beer and quietly kept at his task. Finally the fly was open and his hand slid comfortably down. She bounced as he wiggled like he was trying to jimmy a lock. He used his other hand to peel the jeans from around her waist. She began to help.

Amber had on nothing but a pair of silver string thongs. She was on her knees and Fingers was still sitting on the arm of the faux leather couch. His eyes were closed as Amber inhaled the near-black piece of him protruding from his boxers. She was using two hands. His jeans were unzipped but they hadn't moved from where they were slightly below his hips. She started slow then seemed to get in a zone. She moved her head like a snake being charmed, then began to devour him as if she hadn't eaten in days and he was her only means for survival. Her movements slowed in pace and he held on tight to her shoulders like he was trying to hold her at a distance. He bit his lip and strained to keep his eyes closed. When he relaxed she let go and took two hard gulps. She wiped the evidence from her mouth with the back of her hand, then laughed. He shook his head then looked down to see how quickly he had recovered. He was ready for more. He moved to the couch and sat her on his lap with her back facing him. It was time for me to go. The two lovebirds could enjoy themselves without me. I walked over from the door and handed

Fingers a piece of paper with my name and number on it and said, "This is how we get down at Hustle Hard."

I unlocked the door and stepped out, leaving Amber to her rodeo.

Chapter 6 | Winning Team

I followed Nick into his office.

"I sent off the package to *V* magazine. Lakaya's press release is all set to go. Rob and I proofread it this morning. Promotions has a four o'clock release time. Oh and you have a meeting at noon with Fingers. He'll be looking to accept your offer."

There was no motion for like two and a half seconds. I knew he wanted to drop that bottom lip in awe but he was too cool to let the flies come in. He gathered his thoughts.

"When did you speak to Fingers to make the appointment?"

"This morning."

"Do you know him or something? Because to get any of these artists up before ten in the middle of the week and they're not hustling, is like pulling teeth."

"We've met."

"When?"

"Awhile ago. Like my first week. He's cool peoples. We've talked on the phone every once in a while. Look, you want to sign him or not? He's not even coming with a lawyer or manager."

"How do you know him?"

"I don't know him, know him. I've met him. I figured you'd want to sign him since everyone else does, especially Breeze."

"Of course I want to sign him! But I never made an offer."

"Oh, I took care of that."

I could tell from his eyes his brain was trying to wrap itself around what was happening.

"What did you offer?"

"Three hundred thousand, three albums, and an opportunity to negotiate his own label imprint under Hustle Hard if all three go platinum."

"And he said yes to that?"

"Why wouldn't he? Lakaya is doing great under us. Fingers was going to sign with Breeze, but he said he found out some stuff about Breeze that he didn't want to be associated with. You have a much better reputation for taking care of your artists."

I enjoyed looking at Nick and his effort to try to hide the fact that he was baffled. How could this woman who worked here for three months get the most wanted unsigned artist to agree to a deal that offered at least a hundred thousand dollars less than what the competing bidders were offering?

"Don't get me wrong, it's a good deal, but he would be saying yes to a lot less money than what Breeze or anyone else is offering. I mean, I'm sure they're not including the label imprint in their offer so that could be it, but he's a kid from the streets. I can't see him taking less money for something offered in the future."

"You can offer him more if you want to. I just don't think it's necessary."

"No, the deal you offered protects the company and allows us to make a lot of money. So if I don't have to offer more, then of course I won't! I'm just saying that it's odd someone with no real financial stability and a tenth-grade education would go for the logic and not the money. That's all."

"Well, I think he sees we are a company that cares about all his needs, not just how much we can make off of him."

My grin stayed subtle but Nick saw it. When I looked up from my notepad he was holding his chin with his arms folded, and looking at me. His eyes were deep brown. Normally they seemed lighter, more glassy. This time they were deep, rich, with more meaning.

Fingers came into his meeting with Nick on time. Just like I said, he came alone. It wasn't smart on his part but I guess he trusted me. Or maybe he trusted what he thought I was about. Either way he signed the contract without hesitation. When Fingers left, I saw a smile on Nick that I don't think I ever saw before. His smile seemed so genuine at that moment. His look of appreciation dissolved into another look. One that made me feel soft, but just for a moment. He said we should go to dinner to celebrate. I smiled and rushed to my desk to make a phone call.

"Kessy."

"What's up?"

"Nick wants to take me to dinner. Should I go?"

"What happened? He had his meeting with Fingers already?"

"Yes. He signed and everything was fine. But now Nick is all happy and wants to take me to dinner. The only problem is, I think it'll just be me and him."

"So what? Go, girl. Maybe you might get you some. His sex is kind of good, you know."

"Shut up! Don't be talking like that on this office phone. Remember he has a way to listen. I don't know who else is listening."

"Oh, right. Sorry. Anyway, go."

"But, Kess, you know I don't really do the one-on-one thing. I'd be out of my element."

"Out of your element? Sakia, please! The last boss you had dinner with decided he was going to teach you everything he knew about business to train you to take over. All because he was grateful for some clients you saved him from losing. Sounds to me that this is definitely your element."

My last boss was my uncle and my father taught him everything he knew. Unfortunately my father didn't teach his brother how not to go to jail and get everything taken away from you.

"Kessy . . ."

"Sakia, I know this is different. I know what you want but I also know you look like you're kind of liking Nick. It's okay to like someone. It doesn't make you any less focused. It means you're still a woman."

Nick and I left directly from the office. Everyone left the office about seven and we left a few minutes to eight. We took a car service and pulled up to a building on Sixth Street that looked like an old warehouse. I knew this was the building Nick was renovating for his new restaurant. I had seen the pictures and helped make arrangements for it from the office.

Inside, the round tables in the middle of the floor were stacked with chairs. The booths were cushioned with red velvet pillows and the wood tables were painted black. We walked on the black marble floor to the back of the restaurant as I looked at the high ceiling draped with crystal chandeliers. How did anyone get up that high to put them up there? Nicholas led me by my hand up a back staircase. My palms started to sweat a little. Him grabbing my hand was unexpected. Curiosity barged in and I wondered what was waiting for me. The top of the staircase opened into an area much like a loft and there was a small table set for two in the middle of the floor. We were alone at the top. There were no other tables there. The walls were lined with built-in benches adorned with the same red velvet cushions as downstairs. A small square vase sat in the middle of the small table with three beautiful red roses. I melted just a tiny bit on the inside and smiled a little on the out. The setting was romantic. Were we on a date? I think I was getting nervous.

"I wanted to bring you here to show you my appreciation. You are the first guest and I think you've earned a seat at the owner's table."

He pulled my chair out and I sat down hoping I wouldn't miss the seat. My heart felt as though it was skipping every other beat. I tried to keep my eyes on the roses to avoid Nick's searching eyes. He was looking for a reaction. What could I give him?

"Thank you. I've definitely earned dinner, but this is really nice!"

"Nice to see you're so appreciative. Well, anyway I wanted to thank you and this is how."

Skeptical, that's the word. I was skeptical of how genuine he might be. Normally I wouldn't care if someone was being real or not. All that would matter is my purpose and if I could achieve it. This was uncharted territory.

"This is very sweet of you, thank you. But really I'm just trying to help you win. If you win, I win. That's all."

"Oh, there's more to you than that. I don't believe for one second you are just doing your job. You're a go-getter. I know because I am one, too. I admire that about you."

I was feeling a little more relaxed. If we were going to talk about being sharp and on your toes, I was prepared. For a minute I thought this was going to be more personal. A waiter poured us glasses of wine and left the bottle on the table. He never took our order so I was a bit surprised when he brought our plates.

"Lobster Fra Diavolo for the lady. And for you, Mr. Michaels, your steak well done with baked potato and a side of vegetables."

I was completely caught off guard. I had Lobster Fra Diavolo one time and loved it. But that was only last week. How did he know? What was he trying to show me?

"I heard you tell Kessy how much you loved it."

So now it's my calls he's listening to. Great!

"If you listen to my phone calls, then why didn't you know I have been in contact with Fingers for months?"

"Maybe you speaking to another man isn't the conversation I'm interested in listening to."

Something about his ability to make me blush intrigued me. He accomplished what others in college worked too hard to do. He interested me. I did wonder what else he heard me say on the phone. Had he heard my conversation with Kessy after he asked me to dinner? It didn't take long for me to get the answer.

"So you know, Saks, I'm quite flattered you have an attraction to me."

It was hard swallowing the wine. I needed another glass. When I reached for the bottle he grabbed it and poured. I decided I had to act more confident. I had to be in control. He couldn't think I was one who was able to be embarrassed although the redness in my cheeks didn't help.

The room started to get warm. But no warmer than me when he stood up and asked me to dance. There was no music playing. I wasn't sure if I should be flattered or if there was someone watching somewhere who just wanted to catch me vulnerable. As we slow-danced he whispered in my ear.

"You amaze me, Sakia Sands. You're beautiful and smart. But you're a hustler! You can't deny it. You hustled me. And yes, I am very much attracted to you, too." I didn't know how to respond. The softness of his voice stopped my shaking. When we stopped moving, he broke the embrace. I wanted to be kissed. He looked me dead in my eyes and said, "I'm going to love you."

The butterflies were having a picnic in my stomach. I let his lips press against mine and his tongue find its way. His hands danced around the buttons on my shirt for a while before working to expose my cranberry-colored bra. Our kisses became more aggressive and I let my silk shirt slide off my shoulders. He unzipped my skirt while still holding me captive with his lips. The charcoal fabric glided down my legs. His slacks easily unzipped. I slid out of my heels. Freeing my lips, he kissed my neck, then worked to remove my stockings. Once I stepped out of them, he pulled his ribbed sweater over his head. I noticed how wonderfully the forest-green sweater complemented his chocolate skin. My heart pounded like a drum. His white wife-beater fit like new and highlighted the beauty in his cut shoulders. Still squatting, he kissed my ankles and gently caressed the back of my knees. Using his tongue he traced my thigh up toward that place where he settled and passionately kissed. I watched the waves in his hair move like the ocean. A bit of a rhythm coming close then changing directions. I gripped his fingers and allowed myself to close my eyes. I let out a brief moan. I was all of a sudden aware of my surroundings and what was happening. My legs were shaking and Nick slowly stood up. He kissed my face and read my eyes. Moving the table aside and stepping out of his boxers, he sat on his chair. I walked toward him and he reached down to grab his pants. He took out a condom and handed it to me. I ripped the packaging with my teeth and he watched as I slid the black Magnum on him. My body slowly nestled on top of him, we moved together, close, and embracing. The kisses couldn't stop. He caressed my back like I was his. My breathing was heavy. He was mine.

Chapter 7 | Done in the Dark

Nick and I kept things at the office professional, for the most part. Work itself wasn't an issue because we were both focused on getting our jobs done. We were both dedicated to the continued success of Hustle Hard Records and its president, Nicholas Michaels. In addition, I was still focused on becoming a powerhouse in this company. I started to love Nick, but I needed something to be able to hold on to. I didn't care if all I did was own a piece of the company. I had to own something. If Nick were to leave me or worse, fire me, I needed backup. This was all his. I had to earn mine. It wasn't enough to help him. He needed to see I was a force in my own right. I cared for Nick too much to try and take Hustle Hard from him. He had to see I deserved my own piece of the empire.

If there was one thing I learned from my parents' marriage, it is that a girl needs security. It doesn't matter if the man marries you. You have to make sure if he dies, goes to jail, or leaves you for another woman, you can take care of yourself. Falling in love is nice, but falling off is not an option!

Nick was in Africa meeting with a factory for his new clothing line. He left me in charge and all the business associates needed to see that I was the backbone of the label. Getting results would be my claim to fame. Getting Fingers to sign was only the first step. I brought two other acts through the door. Each act wrote and produced their own music and were already poppin on the streets. The employees at Hustle Hard knew it. This was my time to shine without being in Nick's shadow. No one was going to catch me slipping.

The sky was dark and I was just finishing up revising Nick's calendar. I sent out the guest list for Fingers's album release party. Nick wanted to make sure I handled it directly so it could be clear how dedicated we as a label were to our artists. I thought everyone left the office already. I heard Rob's voice elevate then quiet down. It sounded like he was cursing in Spanish, which was strange because he was usually so laid-back. He loved his job and worked well with the DJs. Everyone in the industry loved him. Rob was Puerto Rican, which helped us win the support of the Spanish radio stations. Every radio jock would play whatever he put in front of him. Who could he be arguing with?

I started to go see what all of the commotion was. It had to be serious. Rob knew how much Nick hated people making scenes near the office. We were the only Black-owned company in the building. Nick was adamant on being professional and not being the ghetto people on the seventh floor.

Only one foot made it out of Nick's office when I heard Rob say Brooke's name. They were loud. I stepped back into the office and took off my shoes. I tiptoed closer to the door and hid my body.

"Brooke, I'm not leaving my wife! You and I are not Saks and Nick. What do you think this is? It's not a soap opera!"

What does he mean by not Saks and Nick?

"But, Rob, just listen. She doesn't understand you or this business. She doesn't even respect you. I hear how she talks to you. When she calls the office and I tell her you're unavailable she says all kinds of things about you."

"I understand that, Brooke, but it's how it is and it's between her and me! I have two kids with her and they need me. We've been over this."

"But, Rob, please, I need you. I'm tired of not being able to hold you at night. I can't take it. She doesn't deserve you!"

I couldn't believe what I was hearing. Rob was cheating on his wife with Brooke? I've met Rob's wife plenty of times. His wife always seemed sweet to me. Then again, I wasn't married to her nor was I his assistant. An assistant catches wind of all kinds of personal stuff. Somehow family members seem to think that having a personal relationship with the assistant will get their messages relayed faster or more efficiently. I met Nick's mom as his assistant first. You should have seen the look on her face when she met me as the girlfriend! Her eyes looked up in the sky trying to figure if she told me anything she probably shouldn't have.

"Maybe we should just end this then."

"No, Rob, please!"

It was obvious Brooke was crying. How could she beg like that? I remember my mother telling me when I was sixteen, "Even when they're raping you, don't beg and don't cry!"

Ever since then I hadn't shed a tear. When I went to see my father in prison, no tears. When they took Uncle Charlie away and we had to close down his business, no tears. No tears, no begging. If they want to give it they will. Principal Allan offered to pay for my college education. Sure he felt pressure knowing I saw him in the parking lot that night with Kessy, but I didn't have to ask him for anything. He knew my mom couldn't afford it. I wouldn't have asked. I might have sent him a little reminder of what happened, but I wouldn't have asked. Even now, when I get what I want, I show I am worth it. I earn it. No begging! No crying!

Nick would die if he heard Brooke and Rob's argument. Rob has been married for eight years and his wife was personally invited by Nick to all the company functions. I think they met at a party for Nick. How can any of us look her in the face if news of this affair ever came out? What would it do to the reputation of our business? You know how some wives are. She might have tried to blame Nick or come up to the office and started acting crazy. Then we would have to call security and cause a big old scene. I can't tell Nick. He doesn't need this kind of thing to think about. Rob has been here longer than anyone. Nick would feel betrayed.

I was midthought when I heard them panting. I peeked out from the side of Nick's office door. The lights were still off on the rest of the floor. I saw the shadow of a man lifting a woman up on top of my desk, her legs wrapped around his waist and him plunging into her like he never had her before and he wanted to make the best of the first time. They enjoyed each other for about eight minutes when her legs dropped and he pulled himself away zipping his pants. I figured this was a good time to turn the lights on and let them know I was standing there. Brooke gasped with surprise and Rob just stood there. He was dumbfounded. It was like the whole room held its breath, but it was only the three of us there. I said nothing. I didn't shake my head, I didn't smile. I just looked them both in their faces. I went back into Nick's office, closed down the computer, put on my shoes, and left the office. To be honest, I didn't know what to say. I kind of wanted to laugh. They watched me as I walked past them. What would I tell Nick? I'm sure they wondered. Nick and my relationship wasn't a secret nor did we try to make it be. However, what wasn't as easy to know was my influence over this business. All they knew was since I'd been here, things had happened. Cassandra was fired, Fingers was signed, the restaurant opened. How much pull did I really have?

Chapter 8 | Unexpected

"I didn't expect you back until tomorrow."

Nick caught me by surprise when he walked into the office that Thursday morning. The past two days Brooke and Rob had been walking around on their toes. Neither of them were sure what I would say or what Nick would do about their incident. We never discussed it and every time either of them looked like they were going into explanation mode I walked away. I'll tell you this though, everything I needed to get done got done.

All the giggling Brooke used to do was over. She was now a serious assistant and quick to complete her tasks. Rob worked diligently, making sure Lakaya and Fingers both had their times in the spotlight. We were an independent company with two of the biggest artists around on our roster. No one wanted to lose their jobs or a spouse over a stupid affair.

"I thought I'd surprise you and come in a day early. Shut the door, I have to talk to you."

Did he go to Angola and find some new singer or something? A new group? Seemed like everyone wanted to find someone overseas to make a great record. Why didn't he call me and tell me the news? It was obvious it was big, very big. The last time I saw him this excited was when Fingers signed on the dotted line. I closed his office door and Nick intercommed the receptionist to tell her to send all calls for him or for me to voice mail. We were having an important meeting. My foot tapped feverishly as I was anxious to know what he had to talk to me about. I hope he didn't go making a business decision without talking to me. That would be foolish. I sat on the mustard-yellow suede couch near the window.

"Why are you so excited? You didn't call before you flew out. I could have had a car pick you up."

"Baby! Stop talking for one second."

He walked around his desk and across the floor to where I sat. Sitting down next to me, he turned to face me, and held my hands.

"Baby, look at me."

I looked at how his eyes smiled while he pulled a black velvet box from his navy blue blazer jacket. The powder-blue rugby shirt he had on underneath nicely complemented the blue diamond cross dangling near the top of his stomach. He stood up, then looked at the black box proudly. My eyes followed his movements as he kneeled before me. My heart was beating so hard it felt like it was going to jump out of my chest.

"Will you marry me?"

The rock was bigger than the one Kessy's mom wore. No tears. I was a little glassy eyed but no tears. My mind started to race. The love we made the night before he left passed visions through my brain. I was still Nick's assistant. For all that I did he hadn't made me vice president, manager, or anything. I could marry him but then what? Do I just sit back and stay home playing the role of wife? Look at him. He's so cute! Do I remain his assistant forever? He makes me feel soft. He's probably going to ask for a prenup. So what happens if we get divorced? I love him. I don't want to divorce him. I don't own anything. I made this company better. I negotiated contracts for his line of clothes, and three acts. Was I just going to be someone's wife with no acknowledgment of my contributions? He remained on one knee.

"Baby, say something."

"Wow, Nick, I don't know what to say. I love you. I want to say yes."

"So say yes!"

"What happens if we do get married? Will I have to quit? Do I move into your house and we ride in together? How does that work with Hustle Hard?"

I tried to smile and not show how much it weighed on my

mind. I mean I really did love him and wanted to marry him. But I couldn't afford to be like my mother and find myself calling my child for money because I needed a husband to take care of me, when he is no longer my husband.

"Is that what you're worried about? I swear you would think you started this business the way you are so committed. It works how you want it to work. You don't see I would do anything for you? If you don't want to work you don't have to. You will be my wife. What's mine is yours. I love you. Hustle Hard is better because of you and so am I. Since you walked in that door you've stood as my partner. I just want you to be my partner at home, too."

No more needed to be said. I was going to become Sakia Sands-Michaels. I couldn't wait to tell Kessy. I, who had vowed to never get married, was going to marry Nicholas Michaels. Maybe it was going to be okay. I did love him. Maybe I wasn't going to be like my mom and dad. We could stay married forever.

The door flung open, exposing Nick and I standing in an embrace and locked in a kiss that had possibilities of leading elsewhere. It was a good kiss! The look on Nick's face told Brooke that she better have a really good reason for not respecting the closed door.

"I'm sorry, Nick, but there's this guy on my line who says he just came from Cassandra's house."

"Yeah, okay! Why is he calling me? Tell him she doesn't work here anymore."

"I did but he says that's not why he's calling."

Nick picked up the line in his office. I stood there with him waiting to hear why this man was calling. I saw a tear trickle down Nicholas's face then I heard him ask, "When did she pass?"

I wasn't sure what to say. I had no idea how to feel. I handed Nick a tissue. The man on the phone said Cassandra passed two days ago and he was collecting some of her things for the funeral home to bury her in. I could hear him crying through the phone. The man was Cassandra's father. He said on the coffee table next to her Bible, Cassandra left a note addressed to Nicholas. It didn't say much, except, "I'm sorry."

In my mind, Cassandra's dark chocolate skin looked less pretty and less soft. I imagined her crying. Her face still looked sad. I imagined her shaking and reading her Bible.

"In other news, the funeral for twenty-eight-year-old Cassandra Brent was held today. She was the former assistant to Nicholas Michaels, the owner and president of Hustle Hard Records. Here, Mr. Michaels is seen with his current assistant who is also rumored to be his current wife as of four days ago. It has been reported the two eloped and will have a more formal ceremony in a few weeks. As a gift to the Brent family, Mr. Michaels paid all expenses for Cassandra Brent's funeral. Apparently, Cassandra was the ex-girlfriend of famed label owner Bernard 'Breeze' King. Her death appears to be a suicide by an overdose on medication prescribed by her doctor. The young lady was being treated for AIDS."

Nick clicked the remote and the reporter's voice came to a stop. The television went black. He sat at the edge of the bed rubbing his forehead. Teardrops slowly dripped down his cheeks and he remained silent. I kneeled on the bed and positioned myself behind him, the white down comforter cushioning my knees. Massaging his shoulders always relaxed him. I knew he was feeling guilty about the way he screamed at her when he fired her. I was feeling guilty myself. I knew what she was doing with giving information to Breeze was wrong, but still I felt like I got her fired. Nicholas and I got married on paper but planning a big ceremony was too hard to think about. That's why it would be in a few weeks rather than a few months. Neither of us wanted the elaborate planning. It seemed selfish in light of the recent event. The sadness was heavy. That's why Nicholas paid for the funeral. I mean, it's not our fault she died. However, that knowledge didn't make any of us feel better. It's a weird thing when someone dies. Your family and friends seem to love you more than they ever did. And the people you violated somehow feel like they violated you. At the funeral, I even saw Breeze crying.

Chapter 9 | My Day

I kept calling Kessy but she wouldn't answer. I let the phone ring eight times every time I called. Where could she be? This was the morning of my wedding and my best friend was nowhere to be found. My strapless knee-length gown was fitting quite snug on my behind. I'm glad the designer made sure I got a girdle built in to this thing. It made my tummy look flatter than what it was and gave my bottom a boost. White was a good color on me. I looked cuter than I did on prom night. I had a professional do my makeup and she made my face look like a model for beautiful skin. My hair was pinned in a French roll with diamonds and pearls attached to the bobby pins. Sophisticated. That's how I looked. Where was Kessy? She said she would be here early.

"Mom, have you seen Kessy?"

My mother was sitting in the living area of the mansion we rented for the ceremony. She barely looked at me over the rim of her martini glass. I don't know why I asked her. She was only smiling because she knew her daughter was marrying someone with some money. I think she had the the surgeon paste her smile there just for this purpose. She could care less about Kessy.

I spotted Rob on his way into where my mom was sitting, coming from the dining area.

"Hi, Rob. Have you seen my friend, Kessy?"

His tux matched Nick's except his had a teal cummerbund. Nick wanted to wear a vest.

"No, I'm sure she's around though."

He held my shoulders as if to tell me to relax. His voice lowered to a whisper. "I just wanted to say thank you for not saying anything about, you know, that whole situation."

At this point I couldn't care less about him and Brooke. Couldn't he see how frantic I was? I couldn't even look at him. I was looking around and trying to peer over his shoulder.

"Yeah, well, I didn't think it would help any of us if I did. So, umm, if you see Kessy, can you let her know I'm looking for her?"

How could she not be here? I knew she should have spent the night here with me. Why did I want to be alone? I don't want to be alone now! Was I the only one looking for her? I didn't want people to see me before the ceremony but what could I do? I needed her. I went outside where the ceremony would be held. Nick stood in the front row of the white fold-up chairs talking to Kessy's parents. It looked like all the guests were present. Even Fingers had on a suit with Lakaya as his date. I don't even know how that happened! The whole crowd held their breath and looked at me in surprise when they saw me running toward Nick. All the chatter ceased. The white lace train was pulling at my hair. It was long and dragging on the grass behind me. I was the only one moving.

"Nick!"

He saw the fear in my eyes. I stopped running. Nick didn't say a word. He was still about ten feet away and he looked worried and shocked to see me. Kessy's mother's eyes were opened wide. The former model put her hand to her mouth and tears rolled down her face. Then I heard a familiar male voice come from behind me. It wasn't me the crowd was watching.

"Worried, are we?"

I turned toward the voice and saw Breeze at the top of the garden stairs I ran down only seconds ago. He had a gun to Kessy's head. Her face was bloody and her lipstick smeared. Mascara ran down her face and her teal halter dress was ripped and speckled with blood. Her legs were shaking and the scratches on Breeze's face showed there had been a struggle earlier.

"So, Nick, this is your plan? You send these two little hoes to cheat me out of my contracts? Nice to see you, Fingers!"

I closed my eyes knowing Nick didn't know what Breeze was talking about. I took a deep breath and turned to see Nick looking confident.

"I never cheated you out of anything. You tried to cheat me for years. Who and what is this about?"

Nick walked toward me slowly. How could he be so confident? It's like he knew Breeze wouldn't shoot. I wished I could explain it all to him. I wish I could tell him how sorry I was.

"Yes, go stand by your woman, Nick! Cassandra told me about the intern who told you about Fingers. Never did I think this ho right here was her. She's good, Nick. I give you that."

For the first time since the police took my father away, I felt helpless. There was nothing I could do to take control of the situation. I was scared. Not just for Kessy, I was scared for us all. Since Cassandra left, Breeze hadn't been able to sign anyone worth listening to. He tried to drop a record himself and it flopped.

I finally spoke.

"Nick has nothing to do with this. And really neither does Kessy. I'm the one who told her what to do. If you came here for anyone, you came here for me."

Nicholas's head tilted to the side when he looked at me. My eyes were getting red and telling him this is all my fault. My mother stood on the side in the background, shaking her head as if this was some regular bull her daughter was always involved in. Kessy's mom was crying hysterically and her husband held her, rocking her like a baby.

"You can't protect him. I know he sent you. You were at my house. You sneaky little ho! Acting like you just wanted to watch. All of sudden this dude ain't taking no phone calls from me, calling me gay and whatnot. You got Cassandra fired and then Nick signed Fingers. I'm not stupid! I see what happened! You got me, Nick!"

His laugh was that of someone who had surrendered their mind a long time ago. His light skin was now burning red. It was like the devil was coming to life. Nick's breaths were deep and calm. He was familiar with the scenario. His eyes showed he remembered how I got my job. He stepped forward.

"You're right, Breeze. I shouldn't have sent them to you for information. It was wrong. But does it really need to go this far?"

"No, Nick, don't."

I couldn't let him take responsibility. He had nothing to do with it. I was dead wrong. He knew it and still tried to protect me. How could I have done this? How will we get past this? Can we? Will any of us get past today? My head started to hurt. I couldn't think of a solution.

Breeze shoved Kessy toward Nick and me. He still held the gun and kept it directed at us. I hugged Kessy and whispered, "I'm so sorry."

She whispered back to me, "He raped me."

The tears flowed from her caramel face like a waterfall. It was now me who was shaking. What did I do to her? I closed my eyes to stop the tears.

It all seemed to happen so fast. The police officers came rushing in. There was one loud shot. I looked up from Kessy's shoulders and saw Nick fall to the ground holding his chest. I fell to my knees over Nick's body. The police grabbed Breeze and put him in handcuffs. Kessy's sobs were louder and I heard my own breaths. My husband, Nick, lay in my arms shivering.

"Don't worry. It's okay. I still love you."

Those were the last words of Nicholas Michaels. The tears flowed freely from my eyes. I begged God to give Nick back to me. I cried, I screamed. I didn't want to let go, but Nick already had. My face was red and swollen. My heart was broken. I couldn't stop shaking. The paramedics tried to pull me away. It was then I realized what love was. He loved me. I loved him but not enough. I put myself before him every time. Now, I lost him and to some degree a part of myself.

My name is Sakia "Saks" Sands-Michaels and I am president and CEO of Hustle Hard Records. My record label is one of the most successful independent labels there are. I sit at the top. This was the story of how I got here.

GUN MUSIC

by Nikki Turner

Chapter 1

 hat's the point?" Crook questioned, shaking the dice in his palm. The corner of Clinton Avenue and Clinton Place was feenin with young hungry wolves packed together, everybody on their own grind, but prepared to come up off the back of anybody weak enough to fall victim. The six men in the circle were huddled together like a football team, watching the dice careen across the broken pavement, money scattered all around six-two.

"Yo, the fuck is my point?" Crook echoed, staggering back slightly from the E&J he had consumed.

"Nigga, if you don't know, I damn sure ain't gonna tell you," the tall slim hustler fading his bet hollered back.

"Just shoot the fuckin' dice." Crook straightened up to his full height, pulled up his sagging pants, and grilled Slim hard. Slim was taller than Crook's five foot eight by several inches and outweighed him by a good forty pounds as well, but Crook wasn't fazed one bit. He was already heated because he was losing the two hundred dollars his girl Sheena gave him to pay the electric bill, and now that he was down to his last fifty, this dude was trying to front on his point?

Crook could see the bulge in Slim's waist, which made Slim smirk like he was safe. Crook wasn't strapped because he had intended to pay the bill and return home, but he got caught up.

He turned to a heavyset cat to his left and asked, "Yo, what the fuck is the point?" He growled, getting madder at himself for even forgetting what he needed to roll to win his money back.

"Don't tell him shit," Slim snarled, silencing the fat cat. "If he don't know, tell him to come off the fuckin' bet."

Crook crouched and kissed his closed fist before letting the dice tumble over and against the brick wall. Five-two.

The circle let out a collective holler at Crook's bad luck.

"Five-Deuce! Come up off that, broke ass nigga," Slim chuckled, referring to the money under Crook's scuffed up left Tim boot.

Crook let his anger assess the situation. This cat had shined on Crook for the last time. It wasn't enough that he had taken Sheena's two hundred, talkin' slick the whole while, but Slim wasn't even from Clinton Avenue. Out there flossin' in his new GS300, wearing the new Carmelo Jordans that Crook wanted but couldn't afford. Above all, it was the way Slim thought his gun could speak for him that made Crook decide, not only wasn't he getting the fifty underfoot, Slim was leaving broke as Crook now felt by his presence. The whole thought process took less than a second, and before Slim could react, Crook's fist cut through the air with lightning-fast intensity and landed squarely against Slim's jaw.

Crack!

Slim stumbled from the blow, dazed but ready to shoot, except Crook didn't give him a chance to get his shit off. Lefts and rights came back-to-back like a swarm of killer bees, stinging Slim into bloody submission. When he slumped against the wall, it was over.

Crook snatched the gun from Slim's waist, yelling, "Oh, you was gonna shoot me, mu'fucka?! Huh?! You was gonna shoot me, bitch?!"

Then the pistol-whipping began. Crook smashed Slim mercilessly until he crumbled to the pavement, beaten and disfigured. Even then Crook wouldn't stop. He had blacked out in a tyrannical spaz. To Crook, Slim represented all that was wrong with his world. Fake-ass niggas like Slim had it, while live niggas like himself starved and struggled.

"Bitch-ass niggas, this is Crook!" he bellowed between stomps. "Muthafuckin Crook!"

The whole corner watched in amused shock, because wolves loved blood as long as it wasn't any of theirs. But Crook was making the spot hot! So it wasn't mercy that saved Slim, but their own greed, because they knew if Crook killed this nigga, police would sweat the block for weeks.

"Yo, Crook, chill! Chill! Po-Po comin'!" someone yelled, even though there were no police in sight. Crook snapped back to reality, then went in Slim's pockets, taking his money, white gold watch, and of course the Carmelo Jordans off his feet. Grimy.

"You wasn't rockin' 'em right," Crook hissed, giving Slim one last kick to the face, which sent his two front teeth flying. Then Crook dipped, taking the alleyway behind the old houses and stores that lined the block and disappeared in the shadows.

Two hours later, Crook sat in the staircase leading up to his and Sheena's apartment. The place smelled of fishy urine and fried chicken, but Crook didn't smell it; he couldn't. His whole body was numb from what was left of the half ounce of coke on his lap. The tip of his nose glistened from the fish scale devouring his senses. He was fucked up and loving the fact he couldn't feel anything but the cool sensation of nothingness. The comfort zone of escape that sniffing coke had become to him.

His life was in shambles, just like the raggedy clothes he had on. The dingy Def Jam University jeans and soiled G-Unit hoody had been his attire for the last three days. His Tims were scuffed to the point that they were on the brink of bursting at the toe. He was a smart nigga that had made a lot of dumb decisions, and now it seemed that he was continuously paying the consequences. He could've stayed in school and made something of himself, but he chose the street, yet, he wasn't a hustler. He couldn't come up in the game because he had a habit and no one trusted him with any substantial amount of weight because he'd crossed all that had extended their hands in the past. Cats had beat him, shot him, and stabbed him, but he always returned shooting, stabbing, and beating, scar for scar, so the money niggas figured he wasn't worth the trouble.

He was a stick-up kid, but he wasn't focused or patient enough to hit any major licks, so he stayed lickin' petty. Then he'd get high, buy Sheena and the kids shit, pay a few bills, and with whatever was left, he got higher. But if anything else, Crook was an emcee. The nigga was that rose growing through concrete that Tupac mused about, because he was that nice. All he wanted to do was rhyme and he tried everything to get on, he just couldn't get right. Regardless, it was in his blood like lava, bubbling to get out, and it was moments like this, filled with pain and anger that made it explode.

> Crook shit be like dope to your bloodstream.
> Fuck when doves cry have you ever heard a thug scream!
> From all this pressure so muthafuck it whatever
> Somebody gotta die when I grab my Beretta.

He gripped the pistol in his lap like a vice and pointed it at the world, pushing the lyrics from his soul through the rage and frustration.

So when I run up on you with the Tech
Crying help is just a waste of breath 'cause all I'm leavin' is scars.
But I'm doin' you a favor, 'cause dyin's easy muthafucka,
It's livin that's hard.

He imagined a gun pointed at his every problem, embodied in a laughing shadow that his cocaine-mesmerized mind had conjured up in front of him. Then he realized that the shadow was his own, and his every problem was inside of himself. It was then when he put the gun to his temple and trembled for a reason not to. *Look at you . . . Look at you, you ain't shit. Fuckin' nothin', a nobody mu'fucka. So broke you gotta rob a nigga for his kicks just to rock?! Go 'head . . . Do it, coward. Who gonna give a fuck? Who, huh, who?!*

His thoughts chided him, but his heart answered with one word.

Sheena.

He closed his eyes tight against the hot tears threatening to run free, just thinking about the only person he had, who stuck by him no matter what. Just on the strength of her commitment, he felt like he should pull the trigger and free her from his bullshit. But the love he felt, and the glimmer of hope it represented, made him lower the gun, take a deep breath, and head upstairs to their apartment.

Crook lumbered up the stairs, wondering what he would tell Sheena. He had been gone since four P.M. and now it was past eleven and the electric bill wasn't paid. He knew she would flip, so he prepared himself for it. Crook slid the key into the door and entered their small one bedroom home. Every time he entered that place, he was reminded of how much he hated it. It was so small, it felt like a prison cell. It didn't matter that Sheena kept what little they had in immaculate condition, there was only so much you could do with flea market furniture and meager means.

"Vic, I'm in the kitchen, baby," Sheena called out, greeting him. He could hear the water sloshing from the dishes she was washing.

"The chicken's cold, but if you're hungry, I could warm it up for you," she offered.

Damn, his mind gasped, relishing the warm welcome but knowing damn well he didn't deserve it. Crook didn't answer. Instead he sunk into the couch and flipped on the TV.

"Vic, you hear me?" Sheena asked, coming out of the kitchen, wiping a plate dry. As soon as she saw him, she knew what was up.

"Again, Vic? You high again, ain't you?"

He rolled his eyes at the screen, then replied, "Naw, I ain't hungry," trying to avoid the question.

Sheena walked closer wearing a frown. Sheena wasn't model gorgeous or video chick thick, but she was definitely pretty with her smooth caramel complexion, big hazel eyes, and kewpie doll nose. Her figure was full, but she wasn't fat and she was the sweetest person in the world, if Crook would let her be.

Sheena sighed hard, then asked, "Did you have any change from the bill? Did you show them the oversight?"

"I ain't pay it!"

She let her eyes flutter closed and back open, thinking she heard him wrong.

"You what?" she said, her tone still even but ready to crack. Crook looked up at her, trying to look menacing, but instead he just looked pitiful.

"I said, I ain't pay that shit, yo. I got caught up, and the shit was closed."

"You what?!" she repeated with intensity.

"I'll pay that shit tomorrow, aiight?" he answered and lit a Newport. Sheena was too frustrated to speak. All she could do was launch the plate she was holding in her hand across the room, and if Crook hadn't seen it, it would have caught him in the face. He moved just in time to feel it whiz past before it shattered against the wall. He jumped up, dropping his cigarette, and grabbed Sheena by her ponytail.

"You out yo fuckin' rabbit-ass mind?!" he barked in her grill. "If that shit woulda hit me—"

She cut his sentence off with a blow that missed its target, but got her point across. Crook pushed her away from him, because he didn't hit women, but he damn sure wanted to at that moment.

"Take yo muthafuckin' ass somewhere and sit the fuck down! I said I'll pay it tomorrow, yo. I still got your money, damn!" he hissed and handed her the rest of the money he took from Slim. It was all balled up, but there was at least six hundred dollars left of the nine hundred and fifty dollars he had taken.

Sheena snatched the money just so she could throw it back at him.

"Why do you always do this?!" she questioned accusingly.

"Why, Vic? All I asked for you to do is pay the damn bill so your children can have a hot meal, so your kids can have heat, and your black ass won't freeze!" Sheena screamed, ready to really let him have it, but her eyes fell on the small fire behind him.

"Vic!" she pointed.

He turned around and saw the flames leaping off the carpet. *My cigarette!* he thought and darted over to the fire with Sheena on his heels. He stomped and stomped until he extinguished the small flame before it could spread. Crook looked down on the smoldering black hole in disgust. Sheena collapsed on the couch and covered her face with her hands.

"We can't have nothing," she sobbed. "I just bought this carpet! Just bought it. Now look at it! I'm tired of this, I can't keep doin' this." She broke down. "I can't, Vic. I'm working two jobs all day and I can't do it anymore. I need you to help me, Vic. Please help me!" Her cries softened his hardened heart and he wanted to soothe her, but since he was the cause of her pain, he didn't see how he could comfort her, too.

"So why don't you just leave me, yo? Just fuckin' bounce and get away," he asked sincerely, feeling like it was the best solution.

Sheena looked up at him with tear-stained eyes and replied, "Is that what you want? You want me to leave you, Victor?"

Crook looked away. "Naw."

"Then why you say it then? Where would I go, huh? I love you, Vic, and we in this together." He dropped to his knees, holding out the gun to her. Sheena looked at it in confusion.

"Then shoot me. Fuckin' kill me. Then you ain't gotta leave but you'll be free of my bullshit," he stated with full conviction.

Sheena threw her arms around his neck and pulled him into her tight embrace.

"Why you say stuff like that? Vic, what's wrong with you, baby? Please, leave that stuff alone. It's killin' you, and if it's killin' you it's killin' me and I swear I don't wanna die. We can't die. We been through too much to give up now." Her words sunk in and took the place of his high. All the thug the world had made him, and all the gangsta life forced him to become, fell back for the moment and allowed him to cry in his woman's arms.

Chapter 2

Crook stepped out onto the streets the next day to a shining sun. He took a draw on his Newport and inhaled the nicotine deeply, then released the smoke in a steady stream to mix with the sounds and sights of the new day. He felt better . . . at least better than the night before. He was still broke, still ain't have shit, but his woman made him feel like the world was his. All he had to do was name it to claim it. It's amazing what good lovin' and sweet pussy will do for a man's outlook on life. Everything else might be fucked up and shitty, but as long as you have a beautiful woman to love you, then shit was bound to get better.

Besides, he had a brand-new, white gold, diamond bezel

watch, not to mention the crisp Carmelos on his feet, courtesy of Slim. He didn't even care that they were a size too big. He just put on an extra pair of socks. Crook checked his watch then headed to see his man Larceny.

Larceny was just as triflin' as Crook was, the only difference being Larceny didn't give a fuck. His mother was constantly reminding him how he was an accident, and she even had an insurance policy taken out on his life. Then, two years ago, she tried to have him murdered.

He and Larceny had grown up together and now at nineteen they both had a similar outlook on life. Basically, fuck the world.

Crook cut through the parking lot off Howard Street and called out for Larceny beneath the fire escape.

"Yo, L! L, get yo ass up!"

He waited a few minutes before a third-floor window shot up and a bare-chested Larceny stuck his head out, smiling.

"Yo, what up, dog? What's good?"

"Melvin!" Crook heard the scratchy female voice from inside the apartment.

"That's that sorry-ass Victor, ain't it? Don't have that sorry-ass nigga round my house!"

"Bitch, shut the fuck up. Don't nobody wanna come in this raggedy-ass hole," Larceny spat over his shoulders as he dipped his head back inside.

Crook didn't necessarily like how Larceny climbed out the window and catted down the fire escape, then dropped to street level. Larceny was brown-skinned with wavy hair and stood a rail-thin six feet even. He had always been wiry, but after he started sniffin' coke, smoking crack blunts and eventually crack, he had shrunk even smaller.

Yet, his size was deceptive. He could thump with the best of niggas and his gun game was treacherous. Larceny was also a Blood. When the gang fever had taken over Newark, he joined a clique of Bloods off High Street, mostly cats he had known for years. Since he didn't have love at home, the Bloods became like a second family, one he would die for. But Crook was his first family, and it was with him that he spent his time. Crook didn't clique up. At first, some of the dudes tried to pressure Crook into affiliation. But he wasn't with it and held fort. They eventually let up because Crook stayed in so much beef, they didn't wanna deal with his bullshit, either.

Larceny walked up and greeted his man with a street hug and a pound. "What's really good, dog? I heard about that kid last night." Larceny smiled proudly showing his gold upper grill that gave his grin a sinister twist.

Crook just shrugged. "Fuck it. Coward was just my size," he boasted, pointing to the sneakers on his feet, making Larceny laugh.

"You shoulda kilt him, on the real. You know them Avon niggas is sneaky!"

"Naw, yo. If I kill 'em, I won't be able to rob his ass no more," Crook replied and Larceny concurred with a pound and an aiight!

The two of them had no job, no hustle, and really no secret pussy laid up, so they had nowhere to go except their spot in the basement of Larceny's building where they got high and spent most of their time. The dark and dingy basement was like home to them, the spot they had grown up in. From breaking down and repainting stolen bikes, to running trains on hoodrats and splitting up licks, everything they ever did, ended up in the basement.

They had been down there for hours, sniffing coke and puffing weed, kicking the willie about this and that. Crook must've told Larceny about the incident the night before, detail by detail, ten times, when Larceny asked, "Yo, you got the pistol on you?" Crook handed him the gun, and Larceny inspected it under the light of the hanging bulb suspended over his head.

"This shit is sweet, dog! I love .40 calibers when they bark. Blow a hole in a nigga big enough to see though. You bust it yet?"

Before he could answer, Larceny pointed the gun out in front of him and squeezed off three rounds in rapid succession. The sound of the gunfire was deafening in the hollow echo of the basement.

"Bitch, is you crazy?!" Crook exclaimed. "All these hot water heaters and boilers down here. Fuck around and blow the whole buildin' up!"

But Larceny was in a zone. He stood up and said, "Man, fuck all these low-life muthafuckas in this building, yo! I don't give a fuck if we all blow up, if the whole world blow up, I had to feel this shit!" He looked at the gun. Larceny was obsessed with guns. He still had every gun they ever used, body or no body on it. Big guns, little guns, fully automatics, and sawed offs—he kept a tight arsenal. He always joked with Crook that if he had a son, he'd show him the guns and say stuff like, "And this one is the one I kilt this nigga with at Ko-Ko's party!"

"Yo," Larceny began, eyes glazed with cocaine madness, "let's go fuckin' do something . . . Fuckin' go rob some niggas and hope they flinch! Let's go rob that nigga with his own gun!" Larceny laughed and Crook joined him.

"Come on then. Somebody makin' money wit our name on it," Crook replied as he stood up, feeling just as pumped as Larceny looked.

"Hold up, hold up, you know the drill," Larceny reminded him. "I gotta hear some of that . . . that . . . Newark shit, nigga. That smack a nigga just for livin' shit you be spittin'." Larceny had already started bobbing to a beat in his head, so Crook just timed his bop and came like:

I love that Newark shit
That Niggah-I-Don't-Wanna talk shit
That if it's beef we in the streets holding court shit
So let me spit a sick sixteen that ain't hard to tell
Just make a choice how you want it, either bars or shells
I'm like a fully automatic, locked and loaded
I hollar Crook, muthafucka! Body dropped shot and folded

Larceny couldn't hold back. He let the .40-caliber bark a full clip salute until it sat back, empty and smoking.

"That's what I'm talking 'bout! That's that shit! That killa shit!"

"Stupid muthafucka," Crook growled with attitude. "Why you empty the clip? I ain't got no more bullets, dumb ass!"

"Never mind all that dog," Larceny replied. "That verse was sick! You gotta get on. Yo, the world need to hear that there, for real!"

Crook pulled out a cigarette and fired it up.

"I'm tellin' you, dog, you know Ike havin' his birthday party Saturday and everybody gonna be there. You gotta get up in there and let niggas hear that fire," Larceny said.

It was definitely a good look if he could get it, because Crook knew whoever was with Ike was the move makers but like he said, "Ike don't fuck wit me like that."

"Damn," Larceny shot back, having a brainstorm. "Let's go holler at him and get you up in there. Ike 'bout that cheddar, and you is platinum. What up? You wit it?" Larceny asked, but didn't even let Crook answer. "Come on, Crook, we goin' to see Ike."

Ike Spencer was an older Newark head that had come up through the game, started promoting plays around the country, and had even opened his own church, all while still getting money in the streets. So at forty-one, he was financially set for life. He was a Blood for "political" reasons. The lay of the land had changed, so in order to capitalize, he changed with the times. The only color that really mattered to Ike was green, so whatever color he had to claim was cool as long as his pockets were his favorite color.

Ike usually held court at his church every Wednesday night, conducting "Sister Services," where he counseled women out of their dough and even their panties. To him, everything was a hustle, so what Larceny had in mind was right up his alley.

Larceny and Crook approached the church on Astor Court and

climbed the stairs. Two cats stood outside and closed ranks when they approached.

"Women only," one of the men told them sternly.

"Naw, we ain't here for that," Larceny answered. "This Larceny, yo. Tell Ike I got that, what we talked about."

Crook looked at Larceny's profile by the light of the setting sun. One of the men went inside the church.

"What you got for Ike?" Crook whispered.

Larceny smirked, speaking out the side of his mouth. "Nothin', but that's what you always tell a nigga you tryin' to see. If he think you got somethin' for him, he always bite."

A few moments later, the man emerged to confirm Larceny's philosophy.

"Ike said go in and wait in his office." Larceny and Crook walked by the man and into the large cathedral Ike had built off to the side. Crook could see a group of women in a side room, and he could hear Ike's voice massaging them with scriptures of game.

Some mu'fuckas do anything for money, Crook thought to himself, but he was too hungry to knock the next man's hustle. They walked into Ike's office, looking around at the pictures of Ike with political figures and famous celebrities. Ike was definitely the man to see. Ike came in minutes later, took off his tailor-made suit jacket, and hung it up on the coatrack. Larceny and Crook turned to him and they all shook hands.

"What's up, Blood?" Larceny greeted Ike and Ike returned his greeting.

"What can I do for you, Larceny? I know you don't owe me nothing. Do you?" Ike chuckled, referring to the game he ran to gain entrance.

"Naw, dog, naw. You know I'm always straight wit you. But I do got somethin' for you. Meet my man Crook." Ike took a seat behind his desk. Since he and Crook had already shook hands, he just nodded a subtle acknowledgment in his direction.

"You family?" he questioned Crook, but Larceny answered.

"Naw, but he's my family, and he nice."

"Nice?" Ike echoed.

"Rhymin', dog. He sick as a mu'fucka, he—"

"Hey, hey," Ike cautioned him, "we in a church."

You drug dealin', gangbangin', bootleg-ass preacher, Crook thought, *talkin' about we in a church.* But he kept his mouth closed.

"My bad, dog. But yo, he fo' real," Larceny explained.

"And?" Ike questioned. "I ain't got no label, dog, you know that."

"You ain't gotta have no label. We just tryin' to get in your party and mingle. Maybe you could introduce him to the right people, you know? Money is money, and I'm tellin' you, Crook is millions waitin' to happen," Larceny boasted.

Ike looked Crook up and down. He knew the name Crook and the trouble it brought, but if he was nice then being the man who put him on couldn't hurt.

"I'm sayin'," Ike began, "I ain't makin' no promises or nothin', but I'll make sure you on the list. I don't want you in there sweatin' me every five minutes or harassin' my guests. Keep yo mouth shut and if I get an opportunity, I'll see what I can do, aiight?"

"No doubt, dog. No doubt. That's all we askin', yo," Larceny assured him.

Ike turned to Crook. "And no guns," he emphasized, pointing to the bulge in Crook's waist.

For the rest of the night, Larceny was so amped about the meeting with Ike and the upcoming party, that Crook had no choice but to share his excitement. He knew he was hot, and all he needed was a chance to prove it, but could it be this simple? After all this time, toiling and struggling, begging just to be on local mix tapes, could one party change all that? Crook couldn't help but let himself hope so.

It didn't even matter that the two dudes they stuck up didn't bring them but a petty $275.00 a piece, or that they were robbing muthafuckas with an empty gun. None of that could kill Crook's spirit.

He decided to go home early to be with Sheena and the kids and tell her about the party. So he cut out and headed to the Chinese restaurant to get Sheena some beef and broccoli, little Tameek and Syasia chicken wings, and some shrimp fried rice and egg rolls for himself. He floated into the restaurant high and day-dreaming about what could be. How he'd jump out of the double-parked G-series BMW with his joint pumping out of the system, all eyes on him.

What he didn't realize was that all eyes were on him. Crook never saw the two dudes in the corner booth start whispering to each other when he came in. He didn't see one of them go out to the car and return a few seconds later. He didn't see any of this until he paid for his food, then grabbed his bags to leave.

Crook never expected to see a man rise up out of the rear booth and start shooting. But he did and he caught Crook slippin' bad. The only thing on Crook's side was that the two cats weren't live enough to just run up on Crook and body him point-blank. They knew his rep and figured he'd be strapped. What they didn't know was that they had picked the right night and the bulge peeking from under his belt had an empty clip.

Plus, they weren't ace shooters so their first two shots rico-cheted off the bulletproof glass that partitioned the counter. People scattered, screamed, and ducked, and Crook ducked right with them. The cats kept coming, emboldened by the fact Crook hadn't fired back. Crook looked around from behind the booth where he was crouched and made a dash for the kitchen door, exploding through and followed by several more shots that peppered the door. The Chinese cooks shouted and yelled as he ran through, knocking over pans and people to make his escape.

He barely got through the back door before the two cats, figur-ing he wasn't strapped, came in hot pursuit. Crook dashed along the rear of the building and leaped for a dangling fire escape ladder. He pulled himself up just as one of the shooters yelled, "Up there! Kill that mu'fucka!!" Crook could feel the heat off the bullets as they whizzed past, causing sparks as they hit the rusted steel of the fire escape.

He threw himself through an apartment window and landed in someone's living room. A woman in the kitchen screamed as he pulled his gun, and ordered, "Shut the fuck up! Shut the fuck up!"

He glanced over his shoulder expecting to see the two cats climbing through the window to murder him in this strange woman's apartment. He jiggled all three lock bolts open, then dashed down the hallway and down the back steps to safety.

Two blocks away, he finally stopped running, but he couldn't stop shaking. He slid down the wall holding his side that ached from all the strenuous exercise. He had been shot or shot at on numerous occasions, but never had he slipped like this. He tried to replay the restaurant in his mind and picture the shooters' faces, but he couldn't. It dawned on him that it could've been anybody. He had robbed so many cats and his name and face were so well-known, beef could come from anyone, anywhere, and at any time, and he'd never see it coming. Crook knew then, if he didn't get on in this rap shit and get out of Newark, he wouldn't last another year alive.

Chapter 3

Crook walked through the door to find Sheena and his two kids on the living room floor, reading a children's book. Tameek, five, and Syasia, six, were the spitting images of their mother. They both had big hazel eyes and her caramel complexion. Their appearance came from her, but their attitudes were entirely Crook's. They were quick-tempered and mischievous, so Sheena definitely had her hands full.

"Daddy!" Syasia cheered as she ran up to Crook to be scooped up in his arms. He gave her a sloppy kiss that made her giggle.

"Have you been good today?" he asked her.

"Have you?" she shot right back, looking and sounding just like her mother. She had heard Sheena and Crook argue many a night about what he was doing in the streets, so she only reflected her mother's concern.

He smiled and playfully hit her on her butt.

"Smart ass, daddy always good. In fact . . . ," he turned to Sheena and said, "Get 'em dressed, we goin' to Chuck E. Cheese."

The kids hoorayed and danced in circles, but Sheena asked, "How? By the time we get there the buses will have stop running."

"Can't you get yo sister car?"

Sheena rolled her eyes and smacked her teeth. "Please, and hear her mouth? I don't think so."

But Crook was persistent. "I'm sayin', it's a special occasion. Never mind, we'll just take a cab."

"All the way to Union? It must really be a special occasion. You musta hit the number or something," Sheena joked.

Crook kissed her, then replied, "Close, yo. I'm 'bout to get on."

"On? You mean music on?" she asked.

"No doubt, ma. Saturday I'ma be at Ike's party and he 'posed to hook me up wit some people. Ain't no way a cat hear this and say no, yo," he explained, hardly controlling his excitement.

Sheena turned to the kids and told them, "Go get ya'll shoes on."

They ran off without hesitation. Sheena turned back to Crook. "Vic, have I ever fronted on you with this music thing?"

"Naw," he responded, like, of course not.

"Every time you come home and somebody said they were gonna do this, that or the third, I was always . . . hopeful for you, right?"

Crook looked at her, wondering where this was going. "No doubt, why?"

"Because, baby, you got that look in your eyes again, and I don't wanna see you get disappointed, because you always go out and end up doin' somethin' crazy."

"So what you sayin', Sheena?" Crook asked defensively, thinking his woman was doubting his shot. She framed his face with her hands, caressing his cheek.

"Baby, I don't ever want you to give up on your dream—ever—but you can't keep chasin' them and runnin' away from your responsibilities." Sheena spoke softly, and when Crook began to speak she cut him off and added, "Just this time"—she paused—"if . . . and I'm stressing the word *if* . . . if whoever don't come through, will you at least try and get a job? I know you be bringin' in money, but the way you do it, sooner or later—" She sighed, closing her eyes against horrible thoughts.

The night's activities flashed through Crook's mind as well. He took her hands from his face, kissed the inside of her fingers, and said, "Ma, for real, I know mad cats be sellin' dreams, but I ain't never had a shot like this. I know we won't look back, but if it is bullshit . . . yeah, ma, I'll get a job."

Sheena smiled and kissed his nose.

"Thank you!"

He squeezed her ass with a smirk.

"Call a cab, let's go breathe a little."

They took the kids to Chuck E. Cheese's, eating and playing video games until the spot closed. It had been awhile since they had gone out together and Sheena really needed to get out, especially with Crook. Seeing him with the kids made her feel good, hoping moments like this convinced him that this is where he needed to be.

"Put your hands in the muthafuckin air!"

The whole arena erupted with delirious cheers.

"Introducing . . . Croook!" the announcer bellowed, and the crowd went crazy. As Crook ran onstage, mic in hand and Larceny by his side, the music was pumping all through him. He was charged and ready. He gripped the mic and started to spit but . . . nothing came out.

He tried again, tried to clear his throat, but still, nothing. The crowd sensed something was wrong and Larceny looked at him like, what? But he couldn't speak. All of a sudden Slim, the cat he had pistol-whipped, rose up in the middle of the crowd and laughed. "What's wrong? Forgot your point, huh?"

Crook looked out into the faces of cats he had stuck up, shot, or killed and they all had guns aimed at him. Infrared beams covered his black fatigue suit. Millions and millions of guns it seemed were all pointed at him. He looked around for Larceny but he had disappeared.

Crook heard the collective cocking of a million shells, locked and loaded, and then one tremendous *boom!* A rain of bullets screamed his name, cutting through the air and filling his flesh simultaneously. Crook's eyes fluttered open, and he found himself in the bed with Sheena wrapped around him. The whole thing was a dream. He hadn't woke up scared or sweating, but he was still relieved it had been a dream. The last word he said before he fell asleep again was, "Saturday."

"What up, dog, you ready?" Larceny wanted to know, looking at him. Crook stared at Club Mirage across the street from where they stood on the other side of Broad Street. They had just gotten off the bus. The front of the club was lined up with sick whips on even sicker chrome, parked and double-parked. The line for Ike's party was around the corner and everyone gawked in awe as limo after limo pulled up, and countless celebrities emerged to the flash of the paparazzi. The shit seemed like a dream to Crook, but he definitely didn't want to wake up.

"Always, yo. Let's go do this," he replied, with the same intensity he had when they were moving on a lick.

Neither was dressed for the occasion. They looked more like they were going to war instead of an A-list party. Both were

dressed in fatigues. Crook in regular green and black while Larceny repped in red and black. As usual, they were skeed up on
coke, but they kept their word and neither one was strapped. They
approached the velvet rope as Larceny proudly announced to the
bouncers, "Crook and Larceny, we on the list."

The bouncer looked them up and down, like yeah right, and
said, "The list? Whose list?"

"Ike, muthafucka," Larceny replied without malice, but his
tone was still harsh.

"Man, get the fuck outta here," the bouncer waved them off,
but Larceny wasn't going anywhere.

"On the real, duke, you need to check that shit, 'cause if Ike
finds out you kept his family waitin' like peasants, you gonna
need all that muscle to keep the shells out yo ass."

The bouncer gritted his teeth as he eyed what looked to be a
ninety pound crackhead. But he checked the list anyway, so if he
had to, he could show them they weren't on it, then smack Larceny for wasting his time. To his dismay, both of them were on the
list. He called on his two-way radio to double-check, but once
verified, he had no choice but to let them in. Once inside, the
place looked like BET's *Access Granted*. Everywhere they looked,
they saw a familiar face. Neither were starstruck, but it felt good
to be in the same room with known muthafuckas. They wandered
through the crowd until they found Ike holding court with a black
politician from Harlem and the politician's wife. Crook and Larceny stood off at a respectful distance until Ike noticed them,
came over, and shook their hands.

"I see ya'll made it," Ike commented.

"Wasn't no way one was gonna miss it. Happy Birthday, dog,"
Larceny told him.

"Yeah, yo, Happy Birthday," Crook echoed.

Ike nodded his appreciation then said, "You remember the
rules? No harassin' my guests. Get you a drink, fall back, and
speak when spoken to, ya'll hear me?" Ike questioned, looking

from Larceny to Crook, getting acknowledgments from both of them. "Okay, enjoy yourselves."

Ike walked off, leaving Larceny and Crook gazing at the crowd, separately thinking the same thought. All the shine up in here, they could stick the spot and retire for life!

Larceny laughed first. "But we ain't here for that," he said, reading Crook's thoughts because mind detects mind. Crook chuckled.

"Maybe next time."

"Shit, next time it's gonna be us up in this piece, flossed the fuck out, ya heard?" Larceny predicted with zeal.

The next few hours, they stayed low-key in a corner booth, while the party moved around them. Larceny was caught up in the industry chicks and the gold diggers sashaying around, but Crook just eyed the rappers who were in attendance. He knew in his heart he was better than most platinum artists that relied on hype or image to sell records. The only hype he had was the head rush he got from the coke in his system. He was a hungry wolf in the midst of an unsuspecting flock of sheep. The only question was, when would the feast begin?

It seemed like it took forever, but a waitress finally approached the table and told them, "Ike would like to see you. Please follow me." She smiled.

Larceny eyed the delectable young tender up and down as he stood up and remarked, "I'll follow you anywhere, sexy. Do me a favor, my drink's dry, why don't you piss in my glass." The waitress ignored the crude remark, but Larceny damn sure didn't ignore her ass as it jiggled like jelly in her napkin of a miniskirt. She led Crook and Larceny over to VIP where Ike was chilling with two Asian chicks and the man he wanted Crook to meet. The super producer Mark Allen was Big Willie Style to Ike's left, neck and wrist flooded with multicolored diamonds, two humongous bodyguards posted on both sides of the booth. Crook and Larceny approached and Crook could feel the importance of the moment.

Mark Allen had produced several of the singles that had the air-waves on lock. One track from him and it was multiplatinum waiting to happen. Everybody wanted him on their album, which made him expensive and arrogant.

Crook didn't expect to meet Mark Allen. He expected an A&R or some big entertainment lawyer, maybe even a small label owner, but to meet Mark Allen was the next best thing to meeting Russell Simmons. But there he was, drunk and looking Crook up and down as Ike introduced him.

"Yeah, Mark, this is the kid I was telling you about," Ike announced. "Crook, I'm sure you know of Mark Allen."

"No doubt," Crook half grinned, trying to keep his composure, and extended his hand to Mark. Mark hesitated, then halfheartedly gave him a weak shake.

"Yo, son, your shit be blazin'," Crook complimented him.

"I know," was Mark's smug reply as he sipped his drink.

"So, ah . . . Crook, right? What up, you rap, sing, what?"

"Naw, I don't sing. I spit that fire, dog. Nobody in here can see me, for real," Crook bragged, ready to prove it against the industry's best, here and now.

"*I spit fire, dog!*" Mark mocked Crook, making the chicks giggle. The comment made Crook a little uncomfortable, but he let it go.

"You know how many cats tell me that exact same thing? But yo, if you so hot, how come I ain't never heard of you on no mix tapes? Who you fuck wit, who's your manager?" Before Crook could say anything, Larceny cut in.

"I'm his manager." Mark looked at Larceny like he didn't know he had been standing there.

"Who the fuck is you? Manager?" Mark laughed, then looked at Ike. "Ike, who is these mu'fuckas?" Ike glanced at Crook and his eyes said, this is your shot. Speak up or lose it. Crook didn't hesitate. He silenced Larceny then turned to Mark and said, "Yo, dog, I'm Victor Crook. I ain't got no demo, no manager, or mix tape 'cause niggas be on some bullshit, so I don't fuck wit but a few. But

I'm nice, the nicest, and all I need is a chance to prove it. I live and die this shit, and I'm gonna make the nigga who give me a chance a very rich mu'fucka."

Mark Allen nodded. "Yeah? Well, I'm already a very rich mu'fucka," he snorted, diamonds sparkling like a light show.

"You can never have enough money," Crook shot right back.

"Mo' money, mo' problems," Mark countered then said, "Look, Crook, or whatever, I ain't lookin' for no acts, yo. So when you get a deal, if you get a deal and a real budget, come see me. Until then, it was nice meetin' me. We'll holler."

Just like that, the door Crook had been waiting to open slammed shut in his face. It seemed like it only opened long enough so the people inside could laugh at him out in the cold, let him feel the warmth, then shut him out, so it felt even colder. He had spoken from the heart, so there was no way he could just walk away.

"I understand that, dog," Crook began, but I'm sayin'—" Mark cut him off.

"And I've said all I'm going say. The fuck outta here, nigga, I'm Mark Allen. Somebody get these clowns the fuck away from my table!"

Larceny moved first out of instinct, but the bodyguard collared him up, so by the time Crook moved on the bodyguard, Ike stood up like, "Okay, ya'll, let it go. Let it go."

Ike felt bad about the way Mark spoke to them and he intended on telling Mark when they left. But first he had to deal with Crook and Larceny. "Go get yourself a drink," he said to the two young gangsters, "and I'll be over to holler at you later."

Crook eyed Mark like a cobra with its hood spread. Mark should've seen it in his eyes, but his vision was clouded with his own importance. Crook nodded.

"Aiight . . . aiight, Ike. It's your party, dog. We cool, come on, Larc, let's go." He and Larceny stepped through the crowd and disappeared. Ike didn't like the vibe they departed with, but never in a million years did he think they'd take it to the level that they did.

Mark Allen made his way to the door of the club with two blond redbones and his five bodyguards, laughing and staggering his hennied-up ass to the limo. It was close to four A.M. and people were still waiting to get into Ike's exclusive party. After Mark dotted the door, the scandalous broads that hadn't made it inside started yelling, "I love you, Mark!" "Let me be your baby mama!" "Let me suck yo dick, Mark!"

After cutting through the crowd, one of Mark's bodyguards opened the door. No one heard or saw a thing until . . .

"Gun music, mu'fucka!" was shouted like a calvary announcement. Automatic gunfire exploded from two opposite directions. Crook and Larceny, both dressed in all black, stood on the roof of two parked cars on both sides of the front door and fired down into Mark Allen's entourage. The big muscle-bound bodyguards, equipped with vests, never had a chance to respond or protect, because they were sending nothing but head shots, watching dome after dome explode like melons.

The bodyguards were the first to drop, then the two chicks. Mark tried to crawl away after being hit in the leg several times. Crook hopped off the car, stood over a crying Mark Allen, and repeated his battle cry.

"Feel this gun music, nigga." Then he lit Mark up while Larceny murdered the bouncer at the door on G.P. for fronting earlier. The street was in a state of pandemonium, people running everywhere making it easier for the two assassins to make their escape.

Meanwhile, inside, Ike had been looking for Crook and Larceny, hoping to introduce them to a few other people in the business. He remembered the cold, hungry look in Crook's eyes, and he felt obligated to salvage the night. When the word reached him, he knew it was too late.

"Yo, Ike," one of his lackeys ran up shouting, "They just killed Mark Allen!"

"What?! Who?!" he asked, as if he didn't know already.

"I don't know, but police is everywhere! Let's go!"

Ike didn't hesitate. They moved swiftly out the back door, his only remark on his way out to another lackey was, "Bring Crook and Larceny to my house, alive or half dead! Just bring 'em!"

Crook crept through the back way to his building in silence. He and Larceny hadn't said a word to each other after the massacre. They drove a stolen Acura through the early morning streets until Larceny let Crook out to creep the rest of the way. Crook didn't know what it meant, but he felt no regrets. He had killed before, but then it was business or in the heat of a robbery, but this . . . this was personal and he relished the feeling. He entered the building through the back door, gun in hand, and went up to his apartment.

He was going to get Sheena and the kids and be out. Where . . . he didn't know, but he knew he had to relocate for a while. As he approached the door, all he heard were cocking automatics and all he saw was red beams all over him like the measles.

"Act like you want it, nigga," one of the gunmen hissed. Crook knew he was outgunned, and he didn't want to bring beef to his door, so he dropped his gun.

"Aiight, dog, you got it. You got a winner."

"Ike wanna see you," was the reply.

They moved up on him cautiously, patted him down thoroughly, then directed him downstairs and into a waiting stretch Humvee. Larceny was already inside when Crook climbed in next to him. Three of the gunmen got in the back with them, then they pulled off heading for Ike's spot in Wayne, New Jersey. When they arrived, they were taken inside and shown to the basement. Ike waited inside and there was plastic all over the floor. When Larceny and Crook saw the plastic they looked at each other. "It all depends on you," Ike said.

The gunmen stood behind them and Ike stood in front like a

general. One word from Ike, a nod even, and the firing squad would silence their madness.

"What the fuck is wrong wit you?! You disrespect my party, my guest, me, matter-of-fact, fuck the guests, you disrespected me! After I brought you in, tried to look out for ya'll dumb asses, this is how you repay me?! Bring me unnecessary heat?!"

The two assassins remained silent.

"Speak!!"

"Yo Ike man, I—" Larceny stumbled over his words. He wasn't scared of death, but he just didn't know what to say. But Crook did.

"He deserved it," Crook told Ike flatly.

"He deserved it?" Ike echoed. "He deserved to be fuckin' splattered all over the fuckin' street 'cause he ain't want to help you rap? Nigga, is you crazy?!" Ike released an aggravated chuckle that said he had heard enough and was ready to see somebody bleed.

"It wasn't about rappin', yo," Crook continued. "You heard the way that bitch-ass nigga talked to me, tried to clown me and all I asked for was a chance. You don't wanna help . . . cool . . . fuck it . . . but he totally disrespected me. We tried to beat his ass right there, but his bodyguards stopped it. Maybe it could've ended there, but wasn't no way I was gonna let this nigga think he was safe 'cause he had the odds. Fuck odds. Fuck 'em then and fuck 'em now. If you kill me right now then you doin' all these industry niggas a favor, 'cause from here on out, anybody tell me no, gonna die the same way."

Ike looked at Crook's stone-faced expression closely, then stepped up to his grill.

"What if I tell you no, huh? Then what?"

"Then I'm a die right where I stand," Crook replied without emotion, as he looked Ike in his eyes. Ike saw that same intense hunger and hopelessness of a man that had nothing to lose.

"You serious, ain't you?" Crook answered with his look. Ike

continued, "The only reason you ain't dead now is because I re-spect what you did. If you woulda came in here tryin' to apologize, talkin' about you lost your head, I woulda shot yo punk asses my damn self, but I respect what you did and I respect the fact you standin' up for it now." Ike stepped away and turned his back as if he was thinking. Then he turned back to him.

"Aiight, I'm a fuck wit you. Let me holler at some people, put something together. But dig . . . we do this my way, you hear me?"

Crook shook his head slowly.

"Naw, Ike, wit all due respect, me and Larceny made the world hear us, we the ones on the front line, so we do it our way. You can holler at who you want, but if they say no, they die. Period."

Ike knew he had a monster on his hands, but being a greedy nigga, he could see the potential in the situation. Crook would probably end up dead, he figured, but he'd be able to cake off his remains for a long time to come.

"Let me talk to a few people," Ike repeated, silently acknowl-edging Crook's terms.

"For now, though, you moving; you, too, Larceny, you'll be wit me."

He looked at Crook. "You got some money?"

"Naw."

"Give him twenty cent," Ike told one of the gunmen who im-mediately left to retrieve the money. "Get a place for you and your family somewhere safe, aiight? Stay off the streets," Ike told him as the man returned with two ten-thousand-dollar stacks of money rubber-banded together, and handed them to Crook.

"That should be enough to keep you outta trouble, and if it ain't, it better be," Ike added.

Crook looked at the money in his hands, heavy like two bricks. Just like that, he had taken his destiny in his own hands and didn't take no for an answer. He put his life on the line and came back with it more abundantly. Crook felt redeemed, because for the first time in his life, he felt like a man.

It didn't take Ike long to pull some strings and get a meeting with another hot producer named T-Beats. T was a Harlemite with that uptown swagger and uptown hustle to match. Ike knew T's people in the other world they dealt in, but in broad daylight, in T's midtown Manhattan studio, the business was music spoken through the mouth of two street niggas. Ike walked in and greeted T-Beats with a bottle of Moët.

"What's that for?" T asked, setting the bottle on the edge of the mix board. Ike sat on a swivel stool across from T.

"Congratulations, past and present. For all that you've done, and hopefully, what we can do together," Ike smirked.

T-Beats sat back in his leather captain's chair, ice in his brown ear gleaming. "Always down for business, Ike, you know how we do, what you got in mind?"

T-Beats already knew about the situation with Mark Allen. Everybody did. T didn't know if Ike was involved, but because it went down the way it did, he was curious to know what Ike was coming with.

"Yo, I'm not gonna beat around the bush. What I say, you may not like, but don't listen as a hustler, listen as a businessman," Ike began, stopping to check T's reaction. T was poker faced, so he continued. "That thing with Mark, I had nothing to do wit, it was unfortunate, but its done and the reason is simple. Niggas want in this business and they ain't wit the politics to do it."

T-Beats nodded, swiveled his chair a little, then replied, "So what's that got to do with me? I'm about paper, not politics."

"Exactly. That's why I'm here. I need you to front a hot track for a couple of hungry niggas," Ike stated, getting to the point.

"Hungry like . . . kill for it hungry? Lay a nigga down in cold blood, hungry?" T-Beats asked, because the industry was buzzin' about the incident.

Ike knew T was a street nigga, and he didn't want to come at him and offend his gangsta, so he asked, "What would you do?

How far was you willing to go to eat? I ain't talking music: I'm talking when you was hungry. What did you do?"

T snickered. "Whatever it took."

"Then would you have wanted to be the nigga on the other side tryin' to stop you from eating?" Ike questioned, turning the tables.

"Naw, but I ain't Mark neither," T countered.

"You don't have to be, T. All you gotta be is the reason all this music shit is out the window for these niggas, and it's back to the streets for real. I'm tellin' you, T, it's beef, regardless if you win, you still lose. And you got a whole lot more to lose than them."

T-Beats stood up and walked around the room, then said, "So you sayin' if I don't give them niggas a track, then the guns comin' out?"

"It ain't just you, T, it's anybody. Anybody they think standin' in they way."

"So these niggas think they can extort T-Beats like a sucka? Like it's sweet?"

T-Beats was getting himself riled up, so Ike stood up to try and calm him down. "You looking at this all wrong, T—one track—that ain't gonna hurt you, yo. But if you let pride make you grab your gun, all you've worked for is out the window over one track, think about it, T," Ike explained.

T-Beats smiled at Ike. "And you, what you got to do with this? You the peacemaker: the diplomat? Nigga, you gonna eat off this shit, too."

Ike kept it gangsta. "You think I'd be here if I wasn't? But I'm lookin' at it like a businessman, same thing I'm tellin' you to do."

T-Beats turned away from Ike, and the room fell into a tense silence for a minute. "It's like this, 'cause I ain't got no time to go to war for no bullshit, I'm a give you a track—one—take it or leave it," T said, then turned back to Ike. "But on the real, Ike, I ain't gonna forget you brought this bullshit to my doorstep. You coulda went anywhere, to anyone, but you brought it here." T-Beats eyed

Ike hard, then handed him a DAT tape. "That's it; I don't want shit off of it. Tell your man, he try some shit like this again, I'ma really see where all ya'll's gansta at."

Ike nodded slowly, letting T's bravado go unchallenged. He had got what he came for, so he left, quietly closing the door behind him.

Chapter 4

It wasn't only the industry that was buzzing, the streets were on fire with the story of what Crook did, and of course, niggas exaggerated.

"Word up. Crook smacked Duke up, the producer mu'fucka, and shot him in the club!" one cat was overheard saying, which later became, "shot Mark Allen, robbed him for fifty g's then killed him!"

Whatever the story, niggas knew the reason. He tried to front on Crook's hunger and got ate. Every hungry nigga understood and respected what Crook had done, because they, too, knew the feelin' of cats trying to shit on their dreams. They had heard all the no's, the can'ts, the won'ts, and had doors slammed on them as well. But Crook wasn't having it, he stood up.

Even the cats Crook had robbed or beefed with saw Crook in a new light. So now, when his name was mentioned, it was usually met with, "Oh, Crook, yeah, that's my mans." Whereas it used to be, "Fuck that bum-ass nigga." Everybody loves that gansta shit! Crook had moved, but not out of Newark. He got his girl a piece of a Honda Accord to go back and forth to work in. While he did what he always did, walked the same streets he always walked.

The day after Ike saw T-Beats, he and Larceny came to Crook's new crib on Hunterdon Avenue, blowing the horn. Inside, Crook was bent over his book of rhymes, putting together what would become his first single, "Gun Music."

"Yo, Crook, Crook!" Larceny yelled, leaning out of the passenger seat of Ike's cocaine-white Escalade, hovering on 24s. The system was blasting the track that T-Beats had given him, and Larceny couldn't wait for him to hear it.

"Yo, Crook!"

Crook came to the window and peered down into Larceny's smiling face. "It's on, dog! Bring yo punk ass down here!" Larceny hollered.

Crook threw on his brand-new Tims and took the steps three at a time until he was out the door.

"You call this safe? You practically moved down the street," Ike chuckled. "Get yo crazy ass in."

Crook climbed in the back and Ike pulled off. Larceny turned around to face Crook. "Nigga, tell me that shit ain't hot!" Larceny exclaimed, referring to the track. "T-Beats is a sick-ass producer."

"That's the track?" Crook gasped. He couldn't believe his ears. The track was so hard it hit you like a fist. It sounded like a premo banger with a twist of RZA's flavor.

"Kick some shit, dog, let me hear some shit," Larceny demanded and Ike laughed.

"For real, you got me out here extortin' niggas for tracks and I ain't even heard you rock yet." You don't have to ask Crook twice, the rhyme was already fighting to be spewed forth. He just sat back and let the beat enter him like a dope feen with a needle. He mentally mainlined T's track then . . .

The slums I'm from is like a hell on earth
Where the only way you leave is in jail or a hearse
Bitches strippin', niggas whippin' in kitchens
Black child runnin' wild, they daddy rottin' in the system
So we ain't the type of niggas to let you eat in our face
Without pullin' the guns out and leave you sleep in your place
So to all you hungry niggas ride wit Crook on this new shit
Fuck this R&B rap, let 'em feel your Gun Music!

After that, all Ike saw was dollar signs. He had the next big thing in his backseat and he planned on capitalizing all the way. He turned the music down and asked, "So what's next? I got you the track, now what?"

"Get the single pressed up," Crook began. "Blaze a mix tape and get some radio spin. The stores will be kickin' in our door, dog, word up!" Crook knew exactly what to do, because he had studied the game for so long.

"Aiight, you just keep bringin' that heat and I'll put up the dough, fifty-fifty. You wit it?" Ike proposed.

"Fifty-fifty," Crook confirmed, and gave Ike dap over the seat. "Our own label. I'm tellin' you, yo, we 'bout to blow!"

"Yo, what we gonna name the label?" Larceny asked.

"Nigga, what else . . . Gun Music Records!"

Once the mix tape hit the streets, it was the only CD cats was pumpin' in their whips. Everybody was on that Crook shit. What made it so gangsta is that it was named "Mark Allen R.I.P." with a newspaper article and photo of the club murder scene and Crook was spittin' over all of Mark's hottest tracks. The streets loved it and Crook and Ike couldn't keep enough CD's before they had to press more. Matter-of-fact, all Larceny did was burn CD's all day. That and get high.

Crook was opening for big name acts as far away as Philly, doing guest appearances on albums and even radio remix singles. Not to mention the labels. It was a bidding war for who would sign the hottest rapper since 50 Cent. The influx of money allowed Crook to get Sheena a 2000 BMW 325i, she quit her jobs and he put down on a house in Irvington, New Jersey. Sheena was in heaven seeing her man finally happy for the first time in her life, but she didn't realize there was much more to come.

"Yo, let's shoot some dice," Crook announced one evening after dinner. He, Sheena, and the kids had just eaten a hefty lasagna meal Crook had whipped up and everyone was stuffed.

"Boy, I don't know how to shoot no dice, and you ain't teachin' my babies no stuff like that," Sheena chuckled.

"Naw, it'll be fun. Besides, it's good to know in a bind," Crook urged her, pulling her out of the chair. "It's like a family fun game . . . in the hood," he joked. "Like Monopoly, that's dice, too!" Crook handed the dice to Tameek. "Aiight, Tameek, roll 'em."

Tameek threw the dice and they landed on two threes. It was Syasia's turn next and she rolled a seven.

"Damn, girl, I need to take you on the block with me." Crook laughed and Sheena hit him. He picked up the dice then turned to Sheena. "Your roll."

"Vic, I don't wanna roll dice," she whined. "Let's watch TV."

"In a minute." He smiled, putting the dice in her palm, and balled her hand. "Now shake 'em up."

Sheena shook the dice but felt something else in her hand. She opened her hand and saw a diamond ring sitting between the dice. Her heart skipped a beat and her eyes got big as plates. Crook took her hand and said, "For real, baby, life is a gamble, make me a winner." Her eyes brimmed with tears as Crook slid the ring on her finger. "It ain't much," he conceded, "but I promise when—"

Sheena silenced him with a "shut up and tongue me"—they kissed—"I'd marry you if it was a rubber band, baby. I love you . . . Crook." She smiled, calling him by his nickname because he had truly stole her heart with the proposal.

"Mommy and Daddy gettin' married!" Syasia cheered and Tameek did, too—mimicking her big sister. That night Sheena put it on Crook's ass, leaving him almost wondering why.

The next morning, Crook was awakened by the phone ringing. He rolled over groggily and picked up the receiver. "What?" His voice crackled.

"We got a problem," Larceny told him. "Come out to Ike's."

"Yeah," was all Crook said, hung up, and went back to sleep.

But Larceny knew him and called right back. "Man, get yo lazy ass up. It's serious."

"Aiight, aiight, I'm comin'." This time, Crook was on his feet. He pulled up to Ike's condo in Sheena's BMW. The same condo Ike had him taken to that night. He hopped out, *chirped* the alarm, and rung the bell. Larceny answered the door in a robe and sweatpants, greeted him wit some slick shit, then took him to the kitchen. Ike was sitting at the table fully dressed and reading the paper, while a cute chocolate chick named Michelle cooked breakfast.

"Hey, Crook, you hungry, baby?" she asked over the frying eggs.

"Naw, boo, I'm good. Wifey don't let me leave without a hot meal in my belly."

Ike put down the paper. "Airplay is dead."

Crook just looked at him, like he didn't understand. They had pressed up over a million singles and sent every major urban station in the country copies. Everybody was on that Crook shit, wasn't no way radio could front.

"What you mean dead?" Crook probed.

"Just what I said. They ain't played the single one time since I sent 'em out," Ike explained, slamming the paper in disgust. "We got over two hundred grand invested in CD's, waitin' to ship and not one single fuckin' spin!"

"They get the CD?"

"Of course they got the damn CD," Ike hissed. "I sent the shit. They just refuse to play it, talkin' about it's controversial, too street."

"Fuckin' cowards," Larceny spit. "It ain't no more controversial than the shit them puppet rappers be sayin', yo." Larceny was hot. Michelle brought the eggs and toast to Ike and Larceny along with some orange juice, then bounced out of the kitchen. Ike took one bite and dropped the fork; it hit the plate with a ceramic clang. "Yo, what the hell is we gonna do wit a million CD's?"

Larceny shrugged. "Sell 'em out the trunk?"

Ike looked at him, like, wrong answer, shut the fuck up.

Crook shook his head. "Man, fuck that. Radio gonna play my shit, yo."

"So what you gonna do, kill every DJ in America?" Ike asked only half sarcastic wondering if this crazy mu'fucka was thinking exactly that.

Crook took a sip of Larceny's juice, then smiled to himself. "Ay, Michelle." he called out. Moments later, she reappeared. "Yo, 'chelle, you ever been to California?" he asked with a mischievous smirk.

Larry Taylor was the VP over urban programming for Clear Channel Communications, the number one radio conglomerate in America. Clear Channel Communications had stations in every urban market in the country, and they basically controlled the daily playlist at every station. Locally, radio had really no control, because in the radio business, the power is centralized. Larry Taylor represented the apex of that power. He was fortyish, an impish black man with a seriously receding hairline. He had graduated from Howard University with a major in communications. Larry had climbed the corporate ladder from DJ to program director on seven different stations in Texas, New York, and Miami, to VP at Clear Channel Communications. He was a man stuck on the cameo era, who didn't care anything about rap or hip-hop, yet it was his word that determined it, when and how many times a record got spun. This was the man Crook sent Michelle to go see.

She posed as a student from his alma mater, doing a paper on the music industry. Michelle said, in her initial email, that she thought his job was exciting, big-upped the influence he had and the power he possessed, and that she would like his opinion on the state of the music business.

Flattery will get you everywhere, but what got her invited to L.A. was her picture that accompanied the email. Larry may have married a white woman, but he couldn't help fantasizing about the young chocolate tender and how she would choose to thank him for his time.

Michelle entered his large office with floor to ceiling windows overlooking the smog-laced panorama of Los Angeles. She was dressed business-like, but the purple silk shirt she wore hugged her curves and accentuated what it was supposed to conceal. She carried a briefcase that she set down by his chair. She shook Larry's hand, then sat and crossed her long sexy legs all in one slow, sensual motion.

Larry tried to hold his composure, wanting to bend her over the desk, but instead, he cleared his throat. "It's very nice to meet you, Ms. Graham, but as you know, I'm extremely busy. So I can only spare fifteen minutes," he stated, but his mind added, *For now.*

"That's fine," Michelle agreed, taking out a blank notepad. "I didn't plan on taking up too much time anyway. I'm interested in knowing how you feel about rap music and the rule Clear Channel Communications set on why and when it is played."

"Well," Larry began. "We here at Clear Channel Communications have a very strict policy on the content of what we endorse. We try to give the listeners a variety yet . . . maintain our integrity," he explained, sounding like a public relations memo.

"Do you have a favorite group?" Michelle asked.

Larry smiled. "No, I must admit, I don't listen to much rap. I'm more of a Billy Ocean type of guy. Do you have a favorite? Maybe I can help you get an interview with them for your paper."

"Thank you, but that won't be necessary. I was sent up here by my favorite group. Have you ever heard of Crook and Larceny?" Michelle quipped, her tone still pleasant and business-like.

Larry's brow furled in thought. "No, not right offhand. Unless you're referring to court charges." He laughed and Michelle joined in politely.

"No, they're a rap group, a very good rap group who can't seem to get any play on any of your stations. They asked me to find out why."

"I don't see what that has to—"

Michelle cut him off. "Really, that's what I'm here for. Crook and Larceny want their record played on your stations." Larry chuckled lightly. Rappers were getting more creative in how they tried to get play. Sending this young hottie up here to fuck him in exchange for spins was definitely original. Pussy was one thing, but his job was another. How he did either didn't affect the other.

"Ms. Graham, if that is your name. Do you even attend Howard?"

"No." Michelle grinned.

"I see . . . so this is all a play just to get me to play Larson Crook or whatever you said?"

"Basically," she admitted, because there was nothing to hide.

"Well, I'm sorry. I give them an 'E' for effort, but, the radio business is much more complicated than that. They, like all the other million and one rap hopefuls, will have to go through the proper channels.

"Now . . . we've wasted enough time . . . so . . ." His tone said goodbye.

"Well," Michelle sighed. "I guess I'll just leave you a little something to remember us by."

Pussy! His dick screamed, but unless she kept hers in a briefcase, that wasn't it. She put a large dusty photo album on his desk.

"What's this?" he asked, recognizing it vaguely, but unable to really place it.

"Oh, that? Well, that's just an old photo album your mother keeps under her bed, next to her nightstand. The one she likes to show on Christmas"—and after seeng his eyes light up—"Yeah, that one. I like your uncle's cabin in Colorado and I hear his ski shop is doing real well. Oh, and your son? He's such a cutie. Think he'll go to Howard, too?" Michelle's voice never lost the sugary tone, but the meaning was unmistakable. Larry sat pale faced and shocked, wondering how they had gotten the photo album and where his mama was right at this moment.

Michelle picked his thoughts and assured him, "Oh, her?

She's fine . . . for now." She giggled. Larry's attitude went from shocked to anger in a split second.

"You think you can threaten me?!" He stood up, trembling with indignation. "I'm calling the police!"

Michelle just studied her freshly done manicure as he picked up the phone to dial and said, "Why, Larry? For communication threats? We'll make bond and then we'll make sure that album is the only thing you'll have left of your family."

"Nine-one-one, may I help you?" Michelle could hear the voice say through the receiver. Larry stood stock-still.

"Hello?"

Michelle placed her finger on the button and cut off the connection. Nine-one-one rung right back.

"Larry, don't do anything crazy, because if you answer that phone, you might as well call the funeral home next for your whole . . . fuckin' . . . family." The venom came out in her threat, and Larry knew she was dead-ass serious.

He absentmindedly picked up the receiver and said, "Everything's okay," then hung up and sat down.

"This is the deal." Michelle leaned forward and folded her hands on the desk. "And please listen closely. Crook and Larceny will get heavy rotation. They will be headliners on your Summer Jam Tour and they will receive full support at every station Clear Channel Communications runs. Any questions?" Michelle closed up her briefcase then looked at Larry as she stood up.

"Wh-what did you say the name was?" the once confident Larry said.

"Crook and Lar-ce-ny." She articulated every syllable clearly through her full strawberry lips. "Your stations already have the single. All they need is your word to make it happen." She blew him a kiss. "That's from Newark, baby, kiss your mama for me," she stated, heading for the door, then added, "As a matter of fact, kiss her goodbye if I don't hear my favorite song before I leave L.A." She laughed and closed the door behind her.

As she drove the rented drop-top Jag back to LAX, she heard the DJ on L.A.'s number one rap station announce, "New music! Hot new music by Crook and Larceny and produced by T-Beats. Check out this banger, 'Gun Music'!"

Michelle smiled to herself, knowing on every station across the country, niggas was hearing the same thing.

Chapter 5

The stores couldn't keep the single on the shelves and the bootleggers couldn't get enough of tracking down the few mix tapes Crook had done back in the day and putting them in circulation. Everywhere you went, Crook and Larceny was that gangsta shit. Ike was constantly fielding phone calls from labels begging to sign Crook and major distributors putting offers on the table for the upcoming album. Money was pouring in. Some cats in the Bronx even wanted Crook to play Akbar Prey in a straight-to-video movie they were doing. Crook kept the BMW he bought Sheena, but copped her a brand-new burgundy BMW 6 Series and the house they were living in. He didn't floss himself out in diamonds and furs and he cut back on the powder habit until it was basically nonexistent in his life. Psychologically, he didn't need it anymore, so the need for it dwindled away. Crook stacked his cheddar, except for an indulgence here and there. But he did remember old debts.

"T, you got a cat out here wanna see you. I think it's that rapper Crook," his man said, sticking his head in the door of the studio.

T-Beats was mixing down a track for Lady Dee, the illest female rapper out, when the word came through the door.

"Fuck he want?"

His man shrugged his shoulders. "Say he got somethin' for you. He's carrying a duffel bag, too."

"You check the bag?" T asked, knowing Crook's MO and not knowing what type of shit he was on.

"He ain't let me," was all his man said.

T-Beats got up and stormed into the front office to face the nigga just in case. When he walked in, Crook was all smiles, sitting in one of the leather lounge chairs. T-Beats looked him up and down when Crook stood up.

"Ay, yo, dog, it's good to finally meet you," Crook greeted.

"Yeah, what you want? I'm busy," T snapped.

Crook understood the hostility, so he got right to the point. "Ay, yo, I know you probably feel like I came at you sideways, but desperate times call for desperate measures. I just came to give you this, to let you know I wasn't tryin' to play you." With that, Crook unzipped the duffel and handed it to T-Beats. He looked in the bag and found himself face-to-face with two hundred thousand dollars.

"I heard you charge fifty thou a track, so the rest is for waitin' so long." Crook smiled.

T-Beats looked up at Crook, and he couldn't front, the gesture was genuine and he felt it, but he said, "It should be half a mil in this bag the way you blowin' off my shit!" Crook laughed and T-Beats did, too. "But, yo, on the real, son, you nice. Your flow fit the track lovely."

Crook shrugged. "That's all I wanted niggas to understand. Good work." Crook turned for the door, but T-Beats stopped him by saying, "What up wit that album? I hope you ain't fuckin' wit no lame niggas to track you."

Crook turned back. "I'm sayin', holla at your man if you know somebody wit that hot shit."

T-Beats opened the door to his studio. "Duke, stop playin'. Who's fuckin' wit T-Beats?"

"Who's fuckin' with this nigga Crook?"

"Then let's go cause problems."

———

Larceny was enjoying his newfound wealth as well, and like Crook, he had a debt to repay.

He hadn't been home in months, staying with Ike and riding with Crook. So coming though the door of his mother's apartment felt awkward. As soon as he closed the door, he saw a gigantic roach run up the wall to welcome him back. Nothing had changed. The place still smelled of dirty clothes and fatback. He could hear the TV on Jerry Springer, so he knew where to find his mother.

Larceny walked in the adjoining living room to see his overweight mother in her soiled blue housedress smoking a Kool 100. She hardly glanced up at him, but snidely remarked, "I see that bitch finally threw your ass out, huh? Go to the store, get me some cigarettes. I ain't got but three left."

Larceny looked at the woman who gave birth to him, and for the first time wondered what a mother was supposed to be. He never remembered her hugging him or celebrating his accomplishments. All he remembered was hating her.

"Naw, yo, I ain't stayin', and once I leave, I ain't comin' back. I just came to give you this." She looked up at him when he said he had something for her. Larceny pulled out a large envelope and tossed it in her lap. A few bills spilled out, all big-faced hundreds. Her eyes never portrayed the inner greed that leaped into her heart.

"What bank you done robbed? 'Cause when they lock yo ass up, don't think I'ma get you out!"

"That's yours, 'cause I don't need you to do shit for me. That's for your fuckin' insurance policy you tried to get me killed over. All twenty-five thousand," Larceny growled. "Now I really am dead to you." He dropped his keys on the table and headed for the door.

She yelled after him. "Nigga, you been dead to me! You shoulda never been born!" All she heard in response was the sound of the closing door. The tears started slow, for what reason she didn't know, but they got heavier and heavier, realizing everything she ever had in the whole fucked up world she made for herself had just walked out of her life forever.

Larceny felt freer than he ever felt. He and Crook were getting paper and loving every minute of it. Larceny performed at the shows as Crook's hype man, but he didn't live for it like Crook. All he wanted to do was party and bullshit. Unlike Crook, Larceny didn't save anything, every dime he got, he spent. He stepped up his wardrobe, platinum jewelry, a brand-new red Viper that he had the doors altered to flip up to open. Larceny tricked on broads he couldn't get before, showing no mercy, even getting one to drink his piss out of a champagne glass. All these chicks were the ones who had dissed him, or he felt would've dissed, had they known him before. Now, he was enjoying every minute of defiling them and went as far as to turn several of them out on crack. He spent thousands getting high until their habit was as big as his, then he cut them off and sent them back, broke and feenin.

Larceny's money grew, too. He spent days butt naked and high in his plush apartment on Chancelor Avenue. Crook came to his crib, banging on the door.

"Yo, Larceny! Bitch, open the door! Open the fuckin' door!"

Larceny was spread eagle with a chick asleep with her head on his thigh, dick in her face and another chick next to him. All of them were butt naked. Crook was so mad he kicked the door in like SWAT, making everyone jump off the floor. "Get out! Get yo ass out!" he barked on the chicks, grabbing handfuls of hair and flinging them to the door. They were so scared, they ran out without their clothes in hand. Larceny knew he was next, and he tried to get up, but Crook lunged at him and caught him with a solid left hook. "You wanna be a fuckin' crackhead, huh?! I'll kill yo ass first!" Larceny rolled off the blow, quickly jumping to his feet. Before Crook knew it, he had caught Crook with a two-piece that staggered him.

"Fuck you, nigga, fuck you think it's sweet?!" Larceny exploded back. Hand for hand, Crook couldn't beat Larceny, but over the years he had won his fair share by grippin' and grabbin'. He took another one of Larceny's blows and absorbed it, just so he could scoop him off his feet, and then slammed him hard on his back. It knocked the wind out of Larceny, then Crook pinned him and rocked his ass silly.

"Why you so fuckin' stupid?! This what you want?! Is it?!" He dragged Larceny to the bathroom, picked him up, and dumped him in the tub.

"Damn!" Larceny winced, hitting his head on the side of the tub." "You coulda broke my neck!"

"Fuck yo neck, you don't give a fuck about your life!" Crook screamed at him, pacing the floor. "Fuck is you doin', man? We go through all this so you can just throw it all away? Huh?! Niggas bled, died, and we steady throwin' bricks at the pen, and this is what you do wit it?!"

Larceny dropped his head in his hands. "Man . . . man, I'm sick, yo, I'm sick and I'm fucked up, I—"

Crook shook him by the shoulders then smacked fire out his ass. "I don't wanna hear that Pookie TV shit! You a soldier, nigga, a live-ass nigga and one of the realest ever born! Fuck yo sorry ass mama, fuck the world, it's always been me and you and we always came through!" He hugged Larceny to his chest and let his man cry on his shoulder.

"I'm sorry, man, Crook, I'm sorry."

"Never say you sorry. Apologize, but never say you sorry."

"I'ma get it together, dog, I swear I am, yo," Larceny mumbled between sobs. Crook sat him back in the tub and turned the shower on in his face.

"Clean up, dog, we celebratin' tonight."

While Crook and Larceny were dealing with all the paper and fame, Ike stayed in the shadows, handling the business side, ne-

gotiating deals. They wanted no part of any of the numerous labels that had been pursuing them. They were strictly for self, the
only question was the sweetest distribution deal they could find.

But one offer was different. It came from Cali, from a real
gangsta of the industry, Big Mike Buddha. Big Mike Buddha was a
three-hundred-pound Jabba the Hutt—looking dude with ice in
his veins to match the ice he sported like baby glaciers. The deals
he made were written in blood, in more ways than one. He was an
OG Blood, respected in the streets and feared in the music business. So when he sent word for Ike to fly to L.A., there was no way
Ike could refuse. Ike didn't tell Crook or Larceny, instead he took
the red-eye to L.A. three days before the platinum party, while
Crook was in Raleigh, North Carolina, doing a show with M.O.P.

He arrived at LAX and was immediately scooped up in a
black Cadillac limousine. Inside were two identical twin chicks.
Their light complexions were peppered with reddish freckles
and their thick curvaceous bodies were clad in tight red dresses.
Their black locs shades hid the murder in their eyes. But tonight,
they had been sent as the welcoming committee and they wel-
comed Ike to L.A. with a twin blowjob that curled the nigga's toes
and had him cumming and farting at the same time. His knees
were weak by the time he stepped out of the limo at Buddha's
Beverly Hills mansion.

He entered the gigantic mansion and was greeted by two white
broads in bikinis that led him out to the pool. There were so many
topless women of all flavors, Ike thought he was at the Playboy
mansion. He found Buddha's big ass in a deck chair sipping on
tequila, watching the sunrise.

"Dog, welcome to L.A.," Buddha greeted him with a shit-
eating grin. "How was your flight?"

Ike sat down and a chick asked him what he was drinking.
"VSOP," he told her and she left to fix it. He turned to Buddha.
"Not as good as the ride over."

Buddha laughed.

"Accommodations, baby, I always make sure my brothers are taken care of.

"So . . ." Buddha swung his legs over the deck chair so he could sit sideways, facing Ike. The girl returned with Ike's drink, then left. "I'm hearin' a lot about the moves you makin', and I gotta be honest, I'm a little offended."

"Offended? Why?"

"Come on, Ike, you ain't no music cat. So why, when you decided to dabble, didn't you come to me? Instead of goin' through all this unnecessary . . . thuggery. You know I coulda handled it," Buddha told him, then sipped his drink, never taking his eyes off Ike.

"Naw, Mike, it wasn't like that. I never really intended to get involved, but shit just happened so fast, so I rolled with it," Ike explained.

Mike nodded. "I can dig it, but, yo . . . this is a crazy business, and you know, two heads is better than one. Black Knights Records is the home of that gangsta shit, dig? I'm sure we can work something out."

Buddha was smiling, but his eyes were of stone. Ike knew he needed to tread lightly. "Mike, I feel you. I do . . . but Crook . . . he ain't feelin' being on a label. I mean, can you blame him? What can a situation like that offer?"

"There's a thousand ways we can make it so Crook can benefit from my expertise, and I can benefit from his creativity. The question is, are all parties willin' to make a deal?" Buddha was persistent. Wasn't no way he wasn't gonna cake off this album after the single alone had moved five million and was still going strong.

Ike sipped his drink casually, concealing the slight jitters. He watched the females as they slithered all around him. "Let me talk to Crook," he replied, since it was Crook who wasn't with it, let him tell Buddha no. "Then I'll be in touch."

"Why don't you," Buddha agreed. "Matter of fact . . . Why don't we both talk to Crook? We could take my G-4, be in Newark for the party, then come back and celebrate the future."

"I don't see any problem wit that."

"Neither do I." Buddha grinned like a cat on his way to a mouse convention.

The platinum party was held at Club Mirage, the same club Crook had walked into months earlier, and walked out to the respect and fear of the whole industry.

Now, the party was for him, and many in attendance then returned to toast his success.

Larceny arrived in a stretch Hummer, with six of his Blood brothers and three sisters all dressed in Blood red and frosted neck to wrist. Ike rolled up in a brand-new champagne-colored Phantom, along with Mike Buddha and the twin chicks, one on each arm.

But Crook killed them all, pulling up in a 1930's style, two-door Cadillac and wearing a black and white pinstriped zoot suit—Capone style—derby, and platinum-tipped cane. He opened the door for Sheena. He lifted her gracefully and she got out with her hair in a '30s style wrap, a gorgeous sequined off-the-shoulder gown, and crystal-beaded mules blessed her feet. She stepped out to the flash of the paparazzi, shyly smiling for the camera. Crook could tell she felt a little uncomfortable because she wasn't model size or as shapely as the gold diggers milling around.

Crook leaned in and whispered in her ear, "Relax, baby, and smile like you're loved. You the prettiest woman in the house." From then on, she floated through the sea of people like a queen.

Everybody was showing Crook and Larceny love. Rappers who Crook didn't know or even want to know treated him like they were the best of friends. The only cats he showed love were M.O.P. and 50, the only cats he respected in the industry.

"Salute," Lil' Fame greeted him.

"Salute," Crook replied and dapped Billy Danze.

M.O.P. and 50 were the only guest appearances he had on his album, so he brought them through to perform at the party. M.O.P. went first, then 50, then it was finally Crook's turn.

He and Larceny took the stage like they owned it, just like in his dream, all eyes were on him, but unlike the dream, he didn't freeze up. Crook ripped through several joints until he was dizzy and he even challenged anyone in the house to battle for fifty thousand on the spot. Nobody stepped up.

After the performance, Crook settled into a booth with Sheena and draped his arm around her while he sipped E&J with the other.

"I'm proud of you, baby," she told him with a kiss. "And I'm so happy that you got what you wanted because you deserve it," she added with teary eyes.

"Naw, ma, we deserve it. You put in most of the work, while I ran crazy. I know I put you through a lot, but the pain is over, we can finally start livin'."

He kissed her deeply, dancing his tongue around hers. The kiss was interrupted with "Ay, yo, dog, Ike wanna see you, he said it's important," Larceny explained.

Crook looked up, annoyed. "Nigga, this important."

Sheena giggled. "It's okay, Vic, I ain't going nowhere," she assured him, meaning every word. Crook pinched her cheek, then rose from his seat and followed Larceny to the VIP section where Ike and Mike Buddha were sitting with their chicks, sipping bubbly. Ike stood up to greet Crook. "What up, dog. Lookin' good, baby! You kilt 'em in that throwback Caddy, looking like a black Al Capone."

Crook grinned. "Fuck that cracker, he look like a white me!" Everyone laughed as Crook added, "I couldn't let nobody outshine me at my own party."

"I want you to meet somebody." Ike turned to Mike Buddha, but Crook cut in.

"No need, Ike, everybody knows Buddha." Crook extended his

hand to Buddha. He shook it firmly. "What up, Buddha? All yo shit is gangsta. I respect yo label and yo hustle, yo."

Mike Buddha nodded with appreciation. "The feeling is mutual. If the single is any indication of what's to come, I see nothing but big things in your future."

"Word."

"So what's the plan? Ike tells me labels been kickin' in your door like whoa. Who you gonna sign wit?" Buddha inquired.

"Gun Music Records," Crook stated proudly. "We got our own label."

Buddha lit a Cuban. "Indo's good, but it's hard for Indo labels these days. You get distribution yet?" Buddha continued with his twenty-one questions.

Crook looked at Ike like, this your department, but answered, "Naw, dog, just a lot of deals on the table; just waitin' on the right offer."

"That's what's up," Buddha agreed. "But what do you think about Inner-Vibe distribution? That's my distributor, and I'm sure we could get something proper on the table. Especially if you merged your label with me."

Crook chuckled. Everybody wanted a piece of the pie. "I'm sure, but for now, I'm feelin' my independence."

Buddha scratched his chin like, "Well, everybody need somebody sometimes. This just happens to be one of those times."

Crook could see the fat cat getting agitated. Buddha wasn't used to any kind of resistance. But Crook wasn't used to giving in, so he said, "Yo, I appreciate your offer, but right now I want to see what Gun Music can do for self. It was good to meet you, but I need to get back to my fiancée." Crook extended his hand to Buddha.

He just looked at it without shaking it. "Have a seat, Crook, let's drink a little. Talk man-to-man, because an offer from Black Knight is never repeated twice."

Buddha's tone turned ominous. To Buddha, Crook was a young

punk, an upstart hardhead that needed to be put in position, one way or another. To Crook, Buddha was a cat he looked up to, but he wasn't gonna let Buddha look down on him because of it. Ike shifted silently, and the twins' body language reflected the tension in the air, so Crook tried to bow out gracefully before the situation totally deteriorated.

"Buddha, on the real, I thank you for comin' to my party. To me, that's respect and I do nothin' but return it, and I give you my word, we'll talk again, but—"

Buddha's famous temper exploded. "No! We'll talk now, you bitch-ass sucka mu'fucka! You think you a real killa, huh?! A live wire?! You fuckin' wit vets now, not these puppet things you been gorilla'n! You better bow yo bitch ass down when I speak to you or find yourself among the unspeakable!"

Buddha felt disrespected because he seldom heard no, and when he did, he never heard it twice. He couldn't accept it, wouldn't accept it, but he didn't realize he'd better be prepared to hold court on the spot.

Ike was the first to see it in Crook. That look in his eyes, the one he had almost in this very same spot, when Mark Allen made his final mistake. He wanted to warn Buddha, tell him to kill him now, on the spot, but before the words came out, it all began to blur too fast for Ike to speak.

Crook turned to Larceny as if he was leaving, pulling his pistol from his waist the whole time in a single motion. He turned and fired twice into Mike Buddha's piglike grill. There was no emotion, no angry words, just a principle being upheld. The twins went into action. Crook hit Buddha once more in the throat before one of the twins pulled a small .380 from her garter belt and hit Crook in the shoulder. The force pushed him into Larceny, who by that time had pulled his pistol and hit the twin dead in her forehead, slumping her onto Buddha's convulsing body. Ike and the second twin dove out of the booth as the crowd went into a frenzy.

"They killed Buddha! Crook killed Buddha!" Ike shouted, and the Bloods in attendance set it off.

Larceny and Crook had been friends for a long time, but Larceny had also made a blood oath with the gang: the Bloods. In the split second it took for Crook to murder Buddha, Larceny's decision was made. He went against the oath he took with his life and rode with his dog.

"You hit, dog! You hit!" he cried to Crook.

"I'm good, yo. Let's just get Sheena and get the fuck outta here!" Crook replied.

Larceny came up firing and cleared a path. As one innocent chick got hit in the exchange, Ike came out of hiding with two burners, both blazing at a ducking and running Larceny and Crook. Crook started to go for Sheena, but thought twice. He didn't want to draw the gunplay anywhere near her.

"Sheena!" he screamed, hoping she'd hear him and get out.

Sheena was still in the booth when the gunfire erupted, and ducked deep in the booth. But when she heard someone shout "Crook killed Buddha," she burst into tears, and crawled along the floor trying to get to her man.

"Vic! Where are you?!" she hollered in anguish, but she got no reply.

Larceny and Crook had made it out of VIP, but more of Buddha's people were waiting and opened up on the two figures as they stumbled out among the fleeing partygoers.

Pop! Pop!

Two shots and a famous rapper from Marcy fell dead. No one was safe. Crook shot back from behind a nearby booth and dropped one of the shooters, then he heard, "Victor! Victor, where are you?!"

"Sheena!"

Her heart leaped when she heard his voice. "Victor!" Crook looked around for Larceny, who was exchanging fire across the floor from behind the bar. "L! Get Sheena outta here!" Larceny nodded and hopped over the counter, taking cover against two fallen bodies. He fired randomly to clear a path, then crawled along the floor until he saw Sheena huddled behind an over-turned table.

"Sheena," he whispered loudly, "Sheena, it's me, Larceny."

"Where's Victor?" she asked trembling, scared of what he might say.

"He's good, but we gotta go." He put his arm around her and led her toward the front door. Once outside, he fumbled for his keys.

"Shit! I ain't drive my shit!"

A burst of automatic gunfire silenced his thoughts. Instinc-tively, Larceny threw Sheena down behind a parked car, and re-turned a blast until his pistol sat back empty. The fire had come from the second twin standing on the door of the Phantom, blast-ing a Mac-11.

While her attention was on Larceny, she never saw Crook creep up behind her and put the gun to her head. "Die slow, bitch!" He snuffed her permanently and snatched up the Mac. It was just in time, because two Bloods came running out on him, firing recklessly. He ducked inside the Phantom, feeling the bro-ken glass from the windshield rain down on him. He came up blazing, catching one of the bloods, the other took off.

When Larceny ran over to the Phantom, Crook asked, "Where's Sheena?"

"Behind that car back there," was his friend's answer.

Crook gave Larceny his keys and told him, "Go get the car, I'll get Sheena."

They split up, Larceny ran down the block to get the Cadillac, while Crook crept down to Sheena. Ike came out and saw Crook dipping across the front of the club and tried to take his head off, but missed several times. Ike heard whimpering to his right, and when he looked over, he saw Sheena. "Blood for blood, nigga!" Ike yelled and Crook knew exactly what he meant.

From his angle Crook couldn't hit Ike and save Sheena at the same time, so without hesitation, he flung himself between Sheena and the impending barrage of shells. His body covered hers as the slugs ate up his back, filling his lungs with blood.

"Noooo!!" she screamed, feeling the jolts Crook's body was taking, but he never made a sound. Larceny was skidding up when he saw Ike on the sidewalk. He hopped the curb in the car and aimed it like a guided missile at him. Ike tried to shoot Larceny through the windshield seconds before he collided with the fender and his body was crushed between the car and the building. Larceny jumped out, snatched Ike's gun out of his lifeless hand, and hit him two times, just to make sure.

"Nooo," Larceny heard Sheena moan.

He turned to see his man sprawled out on top of her, back drenched in his own blood. All Larceny could do was drop his head, then the rage of it all bubbled up. "They killed him! Fuckin' kilt him!!!" he kept repeating.

Sheena rocked Crook's lifeless body in her arms, hearing the approaching sirens. Larceny ran over to hug Crook one last time.

"Damn, dog, why? Why the fuck couldn't they just let us live?? "I love you, dog. I love you." He kissed Sheena on her forehead. "Boo, I gotta go. The police is coming, but I'll be back. On my life, I'll be back."

Sheena heard nothing, she didn't even realize he was there. All she felt was pain so deep, she was scared it would never end. The police found her cradling Crook to her chest.

The club was a mess. Several celebrities besides Crook and Buddha died, and one was paralyzed. The police chalked it up as gang related, determined everyone dead killed everybody else, and left it at that. To them, it was a few less niggas to worry about.

Larceny couldn't take it. Nothing about it made any sense and nothing could justify the fact that Crook was gone forever. All he wanted to do was get high. Maybe even high enough to join Crook, but certainly high enough to forget.

He spent the next few days alone with his pipe and a quarter kilo of coke. While the world mourned and sensationalized the industry murders, he sank deeper into his own depression.

The day of the funeral, Sheena kept calling but all she got was his voice mail. He sat huddled by the picture window, cradling his glass companion. *Beep* . . .

"This Larceny leave a message, unless you naked, then leave an address," his recorded voice said. He expected to hear Sheena again, begging him to pick up, to call but instead he heard Crook say, "Crook and Larceny ain't no gimmick. We ain't just decide in somebody studio that, yo, I'ma be Crook and you gon be Larceny, you know, to sound hard like these studio gangstas. We always been Crook and Larceny 'cause that's how we survived, yo.

"I ain't glorifyin' it, but its reality. Ain't nobody ever give us nothing. We took whatever we got.

"Except—*beep*—" Larceny added and they laughed. It was a recording of a radio interview they had done, and they beeped out the word *pussy*.

"Yeah, we ain't never took no—*beep*—" Crook repeated. "We ain't on no R. Kelly baby rapin'—beep—That's that faggot—*beep.*"

Even though Sheena was just holding the phone to the stereo, Crook's voice sounded so clear to Larceny, like he was right in the room with him, telling him these things live and direct, slapping him back to reality like the day they last fought. Crook's voice made him remember his man. Remember how they met, stealing cigarettes, robbin' together, starvin' together, and finally, on top of the world together. He looked at the pipe in his hands as Crook finished the interview.

"So what's next for ya'll, what else can we expect from Crook and Larceny?"

"What else," Larceny heard him say, recalling the smile when he said it. "We gonna pump the music up and count our money."

He finished, mimicking Rakim's words off "Paid in Full," his theme song.

Larceny knew he had to get to the funeral. He had to be there for Sheena, but especially for Crook. He didn't even bother to get dressed. He threw on his boots and grabbed his keys, wearing only a dingy T-shirt and cut-off sweatpants.

Crook's funeral was packed to capacity. The large church it was held in on Freling Huysen Avenue had so many six-figure whips lined up in its parking lot it looked like an industry party. The fans and media mulled around outside, holding up homemade signs and T-shirts, while the media snapped pic after pic.

Larceny triple-parked his Venom and left the door thrown up like a bat wing. As he pushed his way through, he looked around at all the strange, but celebrated faces. Cats tried to holler at him, chicks tried to console him, but he pushed past them all, heading to the front of the church where Sheena, her sisters, and two daughters, Tameek and Syasia, were sitting. He hugged Sheena, who simply whispered, "Thank you." She embraced him tightly even though she must have smelled his three-day must.

Larceny looked into the kids' faces and knew he had to hold them down, especially Tameek. She was frowned up just like Crook, and Larceny knew one day she'd have the attitude of fuck the world, too. So he had to be around to stop it.

The preacher spoke from the pulpit while Larceny came in, but after a few more words, Larceny grabbed Tameek and Syasia's hands and led them up on stage. He walked right up to the preacher in mid-sermon and interrupted, "I need to say something."

The preacher looked at him like he was crazy, but after he looked at Sheena and she nodded subtly, he relented. Larceny stepped to the mic and said, "Who is all ya'll? What you here for? Ya'll ain't know my man! Half of ya'll glad he dead, because you fake muh"—he caught himself—"fake suckas couldn't stand to see a real cat come through! You wanted to see him dead, probably wanna see me dead, too, but it's all good, see me when you see me. For now, just know, you don't belong here!

"The only people in this room that 'posed to be is the sister over there." He pointed to Sheena. "Baby girl, that nigga loved you. You rode for my dog and you deserved every moment you got wit him. Know in your heart, I'll always ride for my dog's family."

Larceny turned his attention back to the crowd. "But as for ya'll, you think it's over? You think you safe just 'cause Crook gone? It's a million other Crooks out there, waitin' to make you famous. And if the streets don't eat, mark a day on every month for sad songs and eulogies, 'cause that's how we sendin' you! Gun music . . . If you ain't heard it, pray you don't." Larceny lifted his eyes to the ceiling and repeated a line from Crook's song:

" *'Cause that's how it is when you tired of livin'* . . . *Death is parole when your world is a prison.* You free, dog, you free," he whispered through his tears.

Faith Evans stood up to comfort him, then sang her peoples from Newark home.

Larceny and T-Beats got together and put out Crook's album a month after his funeral. The album sold ten million plus, registering it as certified diamond, just like the nigga who made it. Because it takes a lot of heart, time, and pressure to turn black carbon into diamonds, the rest that can't take the pressure end up fuel for the fire.

Crook was a diamond nigga who wouldn't take no for an answer and changed the game. He had let the world feel his pain and they gave him nothing but love in return.

Larceny, on the other hand, had to go hard for his man. Even after his death, but that . . . is another story altogether.

OUTRO

Everyone wants to be backstage but most people don't fully understand what being there really means. I can only give you the perspective of a young black kid who never had anything but a dream that ultimately landed me a spot backstage amongst the stars who are now my peers. What I didn't know then was that that dream would be both a blessing and a curse.

It's a blessing and a curse to have a one hundred, five hundred, ten, twenty, fifty or hundreds of thousands of people chanting your name, showing crazy respect, love, and hate all at the same time. Family and friends asking for tickets to your concerts because they want to see you shine and do your thang because they were there when you were struggling with nothing but a dream, and other family members and so-called friends that just want to be associated with the glitz and the glamour, the fame and fortune, but were nowhere to be found when you were broke and hungry.

I never get comfortable with being backstage because I know that every time I step to the front of that stage and do my thang it could be my last time there—if I don't give a stellar performance, or if the crowd doesn't like me, I may no longer be relevant. I could leave a show and get hit by a car, struck by lightning, or shot. You may ask what's the odds of a nigga getting struck by lightning? With all due respect the odds are probably better than you ripping a performance for over fifty thousand people at the same spot you grew up watching your favorite football team play on Sunday afternoons (Giants Stadium for me), or the same place Jordan scored a double nickel against the Knicks (Madison Square Garden). I don't know much about mind-altering drugs, but I do know that experiences like those have been said to be the greatest high in the world. I can't imagine anything that could compare to the lights, the screams, the love, the music, and the admiration of a packed venue with fans chanting your name in unison.

Backstage is where it all begins and the faces back there are forever changing. The last time I was backstage I didn't see the faces that were there just a few years prior—they weren't even in the building. When you're backstage you may not have everything you think you deserve for the work you put out, but you know there are at least a million other people who wish they were in your position because you are living a dream, your dream. Everybody back there is happy to be there. But if you allow yourself a few extra seconds to take a deep breath and really pay attention to what's going on around you then you will quickly see the snakes, the rats, the knifers, and the sharks of the business. You realize that some of the people who you thought were happy for you really don't give a shit about you. They're just happy that a backstage exists. Backstage can be a mutha fucka.

So the next time you dream about being backstage, think about what that really means. You have to take the backstage seriously in every aspect of life. You gotta be backstage before you can get to the front of the stage. You feel me? Every dream or goal in life begins backstage. So don't be afraid to dream, but don't forget that every dream ain't peaceful.

Peace!
—Styles P

ACKNOWLEDGMENTS

Krista Johns

With God, all things are possible. Thank you, Nikki Turner, for opening up the door for me. Thank you, Ron Slay, for the motivation and the positivity you bring in my life. Thank you, my brothers: Elton, One, and Tank for everything. My kids: Here's to us! Tawuainya (RIP), Tisa, G, and Yummie . . . look at me!

Harold L. Turley II

First, I want to thank God for blessing me with the gift of expression through written word. Through Him, all my blessings are possible. I want to thank Nikki Turner for the opportunity to grace the pages of her blazing hot project. You are a true diva and a valued friend! And finally, I give thanks to my kids, Harold, RaShawn, Malik, and Yhanae. I work so hard now so you won't have to in the future. And to the woman who I will one day call my wife, Tyreasa Sharp. You are my backbone and the beat within my heart. Thanks for standing by my side and supporting me in all that I do. Your love makes my life complete.

Allah Adams

I would first like to thank God for blessing me with a gift, a gift that I want to give to the world! I want to thank Nikki Turner for giving me the opportunity to share my gift with the world. I want to thank my team: Chareice "Cheese" Simpson and Amos Pierre for sticking with me through the bad, knowing that one day things will be good. To all the independent entrepreneurs that I affiliate with, Real Knot Ent., Prolyfic Ent., Street Heat Potent TV. Let's all get together and form a Conglomerate! And last but not least I want to thank all the readers who ever supported me.

Lana Ave

God is good all the time. My aunt Judy and uncle Jon are my examples. My late parents Joe and Irene are my drive. My husband Bryant is my blessing, and my sister Jonay is my inspiration. I love you Cassie, Mariesa, Wade, Deidra, Raven, Rhen, Tiff, and Tam and all uncles, aunts, nieces, nephews, and friends. Thank you to Nikki Turner for the guidance, opportunity, and friendship.

LINER NOTES

KRISTA JOHNS is the author of *I'm Good* and she is currently putting the final touches on *Impressions.* She lives in Cali while raising her two children.

ALLAH ADAMS is a new and upcoming author that currently calls the Big Apple home. *Banana Pudding* and *The Legend of Cagney* are his two self-published novels.

LANA AVE was born and raised in Brooklyn, New York. She is driven by her passion to write the stories she envisions. She is currently working on her first full-length novel.

HAROLD L. TURLEY II is an author and performance poet who thrilled readers with his critically acclaimed novels, *Love's Game, Confessions of a Lonely Soul,* and *Born Dying.* He lives with his wife and children in Brandywine, Maryland. Visit the author at www.myspace.com/haroldlturley2.

ABOUT THE AUTHOR

NIKKI TURNER is a gutsy, gifted, courageous voice taking the urban literary community by storm. Having ascended from the "Princess" of Hip-Hop Lit to "Queen," she is the bestselling author of the novels *Ghetto Superstar, Black Widow, Forever a Hustler's Wife, Riding Dirty on I-95, The Glamorous Life, A Project Chick,* and *A Hustler's Wife,* and is the editor of and a contributing author in her Street Chronicles series. She is also the editor of the Nikki Turner Presents line, featuring novels from fresh voices in the urban literary scene. Visit her website at nikkiturner.com or write her at P.O. Box 28694, Richmond, VA 23228.